A Shroud of Tattered Sails

A SHROUD OF TATTERED SAILS

Scott William Carter

FLYING RAVEN
PRESS

FOR S.K.

THANKS FOR LIGHTING
A FIRE.

A SHROUD OF TATTERED SAILS

For more about Flying Raven Press, please visit our web site at
http://www.flyingravenpress.com

ISBN-10 0692604952
ISBN-13 978-0692604953

Printed in the United States of America
Flying Raven Press paperback edition, December 2015

Chapter 1

They walked side by side, but alone. The beach was deserted, the sun a soft yellow glow behind a vaporous orange film along the horizon. It had been the first day without rain in weeks, overcast and breezy but no rain, the big storm of mid-March already receding into memory.

Gage, carefully navigating the driftwood with his cane as they made their way to the smoother sand near the water's edge, stole a glance at Zoe. Her wool hat was pulled low enough that he could barely see her eyes. Even on a Wednesday in April—not exactly the height of tourist season in Barnacle Bluffs, Oregon—having the beach to themselves was enough of a rarity that one of them should have commented on it, but neither of them did.

He still didn't know how to overcome the hard thing between them. He didn't know what it was. When they actually managed to talk, they argued. When they didn't talk, it seemed uneasy. Uneasy was better than arguing, so most of the time they opted for silence.

"I've got something for you," she finally said.

She sounded timid, her voice disappearing into the crashing surf. It wasn't like her. She went on staring at the ocean and for a moment, in the soft, drowsy light of dusk, he clearly saw the woman she was becoming and not the girl she'd been. All the hard edges of her troubled youth were beginning to fade. Where was the facial jewelry? Where was the spiky black hair? Now she didn't even sport the tiny nose stud she'd been wearing the past few months, and the auburn hair sticking out of the hat had grown long enough that it actually billowed in the wind.

"Oh?" he said.

"I'm not sure you're going to like it," she said.

"Uh oh."

"Actually, I'm pretty sure you're not going to like it. Promise me you'll keep an open mind."

"This conversation is already not starting well."

"Just promise."

"I'm always open-minded," he said. "You know that. That's why they call me Garrison 'Open-Minded' Gage."

He'd been hoping for a smile, but he got a sigh instead. Overhead, through fragmented clouds dappled with bright crimsons and sober violets, glimpses of a more cheery blue could still be seen. To the right, where the beach stretched for miles, the lights of the Golden Eagle Casino far in the distance blinked through the pink haze. To the left, where the bluffs grew taller and the houses more impressive the higher they were, the view ended a few hundred yards away, where the bluff jutted out to some exposed black rocks. Zoe went left. When the tide was low, which it was now, there was a gap in the rocks that allowed passage without requiring them to wade into the surf, but Gage still usually went right. His bad knee—far too bad a knee for a man who could still believably claim to be middle-aged—made him wary of hidden dangers.

The salty air, abrasive yet still somehow welcoming, cleared the dust from his mind, shook off his evening bourbon. He followed Zoe to the rocks, watching her back, wondering what this was all about. Everybody told him that when she became an adult, it would get easier. She was eighteen now. How long did he have to wait?

She hadn't gone far when she turned and thrust something

at him. It was shiny and black, small enough to be cupped completely in her hand.

"Here," she said.

"What is it?" he asked.

She flipped it open, turning the tiny blue-glowing screen so it faced him. A cell phone. He felt a sinking disappointment.

"Ah," he said

"Take it," she said.

"And here I thought you just wanted to walk with me."

"I did! I just, I had this for you, too."

"Zoe ..."

"Come on, Garrison. You can't go through life without a phone anymore."

"I have a phone."

Her hat had inched up far enough on her forehead that he could see her eyebrows raising. Like the rest of her, they had also undergone something of a change, plucked and trimmed to perfection. At some point Goth Girl had decided to become Model Girl. He didn't know why. It seemed to be the opposite of everything she claimed to believe in—nonconformity, individual expression, indifference to other people's opinions.

"I use the pay phone at the gas station down the hill," he explained.

She smirked. "Right. Funny how that's like one of the only pay phones left in Barnacle Bluffs."

"It's a convenient coincidence."

"Or," she said, "it could be because you agreed to pay the owner the monthly bill just so he'd keep it."

"Who told you that?"

"The owner," she said.

"Ah."

"I just don't get it. If you're willing to go that far just to have access to a phone, why don't you just get a cell phone?"

"Call me a conscientious objector."

"I can think of many other words for you."

"Most of those probably apply, too. Look, I appreciate the

sentiment—"

"Just take the damn phone," she said.

"Zoe—"

"Take it!"

Her fiery tone shocked him. He took it. What else could he do? It felt like cheap plastic, inconsequential, hardly worthy of so much drama. She glared at him, squinting at him in the wind with dark eyes, then turned in a huff and marched toward the rocks. He stuffed the cell phone into the pocket of his leather jacket and followed, holding his cane in his effort to keep up. His throbbing right knee threatened to buckle. It never did buckle, though. Somehow, if he could endure the pain, it always seemed to hold. If there was one thing he had proved in his life, even if he had proved nothing else, he could endure a lot of pain.

"Zoe," he said, "what's all this about?"

She hustled for the gap in the rocks. He wondered if this had something to do with her living at the Turret House the past two weeks. His good friend Alex had taken his wife on a long-deserved vacation cruise to the Mediterranean, where they were also visiting some of her relatives in Greece, and Zoe had been staying at the bed and breakfast until they'd returned yesterday. He didn't know why that would make a difference. Since becoming Alex's full-time assistant, she practically lived there most of the time anyway, a fact that annoyed him to no end. She should have been back in school by now.

He caught up with her as she reached the gap, a damp breeze swirling through the shiny black rocks. The air smelled of kelp and dank earth. He reached for her arm, but before he touched her she inhaled sharply.

He thought it might have been because of him until he looked over her shoulder and saw what she saw.

A sailboat, a 30- or 40- footer by the looks of it, was beached a hundred yards from them. Tilted away from the surf that lapped at the white fiberglass hull, the mast a stark black line against the sunset and the wet sand a mirror reflecting all those rich amber and violet hues, the boat looked at first glance like something out of a photographer's dream—as if someone had arranged it just so to get the perfect shot. It was only when Gage stared at it a little longer that he noticed how shredded both the main and jib sails were bunched at the base of the mast. Not much remained of them.

Barnacle Bluffs had no ports. A sailor could find refuge in Newport to the south or Tillamook to the north, as well as a number of other seaside towns that truly catered to the fishing trade, but this part of the Oregon coastline was inhospitable to anything bigger than a kayak. Too many rocks lurked just below the water's surface. Gage assumed the sailboat had been abandoned, washed ashore after weeks or months adrift, the owners rescued by someone who did not have the means to take the broken boat in tow. This had happened before. The ship would be a curiosity for a few days, worthy of an article or two in the weekly *Bugle,* then someone would haul it away and it would be forgotten.

That's what he thought until he saw the woman emerge from the hatch.

From this distance, with the sunset at her back, she was hardly more than a silhouette—tall, stick-figure thin, dressed in a bikini top and tiny shorts, clothes not at all fitting for the cool weather. Her frizzy hair, lots of it, formed a halo around her head. She staggered to the stern, teetered, then swung one unsteady leg over the metal rail. Both Gage and Zoe started for her, hurrying but not running, until the woman slipped and fell.

Then they ran.

The woman lay face down in the water. Zoe reached her first, splashing into the foamy surf, with Gage not far behind. He'd dropped his cane, enduring the excruciating throbbing in his knee to keep pace. Icy water soaked his tennis shoes. Zoe grabbed the woman's shoulder, turning her, and Gage seized the woman under the arms and pulled her out of the water onto the sand. She felt as light as a mannequin.

Already, she was coughing and hacking up salt water, a good sign.

They knelt beside her. The coughing didn't last long, then the woman rolled onto her back, gasping, eyes closed. That mass of reddish brown hair was as thick as dreadlocks, dark and wet around the temples, her face shiny from her dip in the ocean. Her bikini top and shorts, which might have once been yellow with white polka dots, were bleached white with faint patches of yellow. Her skin was a golden bronze in some places, but reddish pink in most of the others, the way someone with pale, freckled skin usually tanned. Judging by the hint of crow's feet around her eyes, he guessed she was in her early 30s.

There really was nothing to her. She made Gage think of those runway models with the physiques that only appealed to the fashion industry—gaunt faces and gaunt bodies, shoulder blades that could have been sharpened like knives. But she was pretty, definitely pretty, with the face of a small-town girl who'd gone to New York or Los Angeles and somehow, even as she lost herself, never lost the *look* of herself, that wholesome Midwestern appeal, before the years passed and the big city turned to younger, more pliant versions that always seemed to be in endless supply.

Gage felt ashamed of himself when he realized he was projecting all of these assumptions onto this poor waif of a woman—a woman who was only now opening her eyes. Green eyes. Aquamarine. A fitting color for a woman from the sea. Janet had eyes that very same color. And what made him think of that? Strange. The woman blinked a few times, staring at the sky, seemingly unaware of Gage or Zoe. He expected to see relief there, or at least some panicked confusion, but there was nothing. She simply stared at the sky.

She did not seem like a woman who'd just climbed out of a beached sailboat. She seemed like a woman who'd decided to lie down for a nap after having one too many margaritas.

"Who are you?" Gage asked.

She peered at him for a long time, blinking slowly, looked at Zoe, then back at Gage. Her cracked lips parted as if she was about to answer, but all that came out was a long, quiet moan. It was only then that a bit of fear crept into her eyes.

"I don't know," she said.

Her voice had the rough quality of someone who hadn't used it in a long time. Gage saw her fear growing, blooming into panic. He figured it was just the shock, that she'd come back to herself in a minute.

"You don't know?" he said.

She shook her head.

"Your name?" he pressed.

"No." The terror was palpable now. Even though her voice was soft, he heard the hysteria emerging. "No … Oh, God. Oh God, no."

"Do you remember the boat? It looks like you really had a rough ride. Do you remember that?"

She rolled her head to the side and gazed at the sailboat as if she not only didn't remember it, she didn't even know what it was. Then, abruptly, she burst into tears. Gage realized he was being an idiot. She was in shock, probably dehydrated. This was no time for twenty questions. He looked at Zoe and she must have been thinking the same thing.

"Use your phone," she said.

It took a second for him to even remember what she was talking about, then he reached into his pocket. It wasn't there. He searched all of his pockets. It wasn't in any of them. He scanned the area around them, and then, when he happened to glance in the direction of the boat, spotted something black and shiny in the shallow water. When the wave retreated, leaving the object caked in sand and sea foam, he saw that it was the cell phone. Zoe saw it too.

"You've got to be kidding," she said.

USING HER OWN PHONE, Zoe called 911. Gage heard the sirens within two minutes, growing louder on the bluffs, and within five minutes two male paramedics charged over the sand with a stretcher between them. By then, the woman had stopped crying. While they checked her vitals, she gaped at them like a rabbit caught in a snare. A state trooper arrived a moment later, a young muscle-bound guy Gage didn't recognize, peppering her with questions like bullets from an automatic rifle. What was her name? What happened on the boat? Who should they call? She didn't answer and Gage told the kid to back off a little, give the woman some time. The paramedics loaded her onto the stretcher and started to haul her away.

"No, no, no!" she cried. She flailed aimlessly about and caught hold of the sleeve of Zoe's windbreaker. Her eyes flew wide open and a vein on her temple pulsed violently. "Please! Don't—don't let them … He'll find me!"

"Who?" Gage said.

If she had been any stronger, the panic would have prompted her to break into a run, but as it was she only had enough energy to lift her head. It was a shuddery, jerky motion that she only managed to maintain for a few seconds before she collapsed on the stretcher—and then she was again crying inconsolably, unresponsive to any of their soothing words. The paramedics started for the stairs, but the woman refused to let go of Zoe's sleeve.

Gage reached to pry her fingers free, but Zoe shook her head.

"I'll go with her," she said.

"You sure?"

"She needs someone."

"Okay. I'll follow in the van."

Gage watched the woman get hauled away, Zoe walking by her side like a dutiful pallbearer. The sun had slipped completely beneath the waves by this point, robbing the sky of all the yellow and turning the blues to violets and the violets to blacks. The state trooper asked Gage a bunch of questions about the woman and the boat, none of which Gage could answer. Two other local cops showed up, a man and a woman, as did Percy Quinn, the sober-faced chief of police.

"What did you do now?" Quinn asked.

The chief, who usually dressed like an undertaker after a

long day, in frumpy white dress shirts and thin wrinkled ties, had tossed his gray trench coat over a ratty blue T-shirt, a packet of cigarettes bulging in the shirt's front pocket. Grease stained his hands and he had a bruise on his forehead almost as dark as his thick eyebrows. His wispy gray hair batted about in the wind.

"Went for a walk," Gage explained.

"Well, you should stop doing that. It always seems to lead to something bad."

"Like talking to you?"

Quinn had his own special brand of smirk he seemed to reserve only for Gage, one heavy with both impatience and burden, and he employed it now. The state trooper who'd been first on the scene caught the chief up with what they knew, which wasn't much, then the whole bunch of them descended on the boat. *Charity Case* was written on the side in stylish black script. Unusual name. Gage wondered about the meaning behind it. Quinn pointed to the license number on the side and asked one of his cops to call it in and get the registration info.

While he was talking, Quinn noticed the cell phone in the water. He picked it up.

"That's mine," Gage said.

Quinn raised those expressive eyebrows. "*You* have a phone?"

"Zoe got it for me."

"And, what, out of spite you tossed it in the ocean?"

"I *dropped* it in the ocean. On accident."

"Maybe you were being passive aggressive. On accident."

Quinn, clearly suppressing a grin, opened the phone, found it dead, and handed it to Gage with a shrug. Gage shoved the stupid thing into his jacket pocket. Meanwhile, the female cop climbed onto the boat on the starboard side and, using the rail for support, made her way to the stern. Her partner, another young male cop, joined her, and the two of them ducked into the cabin. Gage, Quinn, and the state trooper first on the scene waited and watched what remained of the sails flutter in the quickening breeze. Up close, Gage saw how thick the algae was on the hulls, how weathered and beaten the wood trim. He wondered if it was the big storm a couple weeks earlier that had crippled the ship.

The state trooper on the phone clicked off and stepped over to Quinn. "It's registered to a Marcus Koura out of San Jose, California."

"Reported missing?" Quinn asked.

"No, sir," the cop said.

"Hmm. I wonder where Mr. Koura is now."

"I have no idea, sir," the cop said.

"It was a rhetorical question, son," Quinn said.

It may have been rhetorical, but Gage could see where Quinn was going with the line of thought, and it made him uneasy. That he felt uneasy made Gage even more uneasy. He could already see that he was rooting for this woman, that he had some kind of blind spot forming, and he didn't like that at all. When the young male cop poked his head out of the cabin, Gage tensed. He was tall, dark-haired, and athletic, the perfect mold for a police officer, but with a baby-faced innocence that didn't fit—the kind that only reflected back what was good and decent in the world, like a mirror that only revealed your best features and hid the rest. Naturally, Gage feared the worst.

"Nobody else in here," the cop said.

"Men's clothes?" Quinn asked.

He ducked back inside. He returned a few minutes later with the female cop, both of them shaking their heads.

"No clothes at all," the male cop said.

"None?"

"No, sir. Not unless they're stowed somewhere else. I can't find a bag or anything. No food or water or anything either. Not even wrappers and stuff. Weird."

"Weird indeed," Quinn said. He looked at Gage. "Woman shows up in a man's boat, but man isn't in it. She claims to have no memory, but she yells out that someone is after her. What's your brilliant deduction, Mr. Detective?"

"Don't have one," Gage said.

"Really? I figured you'd have it solved by now, being the famous private investigator that you are."

When the male cop on the boat started back inside, Gage spoke up. "You know, you guys might want to hold off on that. Maybe you should think about getting a warrant first."

The cop stopped and looked at the chief questioningly, who, in turn, looked at Gage with a similar expression.

"Really?" Quinn said. "You're going to play this one that way? For a woman you don't even know?"

"You've already determined that there is no one else on the ship," Gage said. "Do you really have enough probable cause to think foul play is involved? I'm just looking out for you here."

"How thoughtful," Quinn said.

"Sir?" the cop on the boat said, still poised at the hatch. "You want me to keep looking or not?"

Quinn's scowl appeared to deepen, but it may have just been the fading light, the shadows accentuating all the many grooves on his face. Behind him, the boat was losing its detail, becoming a solid black silhouette, the sky and the ocean merging together in the gloom. The breeze had died, the air still enough that he smelled the pungent kelp at their feet, quiet enough that he heard the excited murmur of the onlookers on the bluff. Gage didn't glance at them. He kept looking at Quinn instead, waiting for his response to the cop's question.

Finally it came, a slight shake of the head. The cops took it as an answer, climbing down from the boat, but Gage could see that the real shake of the head was aimed at him.

"There could be a logical explanation," Gage said.

"Let's hope," Quinn said.

Chapter 2

Laughter was the last thing Gage expected when he opened the door and stepped into the hospital room, but that's what he heard—and not just from the woman, but from Zoe too.

They already had the woman changed into a blue gown, resting comfortably in a bed, and hooked up to IV fluids. Her hair was still a tangled mess of red vines, but he marveled at how much just a clean face had transformed her from a wasted thing that had washed up on the beach into a young, vibrant woman who might have been in the hospital because she'd fallen asleep by the pool and gotten a bit too much sun. The curtains on the other side of the room were open, the parking lot lights shining on the tops of the firs bordering the parking lot. The room was small, furnished with a big metal bed, soothing taupe walls, and a couple of wooden chairs with thin green cushions. Zoe perched in a chair next to the bed, her own hair showing hints of red that Gage hadn't noticed before but seemed obvious with the woman's hair nearby. They both looked his way, smiling.

"Well, now," he said, leaning his cane against the wall next to the door. "I wasn't expecting such bright spirits. What're you two laughing about?"

"You," Zoe said, with a bit of a mischievous twinkle in her eyes.

"Me? What did I do?"

"Oh, you shouldn't be so hard on him," the woman said. She flashed a smile before she tucked it away, self-conscious, but it was enough for Gage to see how powerfully disarming it was. "This is my man in shining armor. I don't want him mad at me."

Her voice still retained some roughness, but it was already much improved. He also thought he caught a touch of an accent, just a hint in the way she carried her R's, but it was faint and inconsistent. Boston, maybe? It was hard to say.

"Him?" Zoe said. "I was there, too. Without me, we couldn't have even called the ambulance."

"My *two* knights," the woman said. To Gage, she added, "She was just telling me about your cell phone."

"Oh, that," Gage said.

"I'm going to get him another one," Zoe said.

"You'll do no such thing."

"If anyone gets him a replacement," the woman said, "it'll be me. I'm the reason he dropped it in the water. I just, um, I don't have any money right now." She laughed a little, but her face also darkened. "Or even know how to get it, I guess."

"So you don't remember anything yet?" Gage asked.

"No. I'm sorry."

"Does the name Marcus Koura ring a bell?"

Her forehead, more pink than tan, wrinkled. Those thin eyebrows dropped. She pondered it for quite a while, and the pondering seemed authentic to Gage. But then, good acting would seem authentic, wouldn't it? He wanted to believe her, though. That was obvious to him already, and it troubled him, how quickly he was willing to drop his objectivity. Was it just because she was beautiful? My God, she was beautiful, like some rare bird who'd crashed onto his doorstep. Or was it the knight in shining armor bit? He knew he was a sucker for damsels in distress.

"No," she said. "Why? Is that somebody I should know?"

"Apparently he owns the boat."

"Oh. And he … he wasn't in it?"

"No. You don't remember anything at all?"

"I'm sorry," she said.

"Even your childhood?"

"I just … I remember waking up on that boat."

"On the beach, you said, 'He'll find me.' What did you mean by that?"

"I did?"

"You don't remember that either?"

She rubbed her temples with both hands, hard enough to make the skin around her fingers turn white. "No … No, there's nothing there. It's just all dark right now. Fuzzy. I wish I could. I know this must all seem very silly—girl shows up on the beach, has amnesia. I'm sorry. Really, I am."

"Let's make a deal," Gage said. "No more apologies. You've been through a lot and we're just trying to help you. You get some rest, get some fluids in you, it'll probably start coming back to you in the morning."

"Okay. I appreciate it. I really do—both of you, helping me. If I was in your shoes, I don't know if I would believe me."

"You've given me no reason to doubt you."

Zoe snorted. They both looked at her, and her expression, at first bemused, turned sheepish. "Sorry," she said. "It's just, that's so like you. The way you put it."

"And how did I put it?" Gage asked.

"You know."

"No. I don't. Enlighten me."

Instead of answering Gage, Zoe turned to the woman. "Garrison is a private investigator. The best. I mean, he's even been on TV and stuff. If anybody can help you, he can."

"Oh," the woman said.

"He also doesn't ever really turn that part of himself off."

"I see," the woman said. Gage couldn't tell if she sounded pleased or unhappy about this information. "It's almost like fate then, right? I just wish I had some money to pay you. It's not like you should work for free."

"I wouldn't take it even if you had it," Gage said. "Listen, we need to let you get some rest. The cops are going to show up in the morning."

The fear he'd seen in her eyes on the beach flared up again. He watched as her fingers, ever so slightly, clenched the bedspread.

"They are?" she said.

"Not until ten. I asked the chief to give you at least until then to recover. It'll probably all come back to you by then anyway. And in the meantime, they'll do some checking on this Marcus Koura, see what they can find. Maybe he's your husband. Or a friend. Maybe you borrowed the boat and got caught in that bad storm a couple weeks ago, got hit in the head by the mast or something. By tomorrow night, we'll probably have you on a plane headed home."

The woman contemplated her left hand. "No wedding ring," she said. "You'd think I'd remember a husband."

"Give it time," Gage said.

"Will you be here? Tomorrow?"

"I will."

The woman looked at Zoe. "And you?"

"I'll come by later," Zoe said. "I'm working at the Turret House, and, well, I don't like cops very much."

"Who does?" Gage said. "They have no sense of humor, they can't dance, and they give out way too many traffic tickets."

The woman laughed. Something also changed briefly, in her face, a glimmer of awareness.

"What is it?" Gage asked.

"The traffic ticket," she said. "It made me … I thought I remembered something. Getting a ticket. Or somebody with me getting a ticket. There was a nice car, some … some big buildings … Oh, God. It's gone. I thought I had something there. It's like, the more I try to reach for it, the more it pushes away."

The door opened. A woman in a white coat entered brusquely, a pretty blonde focused intently on the iPad in her hand. Gage recognized her. He had seen her at the little market near his house a couple times over the last year, often late, another night owl. They'd exchanged glances, the kind that bordered on flirtation without quite being so. Then, like now, she wore her beauty like an uncomfortable set of clothes, as if she had bought a manual on how to look good as a woman, mastered it merely as a necessity, then moved on to more worthy challenges. Luxurious curls with a golden sheen, just a touch of green eye shadow, a certain kind of compact voluptuousness that could only be gained from just the right series of machines at the gym—it all added up to a well-put-together modern woman.

She looked up, sweeping her gaze across them, a gaze that lingered on Gage an extra second, before she turned her attention to the woman in the bed. A tiny gold pendant with the letters C and K with tiny diamonds hung around her neck. No wedding ring—not that an absence of a ring seemed to mean much these days. He wondered who CK was. Or what it was.

"Hello, I'm Dr. Brunner," she said. There was an accent there. Russian, maybe, faint but still strong enough that he doubted she was born in the United States. "You saw me in the ER, but things were a little hectic. I hope, now that you are not so dehydrated, that you are starting to feel better?"

"Yes," said the woman in the bed. "I am. Thank you. I'm just so … I really appreciate everyone helping me."

"No memory, though?"

"No."

"Well, don't worry about it too much," Dr. Brunner said. Her accent, a little soft on the W's, a slight rolling of the R's, seemed to drift in and out like a faint radio signal. Most of the time it wasn't there at all. "Let us see how you feel in the morning. You have no obvious signs of concussion, but we can do some tests tomorrow if you still don't remember." She looked at Gage and Zoe. "And you two, who are you?"

"I'm a candy striper," Gage said. "Can't you tell by my outfit?"

The doctor did not smile, not even a smirk, so Gage did not

expect her response. "Where are the balloons?" she asked, dead-pan.

"These are my friends," said the woman in the bed. "They found me on the beach. Garrison Gage. He's a private investigator. And his daughter Zoe … or am I wrong? I know I'm assuming. You did call him Garrison, not Dad, so …"

"It's complicated," Zoe said, "but, yeah, I sort of think of him as my dad."

"And I think I'm pretty darn lucky," Gage said, "to be in this room with three beautiful women."

Their reactions to the compliment were all unique, an eye roll from Zoe, a blush from the woman in the bed, and a narrowing of the eyes from Dr. Brunner, a look that might have meant she was pleased, perturbed, or anything in between.

"Interesting," she said. "Does this sort of general flattery usually work for you?"

"Define work," Gage said.

"Hmm. Well, in any case, I think we need to let our patient rest." She smiled at the woman in the bed, and the gesture was like her clothes, practiced, even genuine, but a little too perfect to be completely natural. "Hopefully, I can put something other than 'Jane Doe' in your file tomorrow."

"Doctor," Gage said, "one other thing …"

"Another random compliment?"

"Maybe later. It's about the 'Jane Doe' thing. Her story has quite a human interest element. I know how these things work. When this gets out, we're going to have some press around here wanting to talk to her. Do you think you could …"

"I will make sure she has no visitors," Dr. Brunner said.

"Thank you," Gage said.

"Other than these two!" the woman in the bed said.

"Of course," Dr. Brunner said. She tapped a few times on her tablet, all business, so again her response surprised him. "We always make exceptions for candy stripers and their sort-of daughters around here."

* * *

THE NEXT MORNING, Gage arrived at Books and Oddities a little after eight. The store did not officially open until nine on a Thursday, but Gage was not surprised to find Alex's green Toyota van in the gravel parking lot, the first car there, nor that he had turned on the neon orange open sign.

None of the other dozen shops in the funky Horseshoe Mall bothered to open before ten, even if the owners did show up early, as the tourist crowd that was the lifeblood of the Barnacle Bluffs economy, such as it was, barely ever crawled out of their hotel rooms before then. But the bookstore was more than a job to Gage's longtime friend. Alex may have spent the vast majority of his working life in the FBI—racking up his share of successes along the way—but he'd spent most of those days dreaming of opening a bookshop and a B&B in a quaint coastal town. He would have turned on the open sign even in a monsoon.

There was no monsoon today, the sky a flawless cobalt blue, though it had drizzled briefly during the night as it often did. The rickety boardwalk that connected the stores shimmered with moisture. The United States flag outside the stamp shop billowed in the slight breeze, the air chill enough that Gage kept his chin down until he was safely within the warmth of the bookstore.

Pine bookshelves, buzzing fluorescent lights, and the smell of old books—none of it may have been Gage's dream, but he still loved bookstores, and this one felt like a second home. Something sloughed away whenever he entered, a second skin of stress and worry. The feeling never lasted long, but it was always welcome. A wall of cardboard boxes lined the glass counter, tall enough that Gage could only see the top of his friend's mostly bald head, a shiny scalp visible through thinning gray hair. The swivel chair squeaked.

"That you, Garrison?" Alex said.

Rather than answer, Gage put the white paper sack on the mountain of boxes.

"Chocolate with sprinkles?" Alex said.

"Would I disappoint you?" Gage asked.

"You really want me to answer that?"

Gage stepped past the spinner rack of antique greeting cards to the other side of the counter, where a lighted glass case contained a number of first editions and other rarities—a Civil War era pistol, Indian arrowheads, some baseball cards in Mylar wrappers. Alex, slumped at the computer desk, peered at him over the tops of his reading glasses like a hermit sticking his head out of his hovel. He did not have a mouth so much as a mustache, a thick gray one, and the perpetual bags under his eyes would have seemed darker if not for his already dark complexion. His week cruising in the Mediterranean had made that complexion even darker.

"Figured you'd show up," Alex said. He nodded toward the screen. "There's already a bit about it on the Bugle's website."

Gage leaned his cane against the counter. "They have a website?"

"Yes. A lot of people do now. This Internet thing has really taken off. You should try it sometime."

"Will it work with my manual typewriter?"

"It might. I hear there are even aboriginal tribes in Africa with high-speed satellite access. You know, for when they might want to order loincloths from Amazon.com. Coffee? I've got some of that Irish cream you like so much."

"Of course," Gage said.

Alex shuffled to the back of the store and returned a minute later with two superhero mugs, handing a green one featuring the Hulk to Gage, keeping the blue and red Superman mug for himself. The mug was hot enough that Gage set it on the glass counter, watching the rising tendrils of steam, breathing in the intoxicating aromas of dark coffee and sweet almonds. Alex promptly picked up Gage's coffee mug and slid a paper towel under it, muttering a bit about smudging the glass, then he dipped his hand in the paper sack and retrieved one of the chocolate donuts. With his glasses hanging from their red strap, Alex settled back into his chair, his mug perched on his lap with one hand, his donut in the other.

"Well?" Alex said.

"Well, what?"

"Give me the nitty gritty details."

"There isn't much to tell," Gage said, then explained everything that had happened, from his first encounter with the boat to his last conversation with the woman in the hospital room.

It went so fast that Alex was still nibbling on his donut by the time Gage finished. He ate the last of it, then licked his fingers with great pleasure.

"Amnesia, huh?" Alex said.

"It does seem a little farfetched, doesn't it?"

Alex wiped his hands on a paper towel, tossed it in the trash, then settled back into his squeaky chair. "Depends on what happened to her," he said, taking a long sip of coffee. "I worked a case once where a couple teenage girls completely blacked out all memories of their parents. Talking to them, you'd think they'd raised themselves. Of course, their parents were abusing them in all kinds of terrible ways—until the teens dumped gasoline on them while they were sleeping and lit them on fire. When I saw the bodies in the morgue, there wasn't much left—like they'd been incinerated by flame throwers. The kids didn't have memory of that either."

Gage risked a sip from his own coffee and found it still mildly scalding but at least tolerable. He placed the mug back on the counter. "Sometimes I wonder if you scorch your coffee with a flame thrower. How do you get it so hot?"

"It's my heat vision," Alex said. Grinning, he held up his Superman mug.

"I see. Well, you must have taste buds of steel to drink it like this. So, these kids, how did you know they weren't faking?"

"We didn't. No way to know for sure. Their attorney had two different psychiatrists testify that their memories did appear to be blocked—called it a psychotic break. That and the circumstances of the case got them a pretty light sentence, just time served and probation. Considering what kind of monsters their parents were, nobody was really upset about it … until a year later they set their foster parents on fire, too."

"Yikes," Gage said.

"Yeah. They claimed not to remember that one either. The jury wasn't so forgiving a second time."

"So what are you telling me? That I need to be careful?"

"No, I'm telling you to stop complaining about my coffee. I'm gone two weeks and that's all you can think to say? Of course I'm telling you to be careful. Someone can seem sympathetic, can even be a victim, but still do very bad things. The owner of that boat is missing. Maybe he just fell overboard and the trauma of it made her black the whole thing out."

"And throw out all of their things?"

"It's possible. People do strange things when the primal part of their brain takes over."

"The owner of the boat's name is Marcus Koura. Out of San Jose. You think you can check in with your friends at the FBI, see what they can dig up?"

"I don't have many friends left at the FBI. That's what happens when you stop going to the Christmas parties. But, yes, I'll try. I'll also do some digging of my own on that Internet thing."

"I appreciate it," Gage said. "I'd like to have as much information as possible before the cops run her fingerprints."

"You think they'll do that? Without a warrant?"

"Wouldn't you?"

Alex rubbed his mustache. "Yes, but I wouldn't say anything unless we got something. It wouldn't be the worst thing, I guess. Even if she has a criminal record, at least you'd know who she was."

"I'm concerned about a presumption of guilt before all the facts come in."

"Like the whereabouts of Mr. Koura," Alex said.

"Exactly." Gage took another sip of his coffee and found it had cooled enough that he could actually enjoy the taste. "She's nice, though," he murmured.

"Uh oh," Alex said.

"What?"

"The way you said that. You had a certain tone. I've heard it before. She's a looker, huh?"

"What's that have to do with anything?"

"Everything, if she's your typical love interest."

"I didn't realize I *had* a typical love interest. I've dated blondes, brunettes, redheads—"

"Superficial details," Alex scoffed. "You're drawn to beautiful, broken women who need help being put back together."

"Give me a break."

"It's true. You fix them, or at least help them fix themselves, then you look for the next broken woman. If you had even one ounce of self-awareness, you'd agree with me. Think of all the women who have been in your life. I've known quite a few of them."

"This is ridiculous. I've never liked weak women."

"I didn't say they were weak. Most of them were actually pretty strong, deep down. They just happened to be broken. They needed help getting strong again."

"Janet wasn't broken. I *married* her."

"My point exactly."

"What, you're saying she wasn't my type?"

"No, I think she was exactly your type. You were just wise enough to realize it for once."

"But you just said—"

"I didn't say anything about *type.* I said typical love interest. You fix 'em, then leave 'em."

"Hey! Most of those women left *me.*"

"If that's what you tell yourself," Alex said, taking a sip of his coffee.

Gage hated the smug look on his friend's face. He wasn't willing to concede anything, wasn't even sure he understood what Alex was really saying, but he did know that it was making him angry. Was he really that predictable? He'd never had much interest in sitting in a psychiatrist's chair, or some other silly excuse to waste an hour so that someone who'd spent too much time in college could pay for their trip to Paris each year. What did it matter? He was what he was.

Outside, an eighteen-wheeler rumbled up Highway 101, the vibrations rippling the surface of his coffee. He picked it up to take a sip, then changed his mind and put it back on the paper towel.

He said, "I want to talk to you about Zoe."

"Ah," Alex said.

"I think she's spending way too much time working for you."

"Well, don't beat around the bush, Garrison. Just tell me what you really think."

"I appreciate you giving her a job. I do. After what happened, she needed a bit of a break from college. But it's been six months. It's time for her to get on with her life."

"Maybe this is her life."

"Now you're just *trying* to make me angry."

"I'm not saying she won't go back to school," Alex said. "I'm saying she has to find her own path. We all do, eventually. Knowing Zoe, if you try to force the issue, she'll just push you away."

"I don't know how much more she *can* push me away."

Alex studied Gage's face, steam rising from the mug in his lap. "So that's what this is really about, then."

"Oh no, here we go. You have another diagnosis, Dr. Freud?"

"You're having a hard time letting her go."

"I wanted her to go *away* to college!" Gage insisted. "At least to OSU or U of O, which would have been hours from here. How's that having a hard time letting her go? She would have been in a different city, maybe even a different state. She's so smart, she really needs to go to a school that will give her the best opportunity to succeed."

"Yeah, that would have made it easier for you."

"What?"

"I'm seeing some definite parallels here to the other thing we just talked about."

"Oh God," Gage said.

"If you can send her away, you can consider her all fixed,

then you can move on."

"Jesus! Are you trying to get me to punch you? I'm not going to *move on* from Zoe. How can you even say such a thing? She's like a daughter to me."

"*Like* a daughter?" Alex said.

"What now?"

"Why not just … daughter?"

"Come on, Alex. It's just a way of putting it. It means the same thing."

"Does it?"

Gage sighed. "All right, I've had enough of this. You're obviously going to be no help whatsoever, and I've got to get to the hospital. I want to be there when the police question her. Will you at least think about giving Zoe a nudge? I know you like having your own personal slave, but I think she could do better than changing sheets and shelving romance books."

"Now who's being unfair?"

"Will you talk to her?"

"Nope," Alex said.

Gritting his teeth, Gage snatched up the paper sack. "Fine. I'm not bringing you any more donuts. They seem to make you punchy."

"It's the chocolate," Alex said. "It's like meth to me. Say hello to your new fixer-upper. I look forward to meeting her."

With a snort, Gage grabbed his cane. He needed to make a quick exit before he could no longer restrain himself from beaning Alex on the head. Maybe that would make him a little less flippant, a little less likely to share his homespun psychoanalysis. Gage hadn't hit anyone on the head with his cane in a long time. It would certainly feel good. He opened the door, cool air flitting inside, then turned and glared at Alex over his shoulder.

"You're just lucky I like Eve so much," he growled. "I'd give you a black eye, but I'd feel bad that she'd have to look at your sorry-ass face all day."

"Good to know," Alex said. "Oh, and that reminds me. Eve wants you to come to dinner on Friday. She's making that pistachio baklava you like so much. You up for it?"

"Will I have to listen to more bullshit about my love life?"

"Probably."

"I guess I can't miss it, then."

"Excellent. Oh, if she's able to by then, you can bring your fixer-upper, too."

"I'm leaving," Gage said.

"I love you, Garrison."

"Shut up."

Chapter 3

The police were already questioning their mystery woman by the time Gage arrived at the hospital, a whole half hour before Chief Quinn had said he'd be there.

Gage had no doubt the move was deliberate. Quinn was probably hoping to get her alone. He'd also brought his best detectives with him, Brisbane and Trenton, which, of course, wasn't saying much. The young male cop from the beach, the athletic one with the baby face, was also there, the four of them looming over the bed like buzzards in gray trench coats—even the kid, who wore his coat over his police uniform while the others were all decked out in open-collared shirts and dark slacks.

Irritated at how many of them there were, Gage rounded to the other side of the bed, nudging past Brisbane to stand as close to the woman's bed as possible. The morning chill had gotten to his knee, producing a dull ache, and he leaned against his cane for support. He hated having to rely on the damn thing in front of so many testosterone-driven knuckleheads.

"These bullies bothering you?" he said to her.

She smiled at him, and he was pleased to see that a night's sleep had done her a world of good. The morning light, slanting in from the window, fell in the gap between them and lit up her face like a soft-glow spotlight. She looked even better than yesterday, more color in her cheeks, more shine in her eyes. She'd obviously showered at some point, her red hair fuller, more vibrant.

"Not even a little," she replied. "They're actually very nice."

"Give them time," Gage said.

Brisbane groaned. If there had been a casting call for someone to play the opposite of the baby-faced cop, they'd found their man in Brisbane. Rumpled, wrinkled, and perpetually bedraggled, he always made Gage think he slept in a bus depot. The bags under his eyes were so deep they could have stored loose change. Not once had Gage seen Brisbane make an attempt to comb his thinning gray hair—not that it would have mattered much, there was so little of it. "I was really hoping you wouldn't show up," Brisbane said. "We could do without your smart-ass remarks for once."

"Aw," Gage said, "I think that's the sweetest thing you've ever said to me. Besides, if I'm not here to say smart-ass things, then there wouldn't be anything smart said at all, would there?"

Trenton shook his head. Where his partner resembled a pile of dirty laundry, Trenton was like a stack of shirts that had been washed with too much starch then ironed to a flat dullness. His trench coat, at least six inches too short, made him seem even taller than he was, and that was plenty tall—a full head taller than Gage, who topped out at around six feet on his best days. Trenton also had one thing in common with their mystery woman: bright red hair. It didn't suit him nearly as well. "I don't see why you feel the need to be part of this," he whined. "All you did was find her. It's not like you have anything new to add."

"I *want* him here," the woman said.

They all stared at her, nobody bothering to argue. What could they say? Gage smiled warmly at her.

"Thank you," he said. "If I could, I'd snap my fingers and make them all disappear."

"Oh, don't say that," the woman said. "They want to help, too."

Still smiling, Gage peered across the bed at Quinn. "I'd like to believe that," he said.

The chief sighed. He had also tidied up since last night, his face clean-shaven, the grease-stained T-shirt replaced by a bright white dress shirt and thin blue tie. "We all just want to find out what happened here, Gage. We don't need to make this more difficult than it has to be."

"But making things difficult for you is my purpose in life," Gage said.

"Tell me about it. Anyway, we were just asking ..." Quinn trailed off, looking down at the woman. "You know, until your memory returns, or we get some information about who you are, you're going to have to come up with something for us to call you."

"So still no memory then?" Gage asked.

"No," the woman said, and for the first time since he'd entered the room, her face darkened. "I'm sorry. I've been trying."

"How about we just call you Jane Doe?" Brisbane asked.

"No," Gage said.

"You got something better in mind?" Brisbane said.

"I'll let her decide," Gage said, "but it certainly won't be the name you give to unidentified dead women."

"We could call her Hope," the young cop said.

He'd blurted it out so suddenly that they all gaped at him. He blushed. It was an honest to God blush, not some dusting of pink but a deep crimson that spread like wildfire across his cheeks and down his neck. Gage could only imagine the ribbing that kind of blush elicited from the grizzled cops he worked with every day. He felt sorry for the kid—to a point. The kid was a cop, after all.

"Gage," Quinn said, motioning to the kid, "this is Officer Zachary Gilbert. He's in training to be a detective, so you might see him tagging along now and then."

"I remember you from the beach," Gage said.

"Yes, sir," Zachary said. "Nice to meet you, sir."

"Don't call him sir," Trenton said.

"Yes, sir," Zachary said. "I mean, what should I call him then, sir?"

"Don't call him anything. Pretend like he's not here. Pretend like he's wallpaper."

"Oh, please don't," the woman said. "I really don't want you all arguing. Hope is a very nice name, but I'm ... I'll think of something. Hope is a little too ... I don't know, *cheerful* than I feel right now. I'm trying to stay positive, but I ... I don't know ..."

"Fine," Quinn said, "we'll skip it for now. Maybe it will all come back to you today anyway. As I was saying, we were just asking if she had any memory at all of Marcus Koura."

The woman took a deep breath. "And I don't, unfortunately."

"I imagine," Gage said, "that you've all done your own research into the whereabouts of Marcus Koura?"

Quinn studied the woman's face, as if he was deciding something, then shrugged. "I'm going to be honest with you, ma'am. It doesn't look good right now. Marcus Koura is missing. The last time anyone in San Jose saw him, he was on that boat a month ago, starting what was supposed to be a voyage to Puerto Vallarta, then up to Seattle and back. I guess he was practicing to sail around the world, taking his time about it. That's what his brother told us—Omar. He lives down there, too. They were partners in an e-commerce company, something about money transfers. I don't know. Sounded too much like gobbledygook to me, but apparently they made a ton of money. Any of this ring a bell?"

"No," the woman said.

"Well, I asked Omar about you. He didn't know you. He said Marcus sailed out alone and he was there to see him off. Marcus had broken up with his long-term girlfriend a couple months before he sailed and she didn't look anything like you."

"Strange," the woman murmured.

"Isn't it?" Quinn said. "See, I'm trying to figure out where you entered the picture. And where, exactly, Marcus left it."

"Maybe she hitchhiked aboard," Gage said.

"I don't know," the woman said. "I wish ... I *am* telling you the truth. I really don't know."

"Don't get upset," Quinn said. "I know this is hard. But you have to understand how it looks to us. The sooner we find out what happened, the sooner you can focus completely on your recovery."

"How about she focuses on her recovery first," Gage said, "and then she'll be better able to help you figure out what happened."

"See," Trenton said, pointing at Gage. "See, that's all he does. He just makes things difficult for everybody."

"It's my mission in life," Gage said.

Quinn glared at Gage, which went a lot further than Trenton's schoolboy whine in communicating how seriously the police were taking this situation. "You have two options, Gage. You can be a help or a hindrance. If you're a hindrance, I will make sure you are completely cut out of the loop on this. Are we clear?"

"Clear as salt water," Gage said.

"Gage—"

"Did Omar say where Marcus might have stopped on his way up the coast?" Gage asked.

Quinn sighed. "No. He didn't leave an itinerary."

"He's his brother," Gage said. "They were obviously close if they were partners. He must have some idea where he stopped."

"Well, you can ask him yourself," Quinn said. "He's flying into Portland tonight, then driving over. Should be here Friday morning."

"He's coming here?" the woman said.

There was such a plaintive note of worry in her voice that it stopped the conversation cold. When they all looked at her, she blushed—not quite as red as poor Zachary's, but pretty darn close.

"It's not because I remember him," she said. "It's just—he's going to be angry. Don't you think he'll be angry with me?"

"Come on," Brisbane growled, "why do you think he'd be angry with you unless you know what he's like?"

"I don't, I don't," she insisted.

"I think it's time you cut the crap," Brisbane said.

"I think it's time you back off," Gage said.

"Or what?" Brisbane said. "You going to hit me with your cane like always do when you're pissed off?"

"Only if you ask nicely. I might be able to make your head look a little more even."

"Shut up, you two," Quinn said. "I swear I'm surrounded by children."

"Please stop," the woman begged, "please, please stop. No fighting. I can't have any fighting around me right now. I just can't."

The well-composed woman who'd greeted him when he walked inside was now completely gone, replaced by a nervous, fidgety creature, full of anxious blinking and jerky movements. He counted at least three separate tics. She clutched repeatedly at the bedspread, her little fingers curling as tightly as claws before relaxing, tightening and relaxing over and over again. Her left cheek twitched uncontrollably, and the corner of her lip also spasmed. The tears, only a few at first, turned into a torrent, and she sniffled and blinked, a hot mess now, staring up at them all like a deer who'd been shot might stare at the hunter loping his way toward her.

It was in that moment that Gage realized two things. She wasn't acting. At least, she wasn't acting *now*. There was still a chance that she was withholding the truth from them, either consciously or subconsciously, but nobody was so good they could fake that kind of fearful display. Were they? Fearful was the right word, because that was the other, more important thing that Gage realized.

This woman had been abused. He didn't know how, or by whom, but someone, most likely a man, had physically hurt her in the past. The recent past.

Gage reached over and took her hand, slowly and obviously, letting her see him do it, the way he might try to reach for a whipped dog. Her skin felt warm and clammy, layered with sweat, a bad sign. She did, however, start to calm down immediately, less fidgeting, the tics subsiding. She focused only on him, those big aquamarine eyes wide and bright, and he saw an emotion there that troubled him far more than the fear did: adoration. It wasn't just the adoration. It was how good seeing it made him feel. He thought of his conversation with Alex. She was broken all right and she definitely needed fixing. Why was that so wrong? Why did he feel so uneasy about it?

"We'll get to the bottom of this," he said.

"I want to remember," she said, sniffling.

"I know."

"I'm not trying … trying to play games."

"Things will clear up soon," Gage said.

She wiped away her tears with the bedspread. Stupidly, they all stood and watched, nobody saying anything until finally Quinn cleared his throat.

"Well," he said, "we'll make some calls, see if Koura talked to anyone else before starting his cruise. Maybe someone will know who you are. His brother made it seem like Marcus didn't have a lot of friends, but you never know."

"And maybe she got picked up somewhere else," Zachary said. When he had everybody's attention, he hesitated. "You know, at a port along the way. Maybe he stopped somewhere up the coast."

"That's crazy," Trenton said. "Why would he pick up someone he didn't even know?"

"It's just a theory," Zachary said. "I mean, he'd broken up with his girlfriend not long ago. He was probably lonely. I know what that's like." He blushed again—not a fire-truck red this time, thank God, but still an obvious shade of pink. "I mean, I broke up with my girlfriend a couple months ago. That's all I meant. He might have been open to meeting someone."

Gage was impressed. He'd been thinking the same thing himself, though he had decided not to share it. He wasn't all that eager to help the police find out who the woman was before he did. "It would certainly be worth calling all the ports up and down the coast," he said.

Trenton snorted. "That's a lot of ports."

"Around a hundred," Gage said.

"What are you now, a nautical expert?"

"Nope," Gage said, "just read a bunch. Washington has the most because of all the islands up there, something like seventy. You'd think California would have more, but they only have about a dozen. Oregon's somewhere in the middle with twenty-three. That's without even getting to Alaska or Mexico, which both have a ton."

"How fascinating," Trenton said.

"You read at all, Trenton? I can get you a library card. They have a huge assortment of picture books you might like."

"I hope no one thinks I'm some kind of floozy," the woman said.

Everybody started speaking at once—a mortified Zachary mumbling his apology, an angry Trenton shooting a retort about the kind of people who hang out in libraries, Gage offering some reassuring words to the woman, and Brisbane just generally mumbling to himself—until Quinn raised his hand, silencing them.

"Enough," he said. "We're not accomplishing anything with all this. I think it's time we leave Miss ... well, you need to think of what you want to call yourself. And please do it soon. But we'll let you get some more rest in the meantime. I think it goes without saying that I don't want you leaving town, right? Not until this all gets sorted out."

"Yes, sir," the woman said meekly. "But I can't ... I don't have a place to stay right now. And I know the hospital won't just let me stay here forever."

From the doorway, Zoe said, "You can stay at the Turret House."

Gage had no idea how long she'd been standing there, though from the way she leaned against the door frame with her arms crossed, he guessed it'd been a while. Again, he had to marvel at her transformation. The powder-blue cardigan over the white open-collared shirt, the pleated tan slacks, the matching open-soled sandals that showed off toenails painted the same shade of blue as her sweater—if he hadn't been witness to her change in appearance the past few months and had passed her on the street, he may not have even recognized her. Topping off her outfit with just a touch of pink lipstick and some dangly blue crystal earrings, she looked at least ten years older than her actual age. It broke his heart.

"Alex is okay with it?" Gage asked.

"It was his idea, actually."

"What's the Turret House?" the woman asked.

"A bed and breakfast," Zachary jumped in, before either Zoe or Gage could reply. "The best in town. Really nice people who run the place. You couldn't—couldn't do any better."

He said this to the group, but he was only looking at Zoe when he did. It wasn't just a normal look, either, it was one of *those* looks, the kind a young man gives a woman when he's keenly aware of everything about her that's womanly. That was disturbing enough for Gage, who, despite recognizing Zoe's recent change in appearance and actual age of adulthood, refused to see her as anything but the sixteen-year-old kid she'd been when he'd adopted her. What was even more disturbing was that Zoe was looking right back at Zachary in pretty much the same way.

"That's very nice of you," she said.

"I mean every word."

"I'll … I'll tell Alex."

"It's the truth," Zachary said. "My mom stayed there when she visited. She raved about the place. I think she even wrote a review on Yelp." He glanced at everyone else, apparently realizing that he and Zoe weren't the only ones in the room. "Um, she never does that sort of thing."

"Glad that's sorted out," Quinn said. "All right, everybody, let's leave her in peace. If I don't find you here, ma'am, I expect to find you at the Turret House."

"I won't leave town," the woman said. "But Garrison, Zoe, if you could stay a minute. Just to sort out things."

"Don't worry," Zoe said, "we're not leaving."

She said it defiantly, as if she expected someone to challenge her. Gage cheered inwardly. The tone in her voice, her crossed arms, and the glare in her eyes were all signs that the old Zoe hadn't gone far, and there was no way someone like *that* was going to end up as Alex's assistant her whole life.

Wisely, no one did challenge her, and the cops said their goodbyes and departed. Zachary was the last to go, and there was a bit of an awkward shuffle as he and Zoe passed each other in the doorway, each looking at the other while trying not to make it obvious they were looking. It would have been a comical display to Gage if he didn't find it so disturbing. Please, no, not a cop. She can date anyone but a cop.

Fortunately, there was no exchange of phone numbers, emails, or whatever young people did these days, just a couple of embarrassed smiles. When it was just the three of them in the room, Gage turned his attention back to the woman in the bed.

The woman.

He couldn't go on calling her that. It was too impersonal, too dehumanizing—maybe not as dehumanizing as Jane Doe, but not much better.

"Well," Gage said, "Quinn was right about one thing. Until your memory comes back, we do need to call you something. You got a name in mind?"

"No," she said. "I do like the name Zoe, though. It's very pretty."

"Thank you," Zoe said.

"I suppose Jane would be fine for now. If that's what they want to call me …"

"No, we can do better than that," Zoe said.

"She's kind of like a mermaid," Gage said. "You know, she came from the ocean? You could go by the name of that girl from the Disney movie. What was her name?"

"Ariel?" Zoe said.

"Yeah, that's the one."

"Yuck," Zoe said. "That's the worst idea ever. Do you know how oppressive and subversive that imagery is to girls entering puberty?"

"There's my girl!" Gage said.

"Shut up."

The woman in bed rubbed her temples. "I just wish I could remember," she said. "I don't know why I can't remember. I know the cops think I'm … I'm guilty of something."

"Well," Gage said, "look on the bright side. At least they didn't read you your Miranda rights."

The woman sat up straighter in the bed. "That's it," she said.

"What?"

"The name. Miranda. You can call me Miranda."

Gage thought about it. "Hmm. I'm not thrilled with the legal connection on that one either, but it's a lot better than Jane Doe."

"Shakespeare also had a Miranda," Zoe said. "In *The Tempest*. It kind of fits that way. It was probably that bad storm that brought her to Barnacle Bluffs."

"That's right," Gage said. "Prospero's daughter. He and Miranda were banished to an island. It's a good play, one of my favorites. *We are such stuff as dreams are made on, and our little life is rounded with a sleep.*"

"That's a good one," Zoe said, smiling at him. "There's another one that fits even better. *What's past is prologue.*"

"Ah, yes," Gage said. "How about this one: *Hell is empty and all the devils are here.*"

"Talking about the cops again?" Zoe said *"Full fathom five thy father lies."*

"Misery acquaints a man with strange bedfellows."

"Your tale, sir, would cure deafness."

"My library," Gage said, *"was dukedom large enough."*

Zoe opened her mouth to reply, then shook her head and smiled wryly. "You win this time."

"Well," the woman said, "there's no doubt about *your* memory, at least."

"Sorry," Zoe said sheepishly. "It's a little contest we have sometimes. I know it's probably annoying."

"No, no, it's very cute," the woman hurriedly said and Gage

could already see how she could never stand to let even the possibility that she might have offended someone linger in the air for a second. "I just feel so lucky that it was you two who found me. Miranda it is then—at least, until I figure out who I *really* am."

"Miranda," Gage said, nodding.

"Miranda," Zoe agreed.

"In from the storm," Miranda said.

Chapter 4

Gage took Miranda to the Turret House late that afternoon. Dr. Brunner—whose first name Gage learned was Tatyana—agreed to discharge her only on the condition that Miranda visit a doctor every day until everybody was certain there wasn't some sort of physical trauma that had gone undetected.

When Miranda said she had no insurance or money, and before Gage could jump in to offer to pay, Tatyana said it would be no problem; she would do the checkups herself at no charge. They couldn't be at the hospital, but she would be willing to do the checkups at the Turret House. She scribbled her number on a yellow sticky and handed it to Gage. He wondered if there was something to that, her giving the number to him instead of to Miranda, but he saw nothing in her brusque manner to indicate that she was even remotely flirting with him.

Still, he liked her quite a bit already. House calls? What kind of doctor made house calls, and for free? There was also that faint echo of a Russian accent, a hint of a complicated past. He wanted to know about that past, as well as what the letters CK on her necklace represented.

Was he trying to fix her too? He hated that Alex had gotten into his head.

Since it took some time to get her checked out of the hospital, and Zoe left early to get back to the Turret House to help Eve clean the rooms, it was just Gage and Miranda driving south on Highway 101. The '71 Volkswagen van, which had been completely rebuilt and repainted after the wreck last year, still grumbled and protested at any speed over forty—the floorboards rattling, the wind whistling through all the gaps and cracks.

Gage wouldn't have it any other way. The old van had been with him as long as he had lived in Barnacle Bluffs.

"She likes you," Miranda said.

Gage looked at her. She was gazing ahead rather than at him, and when she realized he was staring at her she glanced at him and smiled furtively before returning her attention to the road. The sun was already low enough in the western sky, shining over the rooftops of the hotels and shops, that he had to squint. The light brightened her hair, brought out hints of blonde; except for her bangs, she had it tied back in a tight ponytail with a rubber band. It made her face seem even more gaunt than it was, but there was a healthy glow now, as if each passing hour brought more life back into her.

The pair of jeans and gray Oregon Coast T-shirt a nurse had rustled up for her were a couple sizes too large. Of course, with how thin she was, just about any clothes would have been too large.

"Who, Zoe?" he said.

"No, the doctor. Tatyana. She's obviously into you."

"I think you're imagining things."

"She's very pretty. And smart, too. You should ask her out."

"Oh, I don't know." Gage shrugged.

"Not your type?" Miranda said, chuckling softly. "I'm sorry, I shouldn't assume. You probably already have a girlfriend."

She said this nonchalantly, but Gage caught something else in a voice, a hint of worry. He noticed her kneading at her jeans with her fingers, something he'd seen her do with the bedspread earlier.

"Not right now," Gage said. "I seem to scare all women away

eventually."

"Oh, I doubt that."

"I'm just too charming for them, I think."

"Hmm."

"There's only so much charm a woman can take. There's like a charm threshold, I've found. You go over that threshold, and it's, 'Hit the road, Jack.' It's why I've vowed to be a lot less charming to women, really embrace my inner rudeness. It's a work in progress, but I think I'm getting better."

"I'm sure that's it," Miranda said, smiling. He was glad to see that the joking had put her at least somewhat at ease, that she'd stopped the gentle clawing at her jeans. "But I'm still willing to bet a few women have stuck around for a while."

"Yeah, one did," Gage said. "I even married her."

"Oh. Is she still—I mean, are you two …"

"No."

"Divorced?"

"Died, actually," Gage said.

"Oh. I'm … I'm so sorry."

"It's okay. It's been over seven years."

She nodded, but didn't seem to know what to say, her face much more grim, full of the kind of sympathy that always made Gage uncomfortable. How did they venture into this territory? Maybe it was because she was a kind of blank slate, but there was something disarming about Miranda, something that made him want to lower his guard and open up to her. He rolled down the window a crack, hoping the cool ocean air would also alter the mood.

"It's a long story," he said. "I still miss her, and it still hurts, but just not as much. I can at least carry on something of a normal life now."

"Well, that's … that's good."

"Her name is Janet. Was Janet."

"I'm sure I would have liked her."

"It was impossible not to like her," he said, which was true. She seemed to have the opposite effect on people that he did.

Everybody liked Janet.

To change the subject, he asked Miranda if she liked salt water taffy, saying that Barnacle Bluffs had some of the best salt water taffy on the whole western coast. She said she didn't know but she'd be glad to try it. He'd been hoping the quick question would jar a memory loose, but no such luck.

They were halfway to the Turret House when he realized he couldn't very well take her there with only a pair of jeans and a T-shirt to her name. Fortunately, they were just coming up on Arrow Shopping Center, the outlet mall in the middle of town that he always thought of as one of Dante's missing circles, and he asked Miranda if she had enough energy to spend an hour in hell with him.

When she looked at him, perplexed, he veered into the sprawling parking lot. She started to protest immediately, saying she didn't have any money, didn't want to burden him or waste his time, but he ignored her. She went on arguing. It was only when they'd parked, gotten out of the van, and were standing outside on the sidewalk that ringed the fifty or so stores that made up the mall that he finally offered a response.

"Look," he said, "you have to have some clothes and whatever else you need. Just pretend you flew in somewhere on vacation and they lost your luggage. It's no big deal."

"I can't—" she began.

"Yes," he said firmly, "you *can*. You can always pay me back later."

"Garrison—"

"Come on, there's a women's clothing store over there."

He took off for it, Miranda following in his wake, still protesting. Only a smattering of people loaded with shopping bags filled the sidewalks—a far cry from the last time he'd braved the mall, when he'd made the mistake of visiting during August back-to-school season and the hordes of people quickly helped him decide that he really didn't need more socks after all. The afternoon sun brightly illuminated the eastern half of the mall and left the western half in shadow. A cool breeze funneled along the sidewalk, skittering tags, receipts, and gum wrappers over otherwise pristine concrete. He smelled grilling hamburgers and baking pizza. They passed a child carrying an ice cream cone and he told Miranda if she was good he'd buy her one, too.

It took her a while to warm up to the idea of shopping, skimming through the racks with only mild interest, clucking about prices, but when he started picking things out himself, saying that if she didn't start choosing some clothes he would do it for her, she became much more focused. It wasn't long before she was loaded up with shirts, pants, shorts, and shoes, enough loot that they had to deposit the bags in the van before heading out again. She was a bit embarrassed about shopping for panties and bras, saying she could take care of that kind of thing later, but he handed her his credit card and told her to buy what she needed while he waited outside on the bench.

He watched people pass, his cane on his lap. A little boy asked him if he needed help. He thought about giving the kid a good rap on the head, but the mother was right behind him and he doubted she would approve. Instead he smiled and said, no, he was just holding the cane for someone else, and fortunately the mother ushered the kid along before he could ask any more questions. When Miranda came out, another bag in tow, she was crying.

"What is it?" he said.

"You're just being so nice," she said.

"Oh. I'll try not to make a habit of it."

"I don't know why you—why you think I deserve this."

"Why do you think you don't?"

"I don't know."

He stood, his balky knee giving him a bit of trouble, causing him to bobble forward just a step. Maybe he should have taken the kid's help after all. Miranda's tear-streaked face was right there, inches away, and before he could back away, she leaned forward and kissed him. It was just a quick peck, more chaste than passionate, but it was directly on the lips. Her eyes flew wide open in the middle of it and she leaned back suddenly, clutching the black shopping bag to her chest.

"I'm sorry," she said.

"It's all right," he said.

"I shouldn't have done that."

"It's no big deal. Really."

"I'm really sorry."

"Was I that bad of a kisser?" Gage asked.

"What?"

"If you say you're sorry one more time, I'm going to slap you. The stress of this place is getting to me and I need an excuse to hit someone. Come on, let's get some ice cream."

They dropped off her last bag and bought ice cream from the shop on the corner, him with a double scoop of peppermint on a big waffle cone and her with a child's size dollop of fudge chocolate in a paper bowl about the size of the tiny cups that fast food restaurants used for ketchup and other condiments. Still, with him chomping away at his and her nibbling tiny bites with her spoon, they finished about the same time. The tears were long gone and she was smiling and laughing at his jokes, none of which were very funny, almost all of which came at the expense of the various people strolling around on the sidewalks.

When they were finished and heading back to the van, they passed an art supply store when she stopped suddenly and gazed at an easel and paints on display. The sun had long since dipped behind the buildings, dusk settling into the mall, and the lights from the store cast a soft yellow glow on her face. She leaned closer, her breath fogging the glass. There was something different in her eyes, something less hesitant and fearful.

"Could we—could we look?" she asked.

"Sure. Do you remember something?"

"I don't ... I don't know."

Inside, she wandered through the narrow, brightly lit aisles with her eyes wide and her hands clasped tightly, as if afraid to touch anything. He caught a whiff of a sharp smell, sharp enough to make his nose prickle; it reminded him of gasoline, some kind of aerosol preservative, maybe.

The store bustled with activity, the clerks busy with customers, an excited chatter in the air. What was the best brush to use with acrylics? What kind of colored pencils worked well with watercolors? The conversations brought back memories of some of the parties Gage used to attend in New York with Janet, who'd spent her life working in museums and often surrounded herself with artists even though she'd insisted she didn't have an artistic bone in her body. She just liked the vibe, she used to say. And even though he never quite got comfortable with the pseudo-intellectual mumbo jumbo that seemed to be the primary mode of communication in that crowd, he'd also liked the vibe—the one coming from Janet.

Gage grabbed a shopping basket and tried to hand it to Miranda. "Knock yourself out," he said.

"Oh no," she said, "I couldn't."

"It might help you remember. You're obviously drawn to the place—sorry, bad pun."

She clenched her hands even tighter, too mesmerized by her surroundings to take note of his meager attempts at humor. She tentatively spun a color pinwheel, but otherwise refused to touch anything else. When she said she was ready to go, her eyes watery and bright, Gage shook his head and quickly filled his basket with a drawing pad, colored pencils, gummy erasers, some acrylic paints, and some brushes, all while she pleaded with him not to spend any more money on her.

"Be quiet," he said, "or I'll buy that easel over in the corner, too."

"But I don't even know if I'm an artist!"

"Guess you'll find out."

She was still arguing even when the clerk rang up the items, not even stopping when the transaction was complete and they were headed to the door. He tried to hand her the bag to go with her others, but she refused to take it, telling him he would just have to return it, this was one gift she wasn't going to accept. He told her that the more she protested, the more convinced he was that she needed to at least try these things.

They continued their animated conversation as they stepped outside, into a brisk wind that hit them full in the face. She glanced forward, then turned back to him, mouth open as if to make her next point, when her expression hardened, the flesh growing tight, the color bleaching out of her skin. She clutched his arm, her fingers digging through his jacket into his skin.

Gage peered ahead and saw a tall man dressed in a dark, navy blue suit approaching. Black sunglasses hid his eyes, and his open-collared blue shirt was buttoned low enough to reveal a silver chain. His black hair, slicked back with just a bit of a wave, contained enough gray to make him look distinguished but not old. He was lean, suave, and handsome, the kind of square-jawed, broad-shouldered man that could have graced the covers of fashion magazines or movie posters.

He was the sort of man that Gage used to see strolling the streets of New York all the time but seldom, if ever, saw in Barnacle Bluffs. He passed without a word.

Miranda peered over her shoulder at him. Gage did too.

"Did you know him?" Gage asked.

"I thought …" she began. "I don't know. Just something about him."

"He looked familiar?"

"Yes," she said.

The way she swallowed, he knew the man had looked more than familiar to her. He had looked terrifying.

Chapter 5

During the drive across town, Miranda hunkered down in her seat as if she expected mortar fire. She twisted her red hair tight around her finger and glanced repeatedly in the rearview mirror, but when Gage asked her what she expected to see back there, she said she didn't know.

He worried about this sudden change in her, the return of this fearful, timid creature that had thankfully retreated during their visit to the outlet mall, but he wasn't sure what he could do about it. Should he keep pressing, hoping that he could dislodge something loose from her memory? Or would pressing cause her to further unravel? By the time they arrived at the Turret House, though, most of the anxiousness had disappeared—and all of it vanished when they rounded the corner on the last street before the ocean and she gazed upon Alex and Eve's bed and breakfast for the first time.

"Wow, what a beautiful place," she gushed.

"Wait until you see the inside," Gage said.

It was at the end of the road, after dozens of similarly expensive houses, nestled against a grassy dune high enough that it hid the ocean just beyond their sight. The Turret House was the most impressive of the bunch, a three-story, castle-like affair with brown shake siding, a wraparound deck on the second and third floors, and the hexagonal turret atop it all, technically a fourth story even if it wasn't quite so. Gage had spent many wonderful evenings in that turret—Alex's study, well-stocked with books and booze—engaging in philosophical arguments that seemed extremely important until they descended the spiral staircase and forgot everything by the time they got to the bottom.

The wind, strong so close to the ocean, flattened the grass on the top of the dune. Sunlight glared on the turret's windows. He parked the Volkswagen in the gravel parking lot, surprised to find Alex's Toyota van parked next to Zoe's little white Corolla, Eve's Prius, and two other cars he didn't recognize. He would have expected Alex to still be at the bookstore. The other cars were probably guests, which was about right for midday on a Thursday.

Eve greeted them at the door, stepping onto the river rock pathway, her black silky hair rippling around her long neck and the high collar of her denim vest. The daffodils on her apron matched the daffodils in the clay pots that lined the path, the same yellow color to a T. That was so like Eve, so much a part of the Turret House, infusing every bit of the place with her personality and her Greek heritage. She smiled warmly at them as they approached, directing her gaze toward Miranda.

"Hello," she said. Few people could infuse one simple word with such warmth, but Eve was such a person. Gage had long since concluded that anyone who didn't like her was somehow defective. "I'm Eve Cortez, one of the owners. We're so glad you're staying with us, Miranda."

She extended a hand, her skin so richly brown she had the appearance of someone who spent a lot of time in the sun even though it was all natural. When Miranda took it, Eve placed her other hand over the top of both of them.

"I'm so sorry about everything that's happened to you," Eve said. "Anything you need, you let us know. You can stay as long as you like."

"Thank … thank you," Miranda said. "I actually don't know

when I'll be able to pay—"

"Not another word about that. There won't be any charge."

"But—"

"No, no, come with me," Eve said, pulling Miranda into the house. "Garrison can get your things. Come, come, I'll show you to your room. Zoe was just changing the sheets on your bed. It's the best room in the house, second floor so it has a nice view of the ocean. We call it the Lavender Room. Do you like lavender? If not, we can put you in a different room."

"I—I love lavender," Miranda said, obviously struggling under the onslaught of kindness. He'd seen Eve's affect on people before and always marveled at it. Some people, when confronted with such pure, overwhelming compassion, even cried.

They disappeared into the house. Gage retrieved the bags from the van and followed them inside. He took the main stairs, the one with a beautiful polished oak banister, and met up with them in the Lavender Room. Zoe was just finishing making the bed and the three women were already chatting like old friends, Zoe and Eve debating about the best time of day to search for seashells on the beach. He smelled lavender mixed with the crisp ocean breeze, flitting in through the cracked-open window. The purple pillows and purple bedspread matched the purple drapes and purple walls; it was so much purple it shouldn't have worked but it somehow did, partly because the ocean that filled the window was so powerful that it required a powerful room decor to give it balance.

Not long after Gage deposited the bags, Alex also showed up—rumpled and wrinkled as always, a coffee stain on the collar of his pinstriped blue shirt. The room, which wasn't all that big to begin with, suddenly seemed a bit crowded.

"Ah, you're here," he said to Miranda. "You like the room? I'm Alex, Eve's assistant, by the way."

"Don't listen to my silly husband," Eve said.

"I didn't say the two were mutually exclusive," Alex said. "Husband, assistant, food tester—I have many roles."

"I *love* the room," Miranda gushed. "It's so, so … well, I can't think of the word. Wonderful, I guess."

"Wonderful will do," Alex said. "It was kind of a fixer-upper to begin with, but I think we've done well with it. I like fixer-uppers—you know, helping something get back to being whole again. Kind of gives my life purpose. You know what I mean?"

"Oh, yes," Miranda said.

The smug bastard glanced at Gage, an annoying twinkle in his eye. Gage would not give him the satisfaction of even the slightest reaction. Instead, he focused on Miranda.

"Anything else you need for now?" he asked her.

"Um …" Miranda began.

"You can leave us be," Eve said, shooing him toward the door. "Go on now, you two. Escape to your little hidey place. Zoe and I will help Miranda settle in." She looked at Miranda, suddenly concerned. "That is what you decided to go by for now, isn't it? Miranda?"

"Yes," Miranda said.

"Good, good. Everyone needs *something* to call you, and I think it's a lovely name."

"Speaking of calling," Zoe said, opening the drawer in the nightstand. "That reminds me, I got you something, Garrison."

"Uh oh," Gage said, "I think I know what's coming."

Sure enough, Zoe had gotten him another cell phone, identical to the first. When she handed it to him, she told him he had to promise not to break this one. He examined the little piece of plastic. Somehow, it seemed even less substantial than the first one.

"What if I don't promise?" Gage said. "Will you take it back?"

"Promise," Zoe said.

"I'll do my best not to break it," Gage said.

Alex chuckled. "Anyone want to take bets on how long this one lasts?"

"I also got one for Miranda," Zoe said. "It's in the night-stand here. All of our numbers are already programmed into both phones."

Miranda also protested, but Zoe wouldn't hear of it. While

Zoe showed Miranda how to use it, Gage and Alex left them and headed to the far end of the hall, the old hardwood creaking. He heard classical music playing softly behind one of the doors, a couple talking softly behind another. Only when they passed through the door that led to the metal staircase, the only one that led to the turret, did Gage release his pent-up irritation.

"Aren't you supposed to be at the store?"

"Closed early," Alex said. "Nobody there."

"Your commitment to customer service never ceases to amaze me."

"Still smarting from that fixer-upper comment, huh?"

"She's *not* a fixer-upper."

"She's very nice. Pretty, too. It seems about time for a red-head, huh?"

"Alex—"

"Come on, let's go to the study. There is something I wanted to talk to you about, but not in front of Miranda. And half the stores in this town close on a whim. It's the coastal way!"

They ascended to the turret, footsteps echoing in the enclosed space, Gage's right knee throbbing. The stairwell smelled slightly dank, but once they passed through the top door, he was greeted by the intoxicating aroma of old leather books. The room was dark, the blinds drawn to protect the books lining the shelves between each of the windows in the little hexagonal room. Alex flicked on the beaded lamp on the end table between the two leather wing-backed chairs, then opened the blinds of the front three windows. When they settled into the chairs, the view was nothing short of sublime, a sweeping vista of bright blue ocean outside, while inside, they were surrounded by pleasant creature comforts and fine literature finely presented.

Gage wasn't sure he believed in heaven. If he did, however, he was pretty sure it would look something like this.

"Shot of bourbon?" Alex offered, gesturing to the liquor cabinet behind them.

"Too early," Gage said.

"You're probably right. I'll drink wine instead. Half a glass, even."

"That's very responsible of you. What's this about, Alex?"

Gage patiently waited while Alex opened a bottle of a California Chardonnay and poured himself a glass. It looked suspiciously like three-quarters of a glass, rather than half, but it was already down to half by the time Alex eased back into his chair.

"Had a few friends in the FBI do some checking on both Marcus and Omar Koura," Alex said.

"Oh? I know from Quinn that they were partners in some sort of e-commerce company, something to do with money transactions."

"Yep. *Were* is the operative word."

"They aren't partners any more?"

Alex, who rested his long-stemmed wine glass on his lap, took a sip. The sunlight glinted off the glass and cast a tiny rainbow on his shirt. "The name of the company is eTransWorld. It's a low-cost financial transaction company—you know, credit card processing, that sort of thing. I'd even heard of them. When I was thinking of switching processors last year, they're one of the outfits I looked into. They had by far the lowest fees."

"You didn't go with them, though?"

"No. Something about them didn't seem quite right. My FBI intuition still acting up now and then, maybe. Kind of like the itch a guy gets in his amputated leg."

"Nice image," Gage said.

"Anyway, I was right to be hesitant. You know about Bitcoin?"

"Sure," Gage said. "That digital currency that's got both Wall Street and the Justice Department all nervous. Wall Street because it's mostly outside their bubble of influence. And the Justice Department because the money can't be tracked ... which makes it a magnet for criminal activity."

"Righty-o," Alex said. "It's totally decentralized."

"Was eTransWorld mixed up with Bitcoin?"

"No, not Bitcoin. Something like it, though, a new kind of financial transaction that is just as dark and just as secure, but supposedly their encryption coding is so good that it makes Bitcoin look like an open cash register on a lemonade stand."

"Lemonade stands have cash registers?" Gage said.

"You get the idea," Alex said, taking another sip of wine. "They started opening it up on a limited basis last year, about the same time that our missing friend, Marcus Koura, decided to sell his shares and get out of the company."

"Do you know *why* he wanted out?"

"That's where it gets interesting. The official story is that Marcus wanted to do something else with his life. The scuttlebutt is that he and his brother had a falling out, because Marcus wanted to sell the company to Facebook or Amazon, both of which were interested, but Omar wanted to hold on and build it up on their own, go public in a few years."

"Interesting," Gage said.

"Yeah, but that's not even the most interesting part. You see, both Omar and Marcus are second-generation Egyptians. Omar is still a devout Muslim, but I guess Marcus lost his religion along the way at some point. Used to be Mohamed Koura, but changed his name to Marcus. What I learned from the FBI is there was an investigation that eTransWorld was channeling funds for certain Middle Eastern organizations that are … how shall we say it, *unfriendly* toward the United States."

"They were laundering money for terrorists?"

Alex downed the rest of his wine. "That's what the FBI was trying to prove. Apparently, they haven't had much luck, which tells you how good eTransWorld is. They were also working on Marcus, trying to get to him through his conscience, hoping he'd turn on his brother. But he didn't crack. Apparently family still comes before country."

"Did you check to see if there were any female FBI agents who were working undercover? If Miranda was—"

"Yeah, I thought of that, but they said all of their undercover operatives who were working on the case are accounted for. Really, though, does Miranda strike you as the FBI type? Wait a minute, I don't know why I'm asking you. You washed out of the

FBI Academy."

"Kicked out, more like," Gage said.

"Details, details."

"And I distinctly remember you playing a part in that."

Alex chuckled. "Best thing that ever happened to you. You were the smartest student I ever had. Too smart, really. The FBI would have ruined you."

"Or I would have ruined the FBI."

"That's probably equally likely, knowing how stubborn you are. When an immovable object meets an unstoppable force …"

"Back to the Koura brothers," Gage said.

"That's it on the Koura brothers, alas. Wish I had more for you. You learn anything else since I last talked to you?"

Gage caught Alex up on what little information he had—first, that Omar was supposedly coming to Barnacle Bluffs on Friday, and second, about Miranda's reaction to the business-man they'd passed at the outlet mall. He added that he didn't think Miranda knew the man himself, just that she'd reacted to his general appearance.

"Did he look Egyptian?" Alex asked.

"Not in the slightest," Gage said. "Square-jawed Caucasian, kind of a taller version of Tom Cruise."

"Interesting. What's your thoughts on how she acted?"

Mulling the question, Gage turned to the ocean. It was the perfect time to look at it. Early afternoon, the sun was not yet low enough in the western sky that it would dip beneath the top of the window and blind him, but it was already well past its zenith and casting distinct shadows on the waves. The water was more silver than blue, but full of hard edges, like rows of knives facing upward. A few seagulls rode the thermals, far enough away that he knew them not by their color but by the shape of their wings. The wind, sometimes a roar up high in the turret, was only a faint whistle against the glass.

"Like an abused woman," he said finally.

"I thought you might say that," Alex said.

"I could be wrong, but it's just the sense I got. It fits some of her other behaviors, too. The jumpiness. She seems desperate to please me."

"You think Marcus was the abuser?"

"Probably not," Gage said. "I don't think she knew him long enough. Unless things change, my hunch is that she didn't meet him in San Jose. She met him somewhere along the way in his sailboat journey."

"And if you find out where …"

"I figure out who she is," Gage said.

"Maybe it won't matter. Maybe she'll remember."

"That's what I'm hoping."

"And you don't think …" Alex began, then trailed off.

"That she's pretending? I don't think so, but I can't be sure. But it doesn't really matter, does it? If she's playing some sort of game, I still have to act like she has no memory anyway. I've got to figure out where Marcus stopped after San Jose."

"You know," Alex said, "there is another more obvious move you can make."

"The press?"

"You've already decided against it?"

"I don't know if I *can* decide against it. It's too good a story. And once that boat washed up on the beach—well, it's not like we could keep it under wraps even if we wanted. The Bugle already had that bit up on their website. As soon as people figure out she's staying here, the reporters will start nosing around. Somebody will take a picture of her. And once that picture is out …"

"Ah," Alex said, "you're afraid that if she really was abused—"

"Exactly. The guy sees her picture, he heads straight here. We might have to make that play eventually, but I'm just trying to delay it as long as possible. Get some more information. Maybe Omar was lying, too, and he really does know who she is. Just too many unknowns right now. No, I'll start by contacting all the marinas up and down the coast, see where it leads."

"Fortunately," Alex said, "you now have a phone."

"Is that what that thing was?"

Alex took his glass back to the liquor cabinet, started to pour himself more wine, then changed his mind and put a cork on the bottle. "So … tell me about this doctor."

"What?"

"Zoe said you were flirting with a doctor at the hospital. She sounded promising. You can get yourself a nice Russian woman without having to order one from the mother country as so many men seem to be doing these days."

Gage sighed. "She's Ukrainian, actually."

"Does she have issues?" Alex asked.

"You never quit, do you?"

"It's my goal in life to marry you off again, my friend."

Gage was trying to think of something to say when someone called his name from the stairwell. It was Zoe. Alex opened the door and the two of them peered over the railing at the landing a floor down, where Zoe stood next to Officer Gilbert, the young cop who was a detective in training. Zachary. That was his name. Zoe and Zachary. Gage didn't like the sound of that. Alliteration was never a good sign.

They stood far enough away from each other that Gage should have been pleased, but it was *too* far apart, as if they were hyper-conscious of each other's presence. The kid, decked out in a standard blue police uniform, had ditched his trench coat.

"Yes?" Gage said.

"Zachary has information for you."

Alex said, "You know, you guys can come up. It's not like you need an exclusive membership or anything. I mean, I let Garrison in. That should tell you something."

"Thank you, sir," Zachary said. "I appreciate it. I just—I've got to get going. I just thought you should know. The techs ran her fingerprints. I just told, um, Miranda, nothing came up. It was just the main database, but—"

"Nothing?" Gage said.

"No, sir."

"Where did they get the fingerprints? Never mind, I don't want to put you on the spot. I'm going to guess that you weren't told to give us this news, were you?"

"Um …"

"You don't have to answer that one either. Your detective buddies find anything else out about where that boat may have docked along the coast?"

"No. I mean, not that I'm aware of, sir. They just looked into where he bought the boat, but nothing came of that. Just a new Catalina he bought from a dealer. But they don't really—I mean, they don't always share everything with me."

"How shocking," Gage said. "Hey, thanks for your help. It's really appreciated."

"Sure. Um …"

"Yes?"

"Well, I think you should know, sir. I mean, I don't want to make trouble or anything, but Miranda, she gave us the finger-prints herself this morning."

"What?"

"That's why it didn't take long to run them through the main database. It's because we had such good prints."

Processing this news, Gage thanked the kid again and Zoe said she'd see him to the door. The way she said it, the warmth in her voice, she didn't even sound like Zoe. It made Gage want to pull out his Beretta and fire a few shots into the ceiling.

His better judgment prevailing, he and Alex retreated back into the study, Alex closing the door behind them. Gage stepped close enough to the front windows that his own breath fogged on the glass. He saw a family in matching red windbreakers on the beach below, and, farther down, an old man dressed in a green camo jacket who was scanning the sand with a metal detector. He wondered how it would be to spend his day like that, listening for the tell-tale beeps, delighting when he found a lost watch or even a few quarters. Could he lose himself completely in the work? His bum knee would make the beach comber's life a tough one for him, but he doubted he would notice the pain if he loved the work enough. That really was the key, finding something so consuming that all your troubles just disappeared.

"Well," Alex said, "I'm going to wager a guess that Zoe and

Officer Friendly there will probably be spending a bit of time together in the near future."

"Just stop," Gage said.

"Aw, you're just sore because the kid is impossible not to like."

"His uniform gives me ample motivation."

"Right. So, can we rule out the possibility of Miranda pretending to have amnesia? If she was pretending, why would she give the cops her fingerprints?"

"Unless she *knew* she wouldn't come up in the system."

"Hmm."

Gage turned around and looked at his friend. "If she knew she had no criminal record, or had any other reason why her fingerprints would come up ... well, that would be a good way to convince us that she wasn't faking it."

Alex made a *tsk tsk* sound. "Such a cynic."

"I learned from the best."

"Hmm. I was never as cynical as you, my friend. What made you such a pessimist?"

"I'm not a pessimist. I'm a realist with an attitude problem."

"That's exactly how a pessimist would think of himself."

Gage turned back to the window. The man with the metal detector was digging at the sand underneath a beached log. Gage watched with anticipation as the man retrieved something metal and shiny, shook off the sand, and held it up into the sun. A beer can. Gage would have liked to say he was disappointed, but really, he expected as much. Did that make him a pessimist?

"Well," he said, "I go on doing the work anyway. I don't know how to do anything else, and how I feel about it doesn't seem to matter one way or the other. I just keep digging around until I find something."

Chapter 6

G age spent most of Friday morning at his kitchen table, calling marinas up and down the coast. Some were friendly, some weren't, and many didn't answer. Nobody knew Marcus Koura's Catalina boat, either based on the license number or on a detailed description. Nobody could remember seeing Marcus or Miranda either, though a few confessed they were so busy and kept such poor records, that even Elvis could have drifted through and they might not have noticed.

After a few dozen calls, Gage snapped the cell phone closed and placed it on the table in front of him. His right ear felt warm, and his fingers actually ached from gripping the plastic for so long. What, exactly, was the appeal of these stupid things? Even looking at it made him want to get a hammer.

Rain tapped on the high arched windows, the light inside the spacious main room of his A-frame gray and diffuse. A storm had blown in overnight, not a big one, but the usual drizzle. It was typical fickle weather for the Oregon coast in April: bright and sunny followed by drab and overcast, often within the same hour. His orange tabby, Carrot, which, like Zoe, he'd also inherited from his one-time housekeeper who'd lost her battle with cancer a few years back, curled up in his recliner. It was the first time Gage could remember seeing Carrot in a week, as Zoe was the one who fed him, and the cat was even less social than Gage; spotting him more than a few times a month was actually a lot.

Maybe he should take a cue from the cat. Why was he so intent on going out all the time? Just look at that recliner. Why should Carrot get first dibs on it?

He was summoning the willpower to call more marinas when the phone suddenly rang, startling him.

It was a high-pitched chirp, one of the most annoying sounds he'd ever heard, and it was made worse by the physical vibrating that accompanied it—like a little black mouse, trembling in terror, the rattle on his walnut table like the clicking of the mouse's claws. Somehow he'd forgotten that people could also call *him*. How depressing.

He flipped open the cell and held it to his ear, unsure if that was all he needed to do to answer it.

"Yes?" he said.

"Garrison." It was Zoe. "You better get over here. There's a guy parked outside."

"What?"

"Some reporter dude. He's … weird. He came in and wanted to know where to find Miranda, but we told him she's out right now. I don't think he believed us."

"Who's he working for?"

"He didn't say."

"Weird, how? Dangerous?"

"No. I don't think so. He's … well, you just gotta see it."

"Where's Miranda?"

"Sleeping. I checked on her a while ago. She's so dead to the world I had to check to make sure she was really breathing. Must have been totally exhausted." She paused, and Gage heard a violin concerto playing faintly in the background, the kind of music Eve usually had playing in the living room after they finished breakfast. "Miranda's so nice, if this guy manages to talk to her, I'm afraid—"

"I know," Gage said. "I'll be right over. Try not to let her near him if you can."

"Uh oh."

"What?"

"He's getting out of his car again."

"Oh geez. I'm on my way."

Even with the extra Friday traffic, Gage made it over to the Turret House in under five minutes. The highway glistened like the back of an eel. The rain, which had already started to ease, still speckled the windshield enough that he had to turn on the wipers.

When he rounded the corner onto Turret House's street, he spotted the strange person he could easily assume Zoe called about pacing along the road in front of the B&B, a short, barrel shaped man in a purple trench coat and matching purple fedora. It was the kind of bright purple that belonged on a woman's fingernails, not a man's clothes. Or a woman's clothes, really. A Pontiac Safari, a big '80s station wagon that had been painted almost exactly the same color as the man's attire, was parked at the curb across the street. Gage, pulling in behind the Pontiac, took a wild guess that the two belonged together.

If the man was trying to look inconspicuous, as if he was just out for a stroll, he wasn't doing a very good job. Gage donned his own fedora—which, alas, was plain brown felt and not purple—and got out of van. His hat may not have been as pretty, but it kept his face dry. He'd brought his cane, too. Maybe he would get to bop someone on the head with it yet this week.

"Points for functionality, at least," Gage said.

When the man turned, Gage realized he had completely underestimated how outrageous his appearance was. The purple color was the tamest thing about him. He sported a massive handlebar mustache, dark and thick and curled, the kind of thing that would have won competitions. It looked so obviously fake that it must have been real. The way it hung firmly in place, and the smoothness of it shining in the damp afternoon air, made it seem more ceramic than hair.

"Sorry?" the man said. "Were you addressing me, dear

chap?"

He spoke in a high-pitched twang, with an accent that was probably meant to sound British but came off as a first-year acting student's feeble attempt. Or maybe it wasn't meant to be British. It wasn't really British at all, just snobbish and affected, with too much lilt and enunciation. The man's head reminded Gage of an inverted traffic cone, with a tiny pointed chin under a massive sloping forehead, the hue of his face a similar orange. Or perhaps it was just the purple, bringing out the orange in the man's skin. His eyes, so tiny they were all pupil, a shiny, unblinking black that made Gage think of buttons used for stuffed animals.

"My fedora," Gage said. "It's not nearly as nice as yours, but I at least get points for functionality, right?"

"Ah," the man said. "You are commenting on the uniqueness of my head garment, I see."

"Head garment?" Gage said.

"The name is Buzz Burgin," the man said. "Actually, I write under the byline Charles E. Burgin, but everyone from the lowest of the low to the highest of the high refers to me as, simply, Buzz. You may too, dear chap. Some have even taken to assigning me the ... the *moniker* Buzz Purple, due to my fondness for that color, but really, Buzz will do. Do you know the owners of this fine establishment? I would like to confer with one of the guests, and I'm afraid they're not being very helpful."

"You should at least walk the length of the street," Gage said.

"Sorry?"

"That's the second time you've apologized," Gage said. "Really, there's no need."

"I'm afraid I don't—"

"To try to blend in," Gage said. "That's what I meant. You should walk a little farther than just the length of the house. You're really calling a lot of attention to yourself. Or was that your purpose?"

Buzz peered at Gage with his tiny black eyes, the pause between blinks so long that Gage actually found it a bit unnerving. The rain slowed and dissipated, turning into more of a mist. The ocean, not visible from this vantage point, could still be heard over the rooftops, a rhythmic rush of air. Buzz's gaze fell on Gage's cane, and he nodded

"Ah," he said, "you must be Garrison Gage."

"I must be," Gage said.

"I heard about you, my good fellow."

"If someone referred to me as a good fellow, they were misinformed."

"The famous detective," Buzz said, chuckling. He touched the corners of his mustache with both hands, not quite twirling it the way a dastardly villain would in an old spaghetti western, but more as if he needed to reassure himself that it was still there. "That business with the God's Wrath cult a couple years back was quite … quite … *captivating*. There was a good series in the *Oregonian* on it. I've thought of that line of work myself, really. All that cloak and dagger. Seems fascinating."

"Cheating housewives don't usually wear cloaks," Gage said, "and runaway teens almost never carry daggers."

"I'm sorry?"

"There you go again, apologizing."

"Oh, I see," Buzz said, "you were referring to the usual … *mundane* business of a private investigator. Good, good, quite droll. You have a sharp wit, dear chap. I admire that. Now, if you could just help me talk to—"

"Not going to happen," Gage said.

Finally, Buzz blinked those dull little eyes of his. "I'm afraid, I'm afraid I don't—"

"There's no one here who's going to talk to you today."

"But—but if I could only explain—"

"You need to be on your way."

"Well, *really*," Buzz said, "I am not sure what I have done to elicit such a … such a … an *insensitive* response. I only ask—"

"Who do you write for?"

"What?"

"You claim to be a journalist. Who do you write for?"

"I *am* a journalist," Buzz replied indignantly, and the orange hue of his face was quickly turning scarlet. "I seldom wish to toot my own horn—"

"Of course not."

"—but I have written for journalistic publications far and wide—"

"Journalistic?"

"—as well as my own blog, *Peering Into Portland,* which, I shall tell you, ranks quite high on all of the search engines—and I have received numerous ... *accolades* for my ... for my ... *incomparable* in-depth investigative pieces—"

"Do you write the same way you speak? With a thesaurus?"

"What?"

"It's quite charming. Look, I don't care who you write for. *The Oregonian, The New York Times,* there's nobody here who will talk to you. There's nothing worth writing about. There's no story, not even one fit for your blog, Peeing in Portland."

"Peering! *Peering!*"

"Whatever. I suggest you get in your purple mobile and head back to the valley."

The little man's face was now almost the same color as his clothes, and as bloated as an inflated balloon. He took a few seconds to gather himself, huffing and puffing a bit, then started shuffling his way to his station wagon. He only made it a few steps before he turned back.

"Now, now, you listen," he sputtered, "I am not a man to be ... to be ... taken lightly. I am a writer of some ... some ... *renown.* Of some merit. I have the power of the pen at my disposal, dear chap. It is a power that even men of ... powerful means—"

"That's the word power twice in the same sentence. Points deducted for redundancy."

"Well, *really!*"

"Yes, really. Now go. And if I see one word about any of this on your blog, Peeping Into Portland—"

"Peering!"

"—I'm going to come find you. Got it?" When the little man didn't answer, Gage used his cane to give Buzz a little push. "Got it? Or should we go look up some words in the thesaurus to see if we can make you understand?"

Gage had barely put any force behind the push at all, but Buzz grasped at his chest and gaped at Gage as if he had been stabbed with a bayonet. It was such an over the top response that Gage couldn't help but give him another push, this one harder. Buzz stumbled backward, arms freewheeling, and barely managed to keep himself upright. His purple fedora spiraled off his head, revealing a bald head that retained a slight purple shade from the hat's dye. As Buzz groped for his hat, Gage thought of one of the sea lions he'd seen on the rocks a while back, bobbing and flopping around on the rocks.

Gathering himself, Buzz tried to protest again, but Gage limped forward and aimed to give him another prod, prompting the little man to flee for his car. Not satisfied his message had truly sunk in yet, Gage followed. The man was not a fast runner. In fact, it really could not even be called running, more of a jittery waddle, and even limping on his bad knee Gage managed a couple more pushes in Buzz's back, each one eliciting a terrified shriek from the reporter, before Buzz escaped into his station wagon. While Gage watched, Buzz fumbled with his keys and finally got the car running.

"You will regret this!" he shouted through the closed window. "I have never—never been treated in such a … such a …"

Gage lifted his cane, aiming it at the glass.

Whatever word Charles E. Burgin was going to come up with in that moment, Gage would never know. The purple man put his purple car in gear and squealed down the street, kicking up some pebbles that pinged against the grille of Gage's van. He watched the man go, watched until he was sure the station wagon disappeared around the bend and he was sure it wasn't coming back, and only then did he turn toward the Turret House. That's when he saw he had an audience standing in the open front door—Zoe and Eve.

Zoe was shaking her head, bemused, and Eve, who couldn't be rude to someone even if she tried, wore the kind of aghast expression that he imagined her children, now grown, had seen on a frequent basis when they got into trouble. *If* they got into trouble. Most people would be hard pressed to disappoint someone like Eve more than once or twice. He imagined it would feel a bit like disappointing Mother Teresa. Tended to stick with you.

Still, there was only one thing to do after such a performance, and with a clearly captivated audience waiting for his response.

He bowed.

AFRAID THE LITTLE purple reporter might return, Gage parked himself by the living room window in one of the rocking chairs and watched the street.

Sunlight pierced the gray cloud cover, and, like hands brushing the clouds aside, the sky began to clear. Alex was already at the store, and Zoe busied herself tidying the rooms, but Eve brought him a cup of coffee and the two made small talk for a few minutes, mostly chatting about the casino's plans to add a second hotel and what that would do for the other hotels in the area. Miranda, her face pink and her hair still wet from a shower, showed up shortly thereafter, and Eve insisted on making breakfast for both of them—ham and cheese omelets, with freshly squeezed orange juice and cranberry scones she'd just baked that morning. The buttery warmth of the scones, just the right combination of sugar and tartness, was so delicious it took all of his will power to stop at two.

Dr. Tatyana Brunner called the Turret House line and asked if she might stop by on her way to work and check on Miranda. She showed up a few minutes later, and, despite Eve's repeated pleas that she join the table, begged off by saying she'd already had a full breakfast.

"It does smell quite wonderful, though," she said. "It reminds me of the *syrniki* my mother used to make."

She wore a white silk scarf tied loosely over a powder-blue V-neck shirt, striking the perfect balance between professional and welcoming. The pleated charcoal gray pants, the pearl earrings, the faint hue of blue eye shadow—just as before, was a technically perfect ensemble, but she wore it as if someone out of central casting had picked it out for her, with little passion or personality. The leather satchel hung on her shoulder as if she had forgotten it was there. Only the diamond and gold CK necklace seemed part of her, and she fidgeted with it while gazing at the scones, as if she was clearly having second thoughts about passing them up.

"Are you sure?" Gage asked. "You haven't lived until you've tried one of these." He grabbed another one, and, making the mistake of thinking it was a bit smaller than it looked, shoved the whole thing in his mouth. "Mmm ... good."

Tatyana arched her left eyebrow at him. "I'm not sure watching you eat makes it more appetizing."

"No?" Gage said, and that was all he could manage, because his mouth was still too full to say anything else.

"We will give you the benefit of the doubt," Tatyana said, "that it is the irresistible nature of Eve's cooking that makes you lose your table manners."

Gage may have made a fool of himself, but he liked the way her eyes lit up when she delivered one of her little zingers. Unlike her clothes, her wit seemed entirely hers, when she was most comfortable with herself and with others. Before he could manage to swallow enough to offer a rejoinder, she'd already asked Miranda if she could perform an exam in private and the two of them disappeared upstairs. Eve, admonishing him, shook her head and retreated to her office to do some paperwork, leaving Gage alone with the rest of the scones. He managed to control himself this time, though his resolve was beginning to fade by the time Miranda and Tatyana returned ten minutes later.

"All square?" he asked.

"I'm fine," Miranda said. "Physically, anyway."

"Yes," Tatyana said. "Nothing wrong with her balance, heart rate, blood pressure, or any other vitals. Her memory ..." She shrugged. "A visit to a psychiatrist might be in order if her memory does not return in a day or two. I know a good one in Eugene who has some past experience with memory issues, but it is a bit of a drive."

"Oh, not yet," Miranda said.

"All right. Well, I better be going. I have a shift starting in just a few—"

"What are you doing for dinner tonight?" Miranda asked.

"Excuse me?"

"Eve and Alex are doing a dinner for family and friends. I'd have to ask, but I bet they'd like you to come."

"Oh, no," Tatyana said, "I really should pass. I have—I have a lot to do, and I—"

"Let me ask."

"No, please—"

"Be right back."

Miranda disappeared through the swinging door, leaving Gage and Tatyana alone in the kitchen. She rested her hand on the oak table, looking at him, and for a moment he sensed the attraction between them, the same attraction he'd sensed when they'd passed each other in the grocery store as strangers. It made him think of the way Zoe and that young cop acted around each other, the hyper-awareness of each other's bodies. Was she aware of it, too?

"You'd be more than welcome," Gage said.

"Are you sure? I would not be ..."

"Imposing? No."

"I'm—I'm not sure why anyone would ... Well, I am just the doctor. It's not like I know anyone here."

"That'll change after tonight."

She let her gaze linger, and he liked the way it lingered. He liked the uncertainty too. It spoke of a vulnerability that she didn't often reveal, a crack in that perfectly composed exterior. Both Miranda and Eve returned, and, as Gage expected, Eve exceeded Miranda's enthusiasm in her invitation to Tatyana to attend dinner. Any remaining resistance on Tatyana's part was no match for Eve's overwhelming hospitality, and Tatyana quickly went from saying no to asking if she could bring anything.

"No, no, no, " Eve said, grabbing Tatyana's arm, "just bring your merry self. But you can bring a guest, too, if you like. Do you have a husband or a, um, a boyfriend?"

"No," Tatyana said. "No, I ... nothing like that, it would just be me. I hope—I hope that's all right."

"Of course it's all right, my dear!" Eve said. "It's more than all right. It's wonderful!"

"All right. Well, I better be going."

"Of course, dear. Let me show you to the door."

Gage couldn't be sure, but he thought he detected a wink from Eve in his direction. Fortunately, Tatyana didn't seem to catch it. Was everyone trying to set him up around here? Gage glanced at Miranda, and she was grinning slyly too, but there was something else in her eyes, a flash of pain or jealousy, an emotion that startled him with how naked and primal it was, even if he couldn't read it entirely.

It was gone so fast he wasn't sure it was even there.

TIRED OF MAKING phone calls, Gage decided to stay with Miranda to see if the two of them could unearth any of her memories. She seemed amenable to the idea, but he sensed hesitancy on her part, perhaps even a bit of trepidation, so he suggested that they just play some games and see what might get jogged loose in her mind if they didn't go at it directly. She'd remembered something about getting a traffic ticket, and, of course, there was her reaction to the man in the suit at the outlet mall. Gage hoped for something similar, perhaps more specific, a clue that would lead him in the right direction.

He suggested chess, and she agreed, but when they set up their pieces at the glass table in the corner of the living room, it was obvious from the start that she had no idea how to play. While he was fine teaching her, he was really hoping that familiarity with something she had played before would connect her to other memories. There was a box of checkers in a little driftwood box, and when he took them out, her eyes lit up with delight. Checkers it was then.

She played well, and with relish, but even three games didn't clear up any of her mental fog. They tried cards. Poker, his game of choice, was a mystery to her, but she seemed intimately familiar with the game of hearts. They played a couple hands and she won them all. With the morning work done, Eve and Zoe joined them for a half hour, and Miranda beat them, too. She was a reluctant winner, though, apologizing each time she won, to the point where it actually began to annoy Gage, especially when he sensed that she was starting to throw games at the end.

They made small talk, but nothing substantial came of it. Current events, politics, she seemed to have some recollection of these things, but when he asked her how she knew about them her face grew cloudy. Eve left to make turkey sandwiches for everyone, despite their insistence that they weren't hungry, but she said it was no bother, she was going to make something for Alex anyway and take it to him at the store. Zoe went to help her.

"Another game?" Gage asked.

"I guess," Miranda said.

"Getting tired of it?"

"A little. I like playing with you, though."

"You want something? A glass of wine?"

"Oh, I don't drink."

He stared at her.

"Huh," she said. "I don't even know how I know that. But it's true. I don't drink."

"Do you think it was for religious reasons? Or maybe you were an alcoholic?"

"I don't know. I'm sorry."

"It's okay. It's something, though. See? We just keep at it, and little bits of your past emerge. How about a board game? We haven't tried any of those. A lot of people played board games as kids. Maybe it will help you remember."

When she agreed, Gage opened the armoire behind him and started reading off some of the board games inside. Monopoly.

Candyland. Scrabble. She was noncommittal to all of these, as well as the other half dozen stacked on top of one another. The lower shelf was packed with puzzles, mostly of Oregon coast scenes, the cardboard boxes chipped and well-worn from all the use. He asked if she wanted to do a puzzle of the lighthouse at Cape Blanco, warning her that there was a good chance a piece or two was missing.

When she didn't answer, he turned and saw that her face had paled and her eyes had flat-lined.

"What is it?" he asked.

"No," she said.

"No puzzles?"

She shook her head.

"You remember something?" he asked.

"I don't ... I don't know."

"Tell me."

She started to say something, then shook her head. Gage prodded her gently, telling if her that if there was even the slightest memory, even an image, she should tell him. She swallowed hard, then said there was no memory. It was just a feeling. What feeling? She didn't know that either, not exactly, but it was like when you'd gotten sick to your stomach after eating a certain kind of food and you saw that food again. It was like that. Gage didn't know what to make it of it. They'd played games for several hours and this was all they could come up with, a strange revulsion to puzzles? She was the puzzle, one with almost all the pieces missing and not even the slightest clue what the image was supposed to look like.

She must have sensed his frustration, because she said, "I'm really sorry."

"Don't apologize," Gage said. "Remember?"

"I know. It's just ..."

"It'll come back in time. Come on, let's go for a walk on the beach. The ocean air does wonders for the soul."

She tossed on the Oregon Coast pullover and the sandals he'd bought her and the two of them ventured out the back door, across the pea-gravel path, and down the many steps to the sand below. The sweatshirt was a good idea, as was Gage's leather jacket. The sky might have cleared, the clouds retreating into the distance like chastened predators, but the wind ripped over the sand with a cold bite. When they got a little distance from the cliff face, where the gusts gathered with greater fervor, the wind died enough that he was at least able to stop holding his fedora to his head.

He smelled smoke—thick smoke, from wet wood. A couple teenagers to the north were doing their best to get a campfire going between a large boulder and a log that had long ago washed ashore. He led Miranda south. A few other people were out and about, a woman jogging barefoot, a man wading in the surf with two little girls, but mostly it was open sand and the occasional seagull awaiting a handout. He saw a silvery flash far out on the ocean and spotted a boat, so tiny it was nothing more than a white speck amidst all the frothy gray water.

Miranda took his arm, then looked at him apprehensively. He patted her hand, her fingers cool to the touch.

"I can use a little extra support myself," he said.

She gripped his arm tighter, searching his eyes. Her red hair streamed across her face and she brushed it aside.

"Is it down there?" she asked.

"What's that?"

"The boat," she said, nodding toward the south. "Is it—is it down that way?"

"Oh. I'm not sure, actually. Probably. The last time a boat washed ashore, it was a month before it was removed. And this time …"

He trailed off, unsure of what might upset her. She was perceptive enough to pick up on it.

"You don't have to walk on eggshells around me," she said.

"Okay."

"I know what you were going to say. You were going to say, and this time the police have reason to think something bad happened on that boat."

"Actually, I was going to say that this time the owner isn't around to do something about it."

"Oh. That too, I guess."

"Did you want to see it? The boat? Maybe seeing it will—"

"No."

They walked a little while without speaking, the wind strong in his ears. She let go of his arm, still close enough that their shoulders brushed, but it felt as if she had increased the distance between them by much more. A continent of space and memory. Gage studied her, wondering if this little spindly thing with the freckled tan was really capable, as she put it, of doing something bad. Could she push a man off a sailboat? In all his years as a private investigator, both in New York and in Oregon, he had occasionally seen very small people do very bad things, but the norm was closer to the stereotype—the strong preying on the weak, whether weak physically or mentally. He did not sense that Miranda was strong in either way.

Still, it would not take a lot of physical strength or mental fortitude to push a man off a boat when his back was turned. All it would take was the opportunity and a few seconds when impulse gave into temptation.

"I wish I could remember," she said.

"You will," he said.

"Do you believe me?"

"Of course."

"Would you say that even if you didn't?"

"Probably."

She laughed. It wasn't a strong, hearty laugh, more a nervous giggle, but it was still better than listening to her wallow in misery. He was glad to hear it, especially as he hadn't meant it as a joke, or even meant to say it at all, and was considering what to say next when her laughter suddenly died and her face darkened.

"I remember something," she said.

"What?"

"About the puzzle thing. Something … It's just, I remember working on a puzzle. It was a picture of a city. A big city, with skyscrapers. I was almost done ... and I was *looking* at the big skyscrapers, too, out a window. So I must have been near a big city. A couple pieces to go. And then ... and then ..."

"Yes?"

"Somebody smashed it."

"What? *Who?*"

She swallowed. "I don't know. I just—I remember a hand sweeping across the table. Pushing it to the floor. Someone ... someone yelling ..."

"A man or a woman?"

She didn't answer.

"Were you in a house? What else was there? What kind of table was it?"

She chewed on her bottom lip. He could see that she was going to cry, so he stepped pressing. They were so close, so close to just the right detail, the one that would open all the doors, and he felt his frustration rising. There had to be *some* way to get inside that addled brain of hers.

He was considering his options, debating whether he should take a stronger approach with her, when a man yelled behind them.

"Hello!"

The word may have been a greeting, but it sounded more like a curse the way the man shouted. They both turned, Miranda clutching Gage's arm. The person who'd shouted—someone he'd never seen before—was still fifty feet away but closing quickly, a bald, brown-skinned man dressed in an expensive slate gray suit, a white silk shirt unbuttoned halfway down his chest, and shiny black wingtip shoes, a stylish outfit more fitting for a high-end business mixer in Miami than the Oregon coast, where Gage often had the impression that both the tourists and the natives dressed in the dark.

The man marched toward them in such a menacing way that Gage positioned Miranda a bit behind him. He already had a pretty good idea who this was, and as the man neared, his appearance only served to confirm it. His skin was smooth and shiny in the misty air like dark-stained oak, the same color from his smooth scalp down to his hairless chest. He was short and slight, but his physical presence still radiated a certain kind of compact power, as if his bones were made of steel and he knew it. Both the man's goatee and his eyebrows were so faint that Gage didn't think he had either until the man stopped a few paces away.

"You are the woman, yes?" he said.

He spoke in a clipped manner, with the accent of someone who had learned English as an adult and not a youth. His face was full of hard angles and flat planes, making Gage think of one of those early computer-animated images of a person that lacked the subtle nature of real human flesh, with all its many imperfect slopes and curves. His nose, tiny as it was, jutted out like a blade.

"And you must be Omar Koura," Gage said.

The man ignored Gage, keeping his dark eyes fixed on Miranda. He took a step closer and Gage got a whiff of the man's cologne, a musky scent powerful enough that Gage could detect it even over the ocean air—like some mixture of a sweaty gym and slightly spoiled fruit, not exactly pleasant. "Where is my brother?" he demanded.

"I'll take that as a yes," Gage said.

"I don't—I don't know," Miranda said.

"You were with him," Omar said. "You must know where he is. Tell me now."

"Whoa," Gage said. "Let's ease up a bit, pal."

"What did you do to him?"

Miranda, gripping Gage's arm even tighter, began a stuttering reply, but Gage put his hand over hers to quiet her. Her fingers felt like ice. Nobody else on the beach was within a hundred yards of them. All along, Omar had refused to acknowledge him, so Gage decided to merely wait him out this time. He patted Miranda's hand and smiled pleasantly at Omar, until the man was finally forced to turn and reckon with him.

"Who are you then?" Omar asked. "The father of this girl?"

"Ouch," Gage said.

"My brother is missing. I want answers."

"Her father?" Gage said. "Really? That one really hurts. How old do you think I am?"

"Where is Marcus?"

"I'm not even fifty yet. I thought I was looking pretty good for my age."

Miranda murmured, "You are, you are."

"Is it the cane?" Gage said. "It's the cane, isn't it? Everybody assumes because I need a cane, I must be old. Nobody assumes I have a cane because a mafia hitman used a baseball bat to turn my knee into crushed ice. I wonder why that is. Or maybe it's the hat." He removed the fedora. "How do I look now? See, I have a full head of hair and everything."

If Omar had any sense of humor at all, he certainly wasn't showing it. He glared at Gage with all the intensity of a man ready to kill someone. This certainly stood in stark contrast with Gage, whose response to such naked hostility was always to make light of it—even if inwardly he was readying himself for the worst. Holding his fedora over his heart, grinning stupidly, he imagined he looked a bit like a drunk at a baseball game listening to the national anthem.

"Your joking manner does not amuse me," Omar said.

"That's too bad," Gage said. "Your amusement was my highest concern."

"You are some kind of ... what? What do they call it? A goodly Samaritan?"

"Close enough."

Miranda said, "He's a private investigator. He's been very kind. He helped me when I—when he found me on the beach. I don't ... I don't have any memory right now. I wish I could help you. I'm sorry. Really, I'm sorry."

Omar eyed Gage suspiciously. "Investigating? What are you investigating?"

"I'm not investigating anything right now. I'm just helping this young lady get back on her feet. And, hopefully, finding your brother in the process."

"Who hired you?"

"I told you—"

"We already know what happened to my brother. This woman, she pushed him off the boat."

"We don't know that at all."

"She killed him."

"I'd be careful making accusations like that, sir. Some people may think you're actually being serious."

"She's a murderer!"

"All right," Gage said, "I've had enough of this crap. Back up a couple steps before you decide to do something stupid."

Omar, his hands balled into fists, didn't move. This was all too much for Miranda, who'd started sniffling when he'd accused her of pushing Marcus off the boat and worked her way up into a sobbing mess by the time he called her a murderer.

"I told you," she said, "I don't remember—"

"Liar!" Omar cried.

He lunged for Miranda as if he intended to grab her throat. Even in his rage, there was something practiced about his movements, something trained, the result of many hours spent repeating the same movements under the watchful gaze of martial arts expert. Gage had seen this kind of thing before. Still, Omar's anger had certainly clouded his judgment. If not for the man's loss of emotional control, it was doubtful he would have put himself in such a compromising position.

Gage had to make this count.

Miranda was on his left, just behind him. Waiting until the last moment, lulling Omar into thinking he was as slow and lumbering as someone with a cane often would be, Gage dropped onto his good knee and plowed his left hand into Omar's gut.

Focused. All the power in his clenched fist.

With a loud *oomph,* Omar doubled over and plowed backwards into the sand.

Miranda shrieked and jumped back a step. Gage had scored a direct hit, but there was something about how slight Omar was that actually worked to his advantage—like punching a feather.

You could put all the power you wanted into a punch, but how much would it really affect a feather? A stronger, bigger man might have washboard abs, with stomach muscles as tough as knotted wood, but at least a punch there would find some resistance, something to work against.

Usually when Gage punched a man like that, he felt it in his fist, a sting that radiated up his arm. This time, he felt as if he'd took a swing at an empty shirt.

Gage knew, even before the kick came, that he was in trouble.

The crash of the waves. The ocean breeze kicking up fine particles of sand. The seagulls, wading in the shallow surf below them, cawing in warning. On his knee, Gage had only a second to take in these sensations before someone hit him on the side of the head with a two by four.

That's what it felt like, and it wasn't until after the left side of his face pulsed with pain and a purple sheen darkened his vision that his mind finally caught up and processed the swing of Omar's leg coming at him.

Gage's own instincts had him moving with the blow, but he still took it hard.

Shoulder crashing into the sand.

Blood in his mouth.

Heart pounding in his ears.

The movie reel of his life skipped a beat, but he hung onto consciousness and rolled away with his cane in hand. It was a good thing, because by the time he'd gotten himself back to a crouch, Omar was on his feet and springing at him with a side kick. Gage saw it coming through a sheen of sweat, the black sole of the man's leather shoe like a tiny anvil dropping out of the sky.

As trained as he was, though, Omar still wasn't thinking clearly. It was all swallowed by emotions Omar could barely control.

Gage ducked to the side, missing the kick by not more than an inch, and brought his cane up so Omar took it right in the crotch.

Omar's own momentum carried him into the cane. He may have been hardly more substantial than his silk shirt, but there were few men alive who could take a blow to the groin like that and keep going.

He shrieked like a man on fire.

Gage, using the cane, directed him to the side and away, making sure to give himself a little more space this time.

It was hardly needed. Omar fell like a lump of wet laundry, curled into a ball, and cupped his hands over his crotch. Even so, Gage knew the man would be up and as enraged as ever—and this time probably without underestimating his opponent.

Using his cane as it was actually intended, Gage staggered to his feet. Pain blasted up his knee straight into his spine, forcing him to pull himself up by brute strength. The left side of his face stung, and he felt the swelling there, the puffiness forming. Sweat stuck his shirt to his back and clumped his hair around his ears. Fortunately, no more blood filled his mouth, but the taste still lingered.

Gage hated the taste of blood. It was one of the few things in life that truly made him mad as hell. Unlike Omar, though, Gage didn't lose control of his emotions. What he lost, instead, was the ability to tell right from wrong—or at least, the ability to care about it one way or another.

Miranda, sobbing quietly, had drifted behind him and to the side, partially covering her face with her hands and peeking out as if witnessing a terrible car accident. There were people far to the north and the south, too far away to really take notice of their little dustup, but even if they *could* have seen them, it would not have stopped Gage from doing what he did next. Just as Gage had predicted, Omar recovered quickly and swung onto all fours, crouching like a panther ready to pounce, the energy and hate all coiled up and his eyes burning bright.

That's when Gage pulled the Beretta out of his side holster.

He'd had his own hand-to-hand combat training back at Quantico, of course, but he also had no illusions about what he could do in his late forties with a bad knee and too many hours spent reading colonial history and sipping bourbon in his re-cliner. The safety lever was flipped, the slide was pulled back to chamber a round, and the gun was aimed in quick succession, the result of hours of practice that made it all happen without Gage consciously thinking about any of it.

Omar's eyes narrowed. For just a moment, Gage thought the man was still going to attack, was sure of it, in fact, and Gage suffered a split second of hesitation. Would he actually shoot this man?

Yes, he would.

Just like that, the doubt was gone—and Omar must have seen it, too. He remained crouching, his posture barely chang-ing, but all that white hot rage began to seep out of his eyes. The Beretta, which had, like usual, first felt slightly foreign in Gage's hand, a cold and heavy lump of steel, now felt like an extension of his own body. Shoulders squared and forward. Right foot slightly behind the left in a boxer's stance. The left hand braced around the right for extra support. Omar's anger may have been fading, but Gage was still ready to squeeze the trigger if the man made even the slightest aggressive move.

"You would shoot me?" Omar said. "For this woman?"

"I would shoot you," Gage said, "because I really don't like you."

"Who *are* you?"

"Right now, I'm the man holding the gun loaded with six-teen rounds. Those are 9 mm bullets, by the way. Just one of them would be enough to turn you into seagull food." The breeze stirred the sand between them, and Gage waited, watching Omar to ensure that the reality of the situation was really dawning on him. When he saw that it was, Gage continued. "Now, I would suggest that you stand up, very slowly, then walk right back the way you came. Get in that nice car you must have rented and drive back to your hotel. Take off your shoes and kick back and watch some television until all that adrenaline fades away. May-be some Wheel of Fortune. Something dumb to let your mind relax. You pretend this didn't happen. I'll do the same. Tomorrow, when I'm sure you've cooled down, maybe we can talk."

Omar, still fuming even if he'd gotten at least a little control of himself, rose to his feet. "Why would I want to talk to *you?*"

"Because otherwise you don't get to talk to anybody. And maybe we can both help each other find your brother. You lost your cool a bit here, pal, but I'm man enough not to go to the police about it. Are you?"

He stared at Gage a long time, trying to maintain some semblance of power, but it was all for show. Gage had won this encounter and they both knew it. Finally, he glanced at Miranda, wrinkled his nose dismissively, then brushed off the sand from his suit. He took his time about it, making him wait, but Gage kept the Beretta aimed squarely at the man's chest. No sense taking chances.

"Inn at Sapphire Head," Omar said, without looking at them, still working on his sleeves. "Room 317."

"Duly noted," Gage said.

"I don't want to wait until tomorrow. Please come see me tonight."

"I have a dinner engagement tonight, but I might be able to come late."

Omar, having finally finished removing the sand from his clothes, fixed his black poker eyes on Gage. "Dinner? With whom?"

"None of your business."

"My brother, he is missing, and a dinner is more important?"

"Will you be there or not?"

Omar sighed. "I will be there. Do you have a number where I can reach you?"

"No," Gage said. Then, remembering he was now a newly minted member of the cell-phone carrying society, corrected himself. "Actually, yes."

"Yes?"

"Yes."

Omar waited. Gage waited along with him.

"Well?" Omar said. "Are you going to give me the number?"

"No."

"No?"

"No."

"But I don't—"

"Listen," Gage said, "I'm getting tired of pointing this gun at you, and when I get tired, I get impatient. When I get impatient, I do stupid things. I suggest you get going. Be in that room tonight. If I decide to come see you, I'll be there late. If not, I won't. Don't tell anyone about our little encounter. Don't talk to the cops. Don't talk to *anyone*. We'll talk tonight and see where things lead."

Omar, standing there in his fine gray suit, looking so polished and dignified that it was hard to imagine that they'd actually come to blows only seconds before, gazed at them for a long time before finally offering a slight nod. He turned to go, then, as if suddenly remembering something, stopped and looked at them again.

"I have no intention of informing the police of our encounter," he said. "I would greatly prefer that what just transpired remain ... private. However, I must inform you that this may no longer be possible."

"What?" Gage said.

Rather than answer with words, Omar directed his gaze above them and to his left. Fearing a trick, Gage kept part of his attention on Omar while following the man's eyes. It took a few seconds to notice what Omar was talking about, to spot the trouble there leaning against the metal fence belonging to one of the houses on the bluff, but there was no mistaking what it was. A man. Not just any man. A man in purple, holding a large camera to his face, the lens glinting in the sun as it pointed in their direction.

Gage, still pointing his Beretta at Omar, could almost hear the shutter clicking.

Chapter 7

It was no use. Before Gage even managed a few steps toward the bluff, Buzz Burgin flitted away as fast as a field mouse.

That sinking feeling settling into Gage's gut was all too familiar. His past experience with the press—other than a wonderful relationship with Carmen Hornbridge, the previous owner of the *Bugle* who'd gone on to better things—already had him fearing the worst. Not just fearing the worst, but *knowing* the worst was about to come to pass. Who knew how long Buzz had been standing there armed with his camera, but it was long enough to snap at least the most damning picture: him pointing his Beretta at Omar, the brother of the missing man, and the mystery amnesia woman standing there looking terrified. Oh yes, it was going to be bad.

Bad for Gage and the police.

Bad for Miranda because of whoever might be looking for her.

Just bad all the way around.

"I will speak to you tonight," Omar said.

Gage turned to reply, but Omar was already a dozen paces away. Hands behind his back, head lowered in contemplation, he could have been a man leaving a boardroom meeting rather than a fistfight. The sand swirled around his black wingtips, and the ocean, ceaseless in its rhythms, continued advancing and retreating upon the shore, ever oblivious to their problems.

The cool breeze soothed Gage's aching face, though he knew by tonight Zoe would be joking about what an improvement the bruise made to his overall appearance. Slipping the Beretta into the side holster inside his leather jacket, he turned to Miranda. She still stood with her hands cupped over her face, eyes wet and bright, her whole body collapsed on itself like a turtle trying to retreat into its shell when its shell was missing. It made for a sad and pathetic sight, worthy of both sympathy and pity, and Gage could see the question in her eyes. *Why?* Not why Omar had attacked, but why was this all happening to her? He did not have an answer. He did not know why—why she was here, where Marcus had gone, or, most of all, why they could not unlock the door to her mind that would most likely lead to all the answers they needed.

Instead, he had only more questions. An endless stream of questions.

He saw that the thing she wanted most was for him to open his arms to her. A hug, that's all. If she was like a turtle without a shell, then he could be that shell. That was what she wanted. Protection. Safety. When the sky was falling all around you, a little safety could go a long ways, even if that safety was mostly an illusion. For now, a simple hug would do. Was that too much to ask?

Yes, it was.

Still seething at Omar's brazen attack, all that pent-up rage having nowhere to go, Gage could not help but direct some of that anger toward Miranda. It may not have been fair, but perhaps it *was* fair; there was still the doubt, after all. It lingered between them, in the gaps between the questions and the answers. No matter how pathetic a figure she made, she could have been playing him for a rube.

"Let's go," he said, turning toward the Turret House.

* * *

TRUDGING UP THE STEPS, Gage endured the trembling agony in his knee in stoic silence. The wind was so loud in their ears it would have been difficult to have a conversation in any case. He had his own shell, and he was happy to retreat into it when offered the chance; focusing on his pain offered its own form of healing.

Back at the Turret House, Eve was in the foyer chatting with some new guests, an elderly couple up from California, and they all gaped at Gage and Miranda when they entered. Glancing in the full-length mirror by the door, he saw why. Dried blood, caked with sand, coated his chin, and the bruise under his eye had already started to swell and turn pink. Eve, after quickly offering her new guests a couple of good restaurants for dinner, hustled both Gage and Miranda into the kitchen. There were lots of questions, of course, and as Gage tried to calm down enough to answer them, Miranda told them in an anguished voice that she needed to go lie down. Eve asked her if there was anything she could do for her, but Miranda was through the swinging doors before Eve finished the question.

"Poor thing," Eve said. "I'll bring her some lemon tea in a little bit. Help calm her nerves."

"A good idea," Gage said.

"Now, from the start, tell me what happened."

He did. While he was talking, she wet a paper towel and cleaned up his face, then got him some ice wrapped in a cotton dish towel. The initial sting gave way to a comforting coolness. The sun, which had already passed its zenith, shined through the porthole window and filled the kitchen with a warm glow, brightening the white cabinets and giving the oak countertops a gauzy, golden glow. He heard the slightly too-perfect crooning of Barry Manilow coming from the dining room, and he decided to forgive her this lapse in musical taste. He would forgive just about anything when it came to Eve.

"You know," Gage said, "if you ever decide to leave Alex, I'll be happy to take his place in a heartbeat."

"Oh, stop, you," she said. She stepped over to the tea kettle on the stove, picked it up, then sighed. "Maybe we should cancel the dinner tonight."

"No, don't do that."

"I don't want to. I just … do you think Miranda is up for it?"

"I think it'll be the best thing for her. Right now, she needs people around her who truly want the best for her, not the worst."

"You don't think this Omar person will come back?"

"No. He'll wait for me at the hotel."

"Okay. If you say so. I just have a bad feeling."

"You have nothing to worry about," Gage said, "because I'll be here. As everybody knows, I'm a good luck charm."

Eve smiled politely at this, but she was too nice to put him in his place. Zoe, however, came down when she heard the whistle of the tea kettle, took one look at Gage, and asked him who he'd managed to piss off this time. A study in contrasts, those two. Eve soon disappeared upstairs with a tray of tea and biscuits, the scent of lemon and apricot jam trailing after her, and Zoe made her daily run to the bank and grocery store, leaving Gage alone downstairs.

Alone and brooding. He didn't want to tell Eve, but he had a bad feeling too, a queasy sense that terrible things were still to come—and maybe soon. He parked himself in one of the wing-backed chairs in the living room, where he had a good view of the front door and street. Nothing out there but a couple of seagulls pecking at the gravel.

Yet there was no way he was leaving these three women alone. Besides, the way he felt at the moment, he wasn't keen on doing a lot of moving around anyway. His face still throbbed, and already he could feel his muscles tightening, the adrenaline that had masked the assorted aches and pains beginning to fade. The chair would be just fine. It was only a few hours until dinner and this was as good a place to recover as any.

He watched the street for a while, but the seagulls soon departed and left him nothing of even moderate interest to hold his attention. He flipped through some recent issues of National Geographic, reading a piece about New Guinea but none of the words stuck. Eventually, he dozed, waking with a start when someone put a hand on his shoulder. He'd already slipped his hand inside his jacket and gripped the handle of the Beretta when he looked up and saw that it was Miranda.

"Sorry," she said.

She blinked bleary eyes at him, and strands of her hair stuck out at odd angles, as if she too had been napping.

"It's all right," he said. "I'm just a little jumpy right now."

"I don't blame you. Are you feeling okay?"

"I've had better days."

"That bruise ..." She reached to touch his cheek, but stopped before her hand reached its destination. "I can't believe that man did that to you."

"He'll have a few black and blue spots himself," Gage said.

"Yes." She swallowed, glanced at where his hand still rested inside his jacket, then asked tentatively, "Would you really have shot him?"

"Yes."

"Just like that? Not even any doubt?"

"I always save the doubt for later. Keeps me alive. Besides, doubt, guilt—those things always go down a bit easier with a shot or two of bourbon."

"Oh. Well, I want to thank you."

"No need."

"I also want to show you something ... in my room."

Either she read something in his expression, or she realized there was a definite implication to what she's said, because she blushed almost immediately—her face and neck turning nearly the same bright red as her hair.

"Oh," she said, "it's not ... I just want to show you something. Something interesting."

"Okay."

"I just ... it's kind of private. I mean—"

"It's all right, Miranda. Let's go."

He followed her upstairs, her blush mostly fading by the time they got there, though she still kept an awkward distance from him and darted quickly to her end table and snatched up the drawing pad there. It was open to the first page. She thrust the pad at him, turning her head slightly away, like a child who'd been caught doing something bad and now feared the consequences.

The drawing pictured a crescent moon over a sailboat, the ocean waves laced with silvery light. There was a hint of a pier in the foreground, the edge of a boardwalk and some posts descending into the water. It was only a sketch, just enough hint of detail to let the mind fill in the rest, but they were the *right* details, done with skill and flair, the practice and training obvious in each little scratch of the pencil.

"Wow," he said, "this is wonderful."

"You really think so?"

"Living on the coast, I see a lot of art. A lot of artists, too. This is as good as anything I've seen. Do you know where it is?"

She shook her head. "I wish I did. I woke up and this was in my head. Before I even realized what I was doing, I was drawing it. It really scared me. I didn't know I could do something like this."

"Well, then you should do more of it. Maybe it'll help you remember."

"I hope so," she said, but when she looked at the drawing, there was something troubling in her eyes—a pained expression, as if part of her *did* remember.

The drawing also sparked something deep in the back of Gage's mind, not a memory exactly, but a flash of meaning that he couldn't quite discern. It was as if he knew he was looking not at a drawing, but some kind of puzzle. Where was this place? There was nothing distinctive, it could have been any of a thousand ports, but still, he sensed it was a particular port and that the details were all in the picture.

Nothing came to him, so he filed it away to think about later. They went downstairs and chatted in the living room. It wasn't long before Alex came home from the store, joining the conversation until about six, when he departed to help Eve prepare. A half hour later, about the time Gage detected some wonderful beef and garlic aromas wafting from the kitchen, Tatyana showed up. She apologized for coming early, but she'd managed to extricate herself from her patients and it didn't make sense to head home only to have to head out again immediately. Mid-apology, she noticed Gage's bruised face and demanded to know what had happened. He let Miranda tell it this time.

Tatyana may come straight from the hospital, and was dressed in the same blue V-neck shirt and charcoal pants as when they'd seen her earlier, but Gage thought he detected a hint of red lipstick that she had not been wearing before. The white scarf was also missing, the V-neck shirt perhaps unbuttoned just a bit lower—still tasteful, but revealing a little more cleavage. Was she flirting with him? He caught a furtive glance from her, and he thought it was the kind of glance that a woman gives a man when she's trying to assess the reaction her appearance has had on him, but what did Gage know? He was wrong about women far more often than he was right.

She did, however, sit next to him on the small couch. Or, to be more accurate, Gage sat next to her. Miranda did not give him a lot of choice, directing her to the couch, and Zoe, who was now off work and had joined them, took the nearest armchair ahead of him. That meant Gage would have had to awkwardly pull one of the wing-backed armchairs closer if he didn't want to sit next to her, but he didn't even consider it. He was perfectly happy to sit next to Tatyana, not quite close enough that their legs touched, but still close enough that he felt her body heat and got a good whiff of her lilac-scented perfume. Had she been wearing that earlier? He didn't think so.

Though the sun had not yet set, it was low enough that the light coming from the living room window—on the eastern side of the house—faded quickly, the sky dissolving, the shadows in the room deepening. They talked for a few minutes, mostly Zoe, who entertained them with a story about a guest at the Turret

House a few weeks back who'd come to Oregon from Boston and had been shocked to find a real civilization and not a scattering of log houses and teepees. Where could he go to find a real live lumberjack, he wanted to know. To Gage, Zoe seemed strangely animated, talking quickly, laughing loudly, not at all her usual edgy, sarcastic self. When the doorbell rang, she jumped out of her chair and flew to the door as if she'd been fired there by a rocket.

It didn't take Gage long to realize what all her nervous energy had been about. In stepped young officer Zachary Gilbert, the two of them grinning at each other like idiots. No police uniform this time, not even a trench coat. He wore dark designer jeans and a blue blazer that was a bit tight in the shoulders, not tight in an I-got-too-fat-for-my-jacket sort of way, but in an I-deliberately-chose-a-jacket-too-small-to-show-off-my-muscular-body way.

"What are *you* doing here?" Gage asked.

"Oh," Zachary said, "sorry, I didn't—"

"Ignore him," Zoe said, and then, pointedly to Gage: "I invited him."

"Actually," Alex said, sweeping into the room, *"I'm* the one who invited him. I just asked Zoe to relay the message. Come in, come in! Ignore the grump on the couch. He's fine as long as he's medicated. You're just in time. Dinner is served!"

There was a bit of an awkward dance as they made their way to the dining room: Zoe trying to stay close to Zachary, as Zachary was obviously trying to keep his distance from Gage. Miranda, who'd done her best to force Gage and Tatyana together on the couch, seemed to do everything she could to position herself between them as they walked. Yet when they got there, and Gage took his seat, Miranda quickly pulled out a chair next to him and gestured for Tatyana to sit. She actually took a chair opposite Gage, next to Zoe and her earnest law-abiding suitor. The way Zoe kept glancing at Zachary, as if she was waiting for him to turn into a butterfly at any moment, was disturbing enough that he barely noticed that magnificent spread before them until his senses were overwhelmed by the sheer goodness of it all.

Chickpea soup, garlic mashed potatoes, creamy cheese baked pasta, Horiatiki Salata, which Eve had explained to him once was the *real* Greek salad since it contained no lettuce—the green silk tablecloth was decked out with a wide array of both Mediterranean and American food, as was Eve's custom. While the living room had grown dark with the onset of dusk, the dining room, located on the western side of the house, was filled with the warm orange light of the setting sun—a copper disc half sunk beneath a flat and tranquil ocean. It gave everyone in the room an ethereal glow, their skin rosier, their eyes brighter, as if the whole scene had been recreated by a Renaissance painter. Even the water inside their crystal glasses shined like liquid gold.

Rare was the time that Gage ate in the dining room and didn't feel like he was eating in a restaurant with a clear view of heaven. Today was no different.

The potatoes were smooth and buttery, with just a touch of garlic. The boiled green beans had just the right mixture of vinegar and salt. The two bottles of a California Chardonnay Alex had opened for the occasion offered just the right combination of tartness and sweetness. The food was so good, in fact, that no one spoke for a good while, and the silence was neither awkward nor even missed. It was not until Miranda let out an involuntary sigh, one obviously prompted by how delicious everything was, that everybody laughed and the conversational gates flew open. Alex talked about an interesting collection of Easton Press leather-bounds he'd bought for the store, which led to questions from Tatyana and Zachary about the book business and how Alex had gotten into it.

"Oh, I was a book lover long before I had any interest in the FBI," Alex explained. "I worked in a used bookstore when I was going to college at UNC at Chapel Hill, not the big one near campus that sold mostly textbooks but a little dusty shop at the edge of town. It was run by a grumpy old guy who taught me a whole lot about the business, both the used paperback trade and the antiquarian side of things. Now most rare books are sold online, but back then it was a totally different business—you'd create a catalog and send it out to other dealers, or you'd put a listing in one of the main trade magazines of stuff you're looking for or selling."

Tatyana took a sip from her wine. "It seems like a very different kind of life than one where you are chasing criminals. Much more … relaxed."

"I didn't chase a whole lot of criminals anyway," Alex said. "For the bulk of my FBI career, I taught at the Academy. But how about you, Dr. Brunner? You must have an interesting story about what led you into medicine, especially way out here on the Oregon coast. You're from Russia, right?"

"Ukraine," Tatyana said. "Though I lived just outside Simferopol in Crimea, quite near Russia, and Russian was the main language spoken."

"Oh, Crimea," Eve said, "such terrible things have happened there recently. So much violence."

"Yes," Tatyana said. "There have always been terrible things in Crimea. It is not like here. It is not peaceful."

"You have lots of family there?" Miranda asked.

Tatyana touched the CK necklace hanging around her neck, the diamonds glinting orange and gold. "Some," she said. "I left a long time ago, though."

She did not elaborate, and the tone of her voice led Gage to believe she had no wish to do so, at least not now. The silence stretched until it became uncomfortable, all of them alone with their thoughts and the clinking of the silverware, before Miranda asked Gage how he became a private investigator. Gage tried to beg off, but since there were three people in the room who had not heard the story, and seemed eager for it, he couldn't hold them at bay for long—especially when Alex, well versed in Gage's past, started to tell the story himself. So Gage told them all about his early beginnings in Montana, his washout at the FBI academy, and how he eventually ended up working for his uncle's private investigation firm in New York before a misunderstanding prompted Gage to hang his own shingle. When they inevitably asked him what kind of misunderstanding, he told them his uncle misunderstood that Gage wouldn't just do what he was told without questioning it.

"Well, that hasn't changed," Alex said.

"Actually," Zoe said, "I find it hard to believe Garrison *ever* did what he was told."

"And your move to Oregon?" Tatyana asked.

Everyone fell silent, most of them taking a sudden interest in their water glasses. Tatyana glanced around nervously.

"I'm sorry," she said, "did I say something that—"

"It's all right," Gage said. "I moved out here after my wife was murdered."

"Oh. I'm sorry. I did not—"

"No, no, it's okay."

And, strangely, it *was* okay, or at least okay enough that Gage could actually tell the story without feeling like he needed to punch someone in the face. Maybe it was Tatyana's presence, the general feeling of welcome in the group, or just the passage of time, but Gage had little problem telling everyone how his wife had died in a mafia revenge hit gone wrong and how this had prompted him to retire to the Oregon coast. When Gage eventually ran out of steam—not because his emotions got the best of him, but because he got tired of hearing himself speak—Alex picked up the slack, regaling them with the story of the young dead woman who had washed up on the beach a couple years ago, and how this had pulled Gage back into his chosen line of work.

He didn't even mind so much when Zoe, as his own story drew to a close, asked Zachary why he became a cop.

"Oh, I don't know," he said. His attempt to look ambivalent about the question clearly failed; the attention from Zoe lit up his eyes and made him straighten in his chair. "I just … it seemed like the thing to do when I was in high school."

"You grew up in Barnacle Bluffs?" Zoe asked.

"Just down the road in Newport. I was born there."

Alex raised his glass. "An Oregon native. I'll drink to that. I think you're the only one in the room."

"Did you have family who were cops?" Zoe asked. "Or close friends or something?"

"No," Zachary said, "nothing like that. My dad is a dentist."

"So you just, what, woke up one day and decided to join the police force?"

"Pretty much."

"Huh."

They all nodded, turning their attention to their food and their wine. Zoe smiled at Zachary reassuringly, but there was clearly disappointment in her eyes, and he could *see* the disappointment there. Everybody could. He glanced around the room. Miranda started to ask about the city of Portland when Zachary suddenly blurted out one word loud enough that most of them flinched.

"Superman!"

They all froze, forks hovering near mouths, water glasses held aloft. He swallowed.

"I mean, he's kind of—kind of why I became a cop," he said. "The comic book, I mean. I read a lot of Superman as a kid. I collected them. Actually, my dad collected comics. I just read them. Superman was my favorite. I had—had posters all over my wall. Green Lantern, Hulk—but mostly Superman. He was just so, you know, *good.* I wanted to be like him. Fight crime, save the world. I couldn't have the powers or anything, but I thought … well, being a cop …"

His voice trailed off, as if it had begun to dawn on him how far he had gone exposing his inner psyche to the group. Any other time, any other place, and such an admission might have provoked some teasing from Gage, but Zachary had been so earnest, no nakedly honest, that it was hard not to at least admire the boldness. He even found himself liking the kid, despite his every effort to prevent the feeling from taking hold.

Zachary slunk into his chair, avoiding their eyes. "Kind of silly, I know."

"No," Zoe said, "it's not silly at all."

"I don't read them anymore. I mean, I *have* them in boxes. But I don't read them. Not much, anyway. I just ..."

He probably would have gone on like that, bumbling forward in an effort to recover from his embarrassment, if Zoe hadn't reached over and touched his forearm reassuringly. It was probably a subconscious gesture, but it was full of such simple, honest intimacy, the kind of gesture that said a lot more than words ever could, that Gage felt a profound gratefulness that Zoe was the kind of person she was, the kind of person he knew he could never really be. He also sat in awe, touched with a poignancy that bordered on the bittersweet, of her journey these past few years from a troubled teenager on the brink of disaster to a young headstrong woman on the cusp of a great life. She'd transformed more in a few months than he had in his entire life.

Zachary looked at her with his own grateful expression, obviously both aware and thankful of her efforts to rescue him. They were in their own little bubble, everyone watching like a mesmerized movie audience, until Zoe seemed to realize what she was doing and pulled her hand back, glancing away like a shy little girl. *Shy.* That was a word that Gage never would have used to describe Zoe before today. It would have been easy enough to embarrass them, and Gage did feel a bit tempted. How much endless ribbing had he endured from Zoe?

"Well," Gage said, "I was always partial to Spider-Man myself. I grant you that Superman is more powerful, but Peter Parker is a much more relatable human being than Clark Kent. He's got normal problems like he rest of us."

He said this without a trace of sarcasm, hoping it would be received the same way. To his delight, it was, though not without a few astonished expressions from those around the table. In any case, after a few silent beats, the comment opened the conversational flood gates, and soon they were all arguing about the ideal superhero. In addition to Spider-Man and Superman, the merits of Wonder Woman, Flash, Batman, and others were hotly debated. Some, like Alex, asserted that a team approach like the Justice League or the Fantastic Four were more akin to a police department's work, but Gage and Tatyana countered that the larger the group, the more bureaucracy would prevent them from responding quickly in a crisis, and that ultimately people wanted to follow one person's story.

Like all such discussions, the central topic was eventually lost in a myriad of tangents and quibbling over details. The purpose wasn't to win the argument, after all; the conversation was merely a mechanism that allowed everyone to feel connected and involved. Usually Gage hated this kind of talking for talking's sake, but this time he didn't mind. In fact, at one point during the discussion, when they were all talking over one another, the energy high, the spirit open and good-natured, he found himself looking at all the beaming faces and realizing something on a deep level that he had never truly realized before.

He was home.

This place, these people—Gage had never felt more at home in his life. At least not since Janet died, and that had been a very different kind of home, a special intimacy that was more about his bond with that one person than it was a feeling of belonging. That's what this was. He felt as if he belonged, with these people, in this place, at this particular point in time. Sure, some of the people were new to the fold, but it didn't matter. They were part of the fabric of this place, too, and their addition to the group did not detract from its appeal but instead add variety and interest. Even Zachary. Gage may have still felt a mild unease at his presence, but he belonged as well. He was making Zoe happy, after all.

Gage felt the sort of deep, inner contentment that was always so elusive to him, even when he'd been married to the love of his life. Always on edge. Always restless. Always wondering when the next shoe would drop. That's how he'd lived his life, both back then and after. This was different. This was living in the moment, with no expectations. For once, he wasn't waiting for everything to go to hell.

Naturally, that's when it did.

If there had been a knock, Gage had not heard it. Their conversation had reached a loud crescendo, loud enough that they might have missed a knock had there been one. Gage simply looked up and there they were: Chief Quinn, Brisbane, Trenton, and two uniformed police officers he did not know by name, standing grimly in the entryway. It took a second or two for everyone to notice them, but when they did, the conversation shriveled and died.

The silence—a terrible and pervasive silence that was somehow more deafening than their conversation had been—lasted only a few seconds. Gage knew, by who they were staring at, what they were going to say, but it did not make hearing it any easier.

"Miranda," Quinn said, "you're under arrest for the murder of Marcus Koura."

Chapter 8

By the time everyone recovered from the shock, Miranda was already in handcuffs. Like a pair of gray buzzards, Brisbane and Trenton swooped down on her and yanked her to her feet, not bothering to hide their glee as they twisted her arms behind her back and slapped the cuffs on her. It was the metallic clink that finally brought everybody to life—everybody except Miranda, who stared blankly like some kind of zombie—and within seconds Gage, Alex, and Zoe were all protesting, the room a cacophony of noise. Zachary sank a few inches lower in his seat. Tatyana and Eve, dumbstruck, watched it all. When Trenton jerked Miranda toward the door, Gage couldn't contain himself. He rose so fast that his chair banged to the hardwood.

Quinn held up a hand. "Hold on there, Gage. Let's not do something stupid."

"You're lecturing me about stupid?" Gage shot back. "You better have a warrant or there's going to be a hell of a lawsuit—"

"Calm down, pal. We don't need a warrant. We have enough probable cause as it is."

"Based on what? You just changed your mind?"

"Based on the body that washed up about an hour ago at Sitka Beach."

"What?"

"Omar ID'd him as Marcus Koura. He was all wrapped up in what was left of the sails. Been in the water a couple weeks at least, so the body's not in good shape, but he's still recognizable. Found by some kids staying at the Northwest Artist Colony and they'd already taken all kinds of pictures with their phones, so I imagine it's already lighting up the Internet."

"That doesn't mean he was murdered!" Gage said. "It could have been an accident. He could have fallen—"

"Right into a gunshot?"

"What?"

"You heard me," Quinn said. "Took a slug right in the heart. And there was no bullet hole in the sails, meaning someone wrapped him up afterwards and tossed him overboard. It also looks like somebody originally tied something to his ankles, an anchor maybe, but it slipped free." He nodded sadly to Eve and Tatyana. "I'm sorry, ladies. I hate to bring this kind of talk to the dinner table. Just couldn't be helped."

Trenton, leering at Gage, clutched Miranda's arm as he might a flagpole he'd used to stake out his territory. "Still want to try to stop us? I'd love to slap some handcuffs on you, too. Maybe you can share a cell."

Focusing on Quinn, Gage said, "Come on, Chief. Are the handcuffs really necessary here? I mean, look at her. My hat weights more than she does."

"There was a murder with a firearm," Quinn said. "We're playing this one by the book."

"Chief—"

"Don't push it, Gage. You want to jeopardize her chances of getting out on bail? I can still put in a good word with the judge."

"Just take it easy on her, will you?"

"We *are* going easy on her."

With that, Quinn signaled to Brisbane and Trenton to escort Miranda to the door. Gage fought the impulse to intervene, knowing it would do no good. Miranda, finally rousing from her near-catatonic state, shot Gage a helpless look so full of desperation and fear that he wished he could think of something to comfort her. Nothing came to him. What could he say? He tried to look sympathetic, but the doubt was there, too. Marcus Koura had been shot, wrapped in a sail, and dumped overboard. While there may have been a justifiable reason for it, right now he could not see it. He also could not see how this little waif of a creature could ever shoot anyone, but the facts were what they were. When his boat came ashore, she was on it and he wasn't.

He followed the police outside, the rest of the group shuffling along behind him in stupefied silence. The sky, devoid of any sunlight, or any sign of the moon or stars, stretched dark and unblemished overhead like the underside of a black vinyl umbrella. Cold gusts of wind leapt over the house and rippled their clothes, stirred the fir trees and the grassy dunes. Trenton lowered her into the back of a police cruiser, a pitiful little shape, and he caught one fleeting glimpse of the whites of her eyes before the door shut and the reflection in the glass showed the front of the Turret House all aglow—as well as a man standing off to Gage's right.

He looked and there was Omar Koura. His face was cast in shadows, so it was impossible to know if he'd watched the whole ordeal with smug satisfaction, but based on his crossed arms and general upright posture, Gage guessed the answer was yes.

After the police pulled away, Omar approached Gage. He dipped his hand inside his jacket and Gage tensed, reaching for his Beretta.

"Do not worry," Omar said. "I do not wish to fight you again."

"Well, that's a relief."

"Only to show you something. A picture. You must see this. You must see this to understand my rage."

Slowly, with great care, Omar pulled a phone out of his jacket. He clicked a button and the screen illuminated. In the darkness, it was so starkly bright that it took a moment for Gage to discern the image itself, but once he saw it there was no mistaking what it was. A body. A body wrapped in what must have been the ragged sails that once belonged to the sailboat *Charity Case*, but from the distance where the shot had been taken it looked more like a shroud—a shroud of tattered sails. A number of people gathered around the body, most of them in police uniform, but Omar had still managed to get a clear shot.

"There lies my brother," Omar said. "That woman, she put him there. She put him there, and now she must pay the price."

Saturday morning—after very little sleep, and more than few calls to some lawyers—Gage showed up at the Barnacle Bluffs Police Station at ten to seven. The squat, nondescript building was on the far side of Big Dipper Lake, sheltered by a ring of Douglas firs, and Gage could just glimpse the smooth blue water down the hill and through the gaps in the trees. The sky was gray, the light dusky. It was a Saturday, and if he'd come a few hours later, Gage knew he would have heard the buzz of motorboats and jet skis, but for now there was just the morning breeze through the fir needles and the chirping of the birds.

Quinn wasn't there, and nobody would let him see Miranda without Quinn's authorization, so Gage waited in the van, shivering, until the Chief showed up at quarter to eight. He drove a black F-150 with mud caked to the side panels and a bumper sticker that read *Watch out for sneaker waves!* Gage got out of the van and met him at the door, leaning hard on his cane. His right knee felt like exposed bones patched together with duct tape, and his left knee wasn't all that much better.

"Do you know what this cool weather does to me?" he said.

"Well, good morning to you, too, Gage."

"It's murder on my bones, that's what. And you kept me waiting for an hour."

"I don't seem to recall agreeing to meet."

"I want her out. Now."

"You know that's not how it's done with a serious felony charge. There will be an arraignment, and that's where bail—"

"This is not a normal situation and you know it. You don't even know who she really is!"

Quinn sighed and ran a hand through his thinning gray hair—hair that still glistened as if he'd just stepped out of a morning shower. "Can I at least get my coffee before we talk about this?"

"She can stay at the Turret House. She's not going anywhere."

"You can have a cup, too. I won't even charge you."

"The kind of coffee you guys make?" Gage said. "You should be paying *me* to drink it."

"There's the Garrison I know. Come on."

He followed Quinn inside. Brisbane and Trenton lurked behind the desk, eyeing him warily. Gage was not at all surprised that they were in on a Saturday; an arrest like Miranda's was big news in a town like Barnacle Bluffs and nobody wanted to miss any of the action. Zachary was there, too, peering over the top of one of the cubicles as if he didn't want Gage to see him. Most of the other cops in the room steadfastly ignored him, a sort of mild passive aggressiveness that he was used to by now. He'd never made their lives easier, after all.

Quinn directed him to a plastic chair outside his office, brought him a cup of coffee in a paper cup and two packets of creamer a few minutes later, and told him to sit tight while Quinn made a few phone calls. The coffee was hot and bitter. The creamer helped with the first part but not the second. Gage flipped through a wrinkled National Geographic, reading about the fight against malaria in Africa, and kept glancing at the big metal door at the back of the room—the one that led to the small jail at the rear of the station. He wondered how Miranda was doing in there, how she was holding up.

Twenty minutes later, Quinn walked out of his office and stood in front of Gage.

"It's a no go," he said. "She's staying put for now."

"What? Why?"

"It's all the publicity. It's got Judge Cooley up in Newport nervous. Bail will be set at her arraignment on Wednesday."

"Wednesday! Most arraignments are next business day, which should be Monday."

"Stop pretending to be dumber than you are. You know as well as I that not all felony charges are arraigned that quickly. And with all the press, he thinks it might be better to take this one a bit slower. Get it right. "

"She's not a flight risk! There's no reason for this."

"You need to lower your voice."

"Chief—"

"Come with me."

With a clenched jaw, Quinn led him into the office and shut the door behind them. The computer was on and humming, the big hulk of a monitor showing a picture of his wife, Ginger, standing on a beach at sunset. When he'd met her, Gage remembered her having red vibrant hair, much like Miranda's; now it was gray and flat. Stacks of paper, manila folders, and other files covered the metal desk. Taking his time, Quinn settled himself into the squeaky swivel chair, clasping his hands under his lips and staring up at Gage. The way his hands were pointed, with his big black eyebrows over them, his face seemed to form a question mark.

"Not a flight risk" he said. "And you know this ... how? Based on a couple meals you spent with her? We don't even know who she is, Gage."

"You have a body, but no murder weapon."

"True," Quinn said. "We certainly have ample reason to believe a murder took place, though."

"If she hadn't stepped off that boat, she wouldn't even be a suspect."

"Also true. But she *did* step off that boat. Facts are facts."

"You have no motive."

"I imagine when we find out who she is, that will come out. Come on, Gage. The owner of the boat was shot, dead center in the chest, pretty much an impossible angle for a suicide. Somebody wrapped him in a sail and tossed him overboard, tying on something heavy for good measure. Who else could have done this?"

Gage knew he was grasping, but he didn't care. "Maybe she wasn't the only one on the boat. Maybe someone else was on there and got out before Zoe and I came along."

Quinn sighed. "Gage, come on."

"It's possible."

"Really? Did you see any other footprints in the area?"

"They could have walked through the surf."

"Sure, and maybe Michael Jackson and Elvis were on there, too. Let's throw in Jimmy Hoffa. Plenty of room."

"You're making jokes," Gage said, "but you know the case here is flimsy."

"Yep, and she'd help herself by telling us who she is." Before Gage could object, Quinn held up his hand. "I'm willing to go with the amnesia thing until proven otherwise. But come on, pal, you have to admit it doesn't look good. Have you seen what's all over the news this morning?"

When Gage didn't answer, Quinn swiveled around in his chair and moved his mouse. The picture of his wife vanished, replaced by the *Oregonian*'s homepage. The first picture Gage saw, taking up half the screen, was a split image: one half showed the sailboat washed up on the beach, the other half was a head and shoulders shot of Miranda. Based on the Oregon Coast sweatshirt she was wearing, the picture was obviously from the previous day. There was something menacing about her expression; she wasn't quite scowling, but there was a dark, contemplative look about her. No surprise that Buzz Burgin had chosen that particular picture—it made her look guilty.

Below the split photo, with the article text wrapping around it, was the one Gage had feared. It pictured Gage pointing his Beretta at Omar. Buzz had managed to snap the photo at just the right instant, when Gage appeared menacing and Omar helpless.

"Must be a fascinating story behind that photo of you," Quinn said.

"Must be," Gage said.

"Care to tell me about it?"

"We were practicing for the local community theater."

"Uh huh. Maybe I'll ask Omar. Interesting he didn't mention it."

"It's his first play," Gage said. "He's a bit self-conscious about his acting."

"Yeah, well, maybe I'll let sleeping dogs lie on this one. The point is, Miranda's case is already high profile in Oregon. I'd be willing to bet good money that by the end of the day, it'll have a high profile across the nation, maybe even worldwide. The woman washing up on the beach with amnesia was fascinating enough. But a murder on top of it? Hard to see how this doesn't get some national attention. The last thing Judge Cooley wants is for some east-coast journalist with a stick up his butt to start writing about the backwards judicial system out here in the wild west."

"We'd hate for them to get the wrong idea," Gage said. Thinking about it now, he realized that a jail cell wasn't exactly the worst place for Miranda, at least temporarily. If the story did go viral, then whatever man she'd fled—if that was indeed what had happened—would soon see her picture and know exactly where she was. There was also Omar. When he'd said that Miranda would have to pay for what she'd done, there was a fair chance he wasn't talking about prison, but exacting a more personal form of revenge. "All right, whatever. Can I at least see her?"

"That I can do," Quinn said. "Judge Cooley does want to keep her here, not at the county lockup."

He took Gage to the back of the station. They stepped through the metal door, into a tiny waiting area before two other doors—one that led outside, so the cops had easy access for dropping off prisoners, and another that led to the handful of jail cells. It was cool and musty. A burly cop came out of a room and had them sign the logbook. Gage surrendered his Beretta. The cop unlocked the second door and let them into the cells, closing the door behind them with a loud clank.

The ceiling lights, behind metal webs, cast a net of shadows on the concrete floor. They passed four cells, two on each side, none of them occupied. The clap of their footsteps were the only sounds. Miranda was in the last cell on the right, clutching the bars and pressing her body as close to them as she could, as if she was trying to get as much of herself outside the cell. She still wore the white blouse and tan capris she'd worn at dinner, the ones he'd bought her, though they were noticeably wrinkled. Her hair was a tangled mop, her mascara was a dark smear, and her cheeks were splotchy and red.

"I was hoping you'd come to see me," she said.

"Of course I'd come," Gage said. "We're going to get you out of here in no time."

"Today?"

"I'm afraid not. Soon, though."

She started to tear up, then gave her head a hard shake, as if trying to ward off the feeling. "It's okay. I'll be okay."

"I know."

"I've just ... I've never been in jail. At least I don't think I have. I don't know. Um, Garrison?"

"Yes?"

She started to speak, then looked at Quinn. "Can I speak to him a second? I mean, a little privacy?"

Quinn's face soured. Usually he looked a bit like Mr. Rogers, exuding a kind of sober but still somewhat kindly demeanor, but every now and then his patient facade fell away and he revealed the grizzled, embattled small-town police chief he really was, one who'd suffered and seen far too much. "I can't take you out," he said. Then, after barely getting the words out, he sighed. "Sorry. I know it's no picnic being in here. I can wait on the other side for five minutes. Is that all right?"

When Miranda nodded, he tipped his head and retreated back the way they came, taking position by the metal door. Gage stepped up to the bars, close enough that he caught a whiff of the perfume she'd worn yesterday, weaker and mixed with sweat. It smelled like the ocean, and he knew where he'd smelled it before. Eve must have given her some.

"Miranda," he said, "you should know that anything you say

to me in here could potentially be used against you. I'm not a lawyer, so there's no attorney-client confidentiality that covers us."

"No, no, it's okay," she said. "I'm not going to … Oh, Garrison, you don't believe it, do you? I mean, you don't believe that I'm … that I would have …"

"Of course not," he said.

"Because I wouldn't. I would never."

"I know."

"I mean, how would you believe me, right? I know. I don't remember, so how would I know? But I wouldn't do that. I can't even imagine … It makes me shake, just thinking about it. Please believe me. I need at least one person to believe me."

"I do," Gage said.

She sniffled, then wiped away the tears that had begun to form. "Thank you. Even if you're lying, it still means something. You're not lying, are you?"

There must have been something in his eyes, or in his expression, or perhaps just in the hesitancy of his reply, because he saw something crumple inside her, some of her hope wilting under the glare of his own doubt. He could not deny the doubt. The truth was, he *wanted* to believe her, wanted it very much, and that was enough for him. It would keep him going. For her? So scared and alone? He knew she wanted more, but he was only so good an actor. All he could give her was his best effort in doing his job and hope that was enough.

"Miranda," he said, "I'm going to prove you didn't do this."

Chapter 9

Gage may have wanted to prove that Miranda was innocent, but he was still at a loss about how to do it. How could he prove she was innocent when he didn't even know who she was?

He stopped at The Diner and pondered the question over breakfast. The pancakes tasted doughy, the eggs were on the runny side, and the coffee could have doubled as motor oil for his van, but he still loved the cramped but cozy restaurant, as a lot of the locals did. Its real name was McAllister's Family Diner, but that had been just one of its many names in its storied history of varied owners and even more varied cooking, and most everybody around Barnacle Bluffs just knew it as The Diner. The black-and-white checkered floor may have been scuffed and peeling, the red vinyl booths sagging and patched with duct tape, and the jukebox may have only been able to play a half-dozen songs without skipping, but there was still a heart and soul to the place that most of the touristy restaurants on the coast lacked.

As a rule, Gage didn't eat out much—he didn't get out much period—but when he did, it was usually at The Diner.

It wasn't until he was halfway through his breakfast that it dawned on him that he might have made a mistake. As he was forcing down another sip of the sludge-like coffee, he realized that most of the conversation in the room had ceased. A young couple in a corner booth chatted away, oblivious, but most of the other dozen people were looking at him, some with thin *Bugle* newspapers open on their tables, others alternating between peering at their smartphones and staring at Gage. One of them, an old man wearing rainbow suspenders over a blue plaid shirt, a regular Gage recognized but didn't know by name, leaned over on his stool and whispered to Gage.

"Hey," he said, "you that fella on the beach, ain't ya? The one protecting that woman."

Gage, seated at one of the little tables between the booths and the counter, debated how to respond. Ignoring the comment was probably not an option. "Word travels fast," he said.

"Saw your picture in the paper. You're that private investigator."

The guy might have been whispering, but there was no need. Even if the majority of the people didn't look at him, most of their heads turned, ears perked to pick up the conversation. Gage dabbed at his lips with a napkin and took his time before answering.

"Right now I'm just a guy trying to eat his breakfast," he said.

"She really a killer?"

"No."

"Huh. Really seems that way."

"Doesn't matter how it seems. Matters how it *is*."

"What, you her boyfriend or something?"

"Just somebody trying to help."

Gage took a bite of his pancakes, not because he was hungry but because he was trying to signal that the conversation was over. But the old man wasn't finished.

"I read about you before," the old man said. "You're always stirring up trouble around here, ain't ya?"

Gage had left his cane leaning against the other chair, and he looked at it, wondering if he should use it to get the old man to shut up. He'd lived here for over six years and he still felt like

114

an outsider. When would that ever change? Probably never. It wasn't like he needed any of these people. He was still contemplating his response when Judy, a bosomy waitress who'd been working at The Diner for over a year, bustled over to his table with a pot of coffee and refilled his cup.

"You leave poor Garrison alone, Ed," she said. The steam curled around her hand. "You seem to forget all the good he's done around here."

"Aw, whatever," Ed said, dismissing them all with a wave of his hand and turning back to the counter. "

Judy, a stout woman who'd barely exchanged more than pleasantries with Gage, leaned over and winked at him. "Some of us do more than just read the paper," she said. "Some of us even manage to think for ourselves."

"I appreciate it," Gage said.

"It's not just that. One of my girlfriends told me a few years back how you helped find her daughter years ago, after she was kidnapped by those bank robbers. She said you didn't even accept any money. I never forgot that. She said you weren't even in the paper for that one, like you didn't want no publicity."

"Oh."

"You just keep doing what you're doing. If you think that woman is innocent, well, then she probably is. And ignore all the gossipy busybodies in this town."

She said the last part loud enough for most of the people around them to hear, before patting him on the shoulder and heading to a booth at the back. Some of the other diners shot him a wary glance before returning to their food. Nobody said a word to him afterwards.

Maybe he had a few friends in this town after all.

But only a few.

WITH NO OTHER idea what to do at the moment, Gage swung by the Turret House, picked up the drawing of the ocean Miranda had created, and took it up to Books and Oddities to get

Alex's opinion. They batted ideas around for over an hour, interrupted occasionally by a customer, but even working together didn't glean any special clues from the drawing. A moon, a pier, and whole lot of ocean—it really could have been anywhere. After a while, Gage resorted to sitting glumly behind the counter, perched on a stool like a grumpy parrot, while Alex disappeared to help a young woman find some books for her hard-to-please kindergartner.

When Zoe showed up a little before noon with a sack lunch for Alex, Gage's mood darkened. Part of this was due to the hour of the day, which meant he'd burned up the entire morning and made no progress. The other part was Zoe herself, decked out in a tea-green cardigan over a white open-collared shirt, her sharply dressed presence a reminder of the feud that still simmered between them about what she was doing with her life.

Afraid of what he might say to her in his present state of mind, Gage offered a sullen goodbye and fled for his house. There were two reporters waiting for him, a young man from the local *Bugle* and a chain-smoking middle-aged woman from Eugene's *Register Guard.* They fired questions at him as soon as he stepped out of the van. He patiently told them that if they didn't get off his property in ten seconds, he would assume they were trespassers and take appropriate action.

The picture of him brandishing his Beretta must have been fresh in their minds, because they beat a hasty retreat without the need for a second warning.

He spent the rest of the afternoon doing chores and running errands—laundry, grocery shopping, forgetting, as usual, that it was a weekend and weekends meant tourists everywhere—in the hopes that if he focused on trivial matters, his subconscious might chew on the Miranda problem and offer up some kind of lead. No such luck. His frustration continued to mount. The bank of storm clouds moving in from the west, gray and menacing, matched his mood. Even inside his house, as he worked on the leaky sink in his bathroom and kept the little window cracked open, he felt the air thickening, growing heavy with moisture. Long before dusk, he watched the fuzzy sun disappear into the clouds, breaking apart like a cherry gum drop and taking most of the light along with it.

It was about that time his cell phone rang for the first time that night.

Startled, he dropped the wrench and banged his knuckles against the pipe. He cursed and went looking for the phone, found it in his leather jacket. It was Zoe, telling him that a friend of hers was home for the weekend and wanted to know if Zoe could hang out for the night. Home from college? That's what Gage asked, putting more emphasis on the word college than was necessary, which led to some terse silence followed by an even more terse "fine" and "see you later." He wondered why she even called. It wasn't like she needed his permission.

Twenty minutes later, the phone rang again, and for a second time Gage banged his fist against the pipe. He marched back to the kitchen, where he'd left the phone on the counter. From where he stood in the kitchen, he could see out the big west window, over the rooftops of the houses below and the ocean beyond. The black plastic vibrated across the white tiles like an angry cockroach, the display on the front glowing like a pulsating eyeball, and Gage lifted his fist to smash it. At the last second, he managed to stop himself, snapping it open and shouting into it instead.

"What *is* it?"

He heard a faint buzzing, and the sound of his own breathing, before a woman answered in a quiet voice.

"Hi," she said. "Did I call at a bad time?"

It was Tatyana. He might not have known her, the way the phone changes a person's voice, except for the tinge of Russian accent.

"Oh," he said. "Hello."

"I hope I'm not bothering you."

"Oh, no. No, that's okay. I've just—it's been a long day."

"Everything all right?"

He sighed. "Not really. Miranda's going to have to sit in jail until Wednesday. And I don't have any idea how to go about helping her right now."

"I know," Tatyana said. "She told me. I'm very sorry about that."

"She told you?"

"Yes. She called me a little while ago. She—she also asked me to call you. That is how I have your number. I hope that's okay."

Holding the little piece of plastic to his ear, gazing out at the last remnants of dusky purple light over the much darker swath of the ocean, Gage digested this news. Miranda would not have been allowed many phone calls, and she'd used one to call Tatyana. If Miranda had been concerned about him, why not call herself? Or was she trying to play matchmaker again? All along, based on her flirting, he'd sensed that Miranda had been interested in him herself, which made her clumsy attempts to bring him and Tatyana together all the more strange.

"Are you still there?" Tatyana asked.

"Oh, yes. Sorry, just thinking."

"Okay."

There was another pause.

"Well," she said, "if everything is really all right, I suppose I should—"

"Would you like to go to dinner?"

"Dinner?"

"Yes, you know that thing people do when they're hungry in the evening. Sometimes they even do it with others."

She chuckled so softly he barely caught it, but it was there. Thank God. So she wasn't completely impervious to his charms. Somehow, just hearing that laugh, it made him want to try that much harder to win her over.

She said, "You really like making jokes, don't you?"

"When they make people laugh, yes. When they don't, I think I die a little inside."

"We don't want that. But I warn you, I really am not much for laughing."

"I've kind of gathered that," he said. "I've also gathered that

118

you have a very good sense of humor, even if you don't laugh all that much."

"Hmm."

"Dinner, then? My treat."

There was a pause. He felt his pulse in the fingers clutching the phone, a steady tapping. He didn't realize until he'd asked her to dinner how much he wanted her to say yes.

"Yes," she said.

"Yes?"

"Yes, I will go to dinner. But I pay for my meal."

He offered up a melodramatic sigh. "If you insist. But it really does hurt my chivalrous heart not being able to pick up the tab."

"Somehow," she said, "I think your heart will survive the experience."

"Ah! See, there's that humorous side of you. Can I at least pick you up?"

"Will it hurt your heart if I say no?"

"Very much. I don't know how much more hurt it can take."

"Then I will not test it this time. "

She gave him her address—she lived in one of the condos that overlooked Big Dipper Lake—and he told her that he'd be there at eight o'clock. He shaved, showered, and took his time about it, but still he was dressed and ready to go at half past seven. He left anyway, thinking there might be traffic. There wasn't. He didn't want to seem too eager, showing up twenty minutes early, so he looped around the lake to the boat dock on the north side. The lake was dark and silent, the lights off the houses shining brightly on a clear night. A sliver of a moon hung high overhead, clothed in wispy clouds like an old woman wearing a lace shawl. He parked and rolled down his window, hoping to take in the fresh air but catching a disturbing whiff of something rotten. His sharp investigative powers determined the source to be an overflowing trash can by the playground not far away.

So much for a peaceful interlude. He waited a few more minutes, then drove slowly back to the condos on the south side. The complex, three modern-looking buildings nestled in the trees, all mirrored glass, polished steel, and gray stone, had been built three years ago but he'd heard the condos were priced on the high side and only half had sold. Judging by how few of them were lit and how many parking spaces were empty, he wondered if half was being generous.

Still ten minutes early, he decided to wait in the van. His plan was foiled when Tatyana emerged from the glass lobby in a trim red leather jacket, tight designer jeans, and matching red sandals and handbag. Again, it was as if she'd chosen the outfit out of a catalog, but Gage didn't mind. He'd noted her figure before, but those jeans gave him an appreciation on a much more primal level.

He'd no sooner recognized his attraction than he felt a stirring of guilt. Here he was going out with a beautiful woman while another beautiful woman—one he considered his responsibility—sat alone in a jail cell. What was he thinking?

Then the beautiful woman with the luxurious blonde hair climbed into his passenger seat and he remembered exactly what he'd been thinking. He'd been thinking about what Tatyana might look like naked. Was that so wrong? There was no doubt that Miranda was attractive, and he might have been attracted to her as well, but he would never pursue someone who couldn't even remember who they were. It struck him as sleazy, on par with a man who'd slip a date-rape drug into a women's drink.

Besides, he wanted to talk with Tatyana about Miranda, get her professional opinion. That's what he told himself anyway, and he almost believed it.

Tatyana flashed him a fleeting smile, eyes wide and pupils dark, before she turned forward. There was something different about her, something not so composed and contained, and he realized she was nervous. It encouraged him.

"How did you know I was here?" Gage asked.

"I heard your van," she said.

"Ah. It has a very distinctive sound, doesn't it?"

"It does," she said.

"Kind of like a dying moose."

She looked at him. "Why didn't you come up? Were you afraid of being too early?"

"Hmm. You're a perceptive one."

"You should not worry about that sort of thing with me. I don't worry about things like that. What do you call them? Social norms."

"Well, that's good," Gage said, "because I generally have a hard time with social norms. Social anything, really."

She looked forward again. Her hair, her make-up—everything was just perfect, but there was also a pale and strained quality to her. He got the sense she might throw up. Or that she might rip open that purse, the way she gripped it so tightly.

"Are you okay?" he asked.

She turned toward him abruptly, as if he'd startled her. "What?"

"We don't have to do this tonight, you know. I can take a rain—"

"No, no, I'm fine," she insisted.

"Okay."

"Please. I want to." *Vant* to. There it was again, the accent coming on a little stronger. Perhaps because she'd put a little too much emphasis on that last sentence, she glanced at him. "I'm sorry if I … if I don't seem like myself. I have not done something like this in a very long time. That's all."

"Hey, you can't be any more nervous than me."

That seemed to relax her. She dropped her shoulders and at least some of the tightness in her face melted away. He wanted to ask her what she meant by a long time, and why, but he knew those questions were premature. Instead he asked her if the Inn at Sapphire Head would be all right for dinner. She said she'd never eaten there but that she'd heard good things about it.

Ten minutes later, they parked in the expansive lot next to the golf course and walked through the tunnel under the highway, the wind swirling. The way she walked next to him, there was something very closed and contained about her, but also radiating an electric buzz. They weren't comfortable with one another yet, the walls of their castles still heavily guarded, but there was an expectation that things would change, that they both *wanted* things to change. In the elevator, on the way up to the top floor, she stood close enough that he breathed in the scent of whatever shampoo she'd used, like the smell of wildflowers after a spring rain. He wanted to lay his chin on her head, nuzzle her against him.

After they were seated, at a cozy two-person table overlooking the dark ocean, they both looked at each other and started to speak at once.

"How long have you—" he began.

"Why do you—" she said.

They both smiled and that broke the tension, at least enough that some of the awkwardness disappeared.

"You first," he said.

"No, no, you should—"

"Come on now. We could be at this all night otherwise."

"All right. I was just going to ask why you like being a private investigator. I heard how you became one the other night, but not why you like it."

"Oh, many things. Mostly because I heard it was a good way to meet women."

"Hmm. Did that work for you?"

"No, I was misinformed."

"I see. Well, it is the same reason I became a doctor. I heard it was a good way to meet women."

Gage, reaching for his water glass, froze. "Women?"

"Yes," she said. "I'm sorry. I thought … I thought you knew."

"You're … um …"

"Gay," she said, nodding.

She let him dangle in the wind, her eyes wide and bright, while he revisited everything that had happened between them the past few days. Had he completely misread the signs? He was trying to summon some kind of response, one that wouldn't reveal any of the deep disappointment he felt, when she finally smiled.

"You're joking," he said.

"What if I said I liked girls *and* boys?"

"Um ..."

"Joking again."

"Oh."

"Are you always this easy to fool?"

"Only by beautiful women."

"Ah, there you go," she said, laughing, "a very good response, I think."

"And you, ma'am, are a liar."

"What?"

"You said you didn't laugh much, and I've heard you laugh several times now. It's a very good laugh, too."

She smiled. "Maybe I just laugh at you."

"I'll try to take that as a compliment."

"You should."

She took a sip from her water, looking at him over the top of the glass. Her wit was so dry, she was hard to read. He loved it. He loved many things about her. How odd it was, to have lived in the same town, to have passed each other in the grocery store so many times, and all along this wonderful possibility existed between them.

"It's very strange, isn't it?" she said, putting down her glass. He thought maybe she'd read his mind until he saw the troubled expression she wore. "Here we are, having dinner for the first time, when the person who brought us together is sitting in prison."

"Ah, the elephant in the room," he said. "Does it bother you? That we're here together?"

"A little," she said.

"Me too."

"Maybe we shouldn't be doing this."

"Maybe," he said, nodding.

"Or ... we could simply acknowledge the fact that ... that the timing is unusual, as are the circumstances of our meeting, and then both decide that despite the, um, awkwardness of it, there is nothing wrong with two people having dinner."

"Boy, you are a smart lady," Gage said.

"Yes, I am. Now I have another question, and I want you to answer it without jokes. How did you end up taking care of Zoe?"

As much as Gage preferred to avoid talking about his past, even his fairly recent past, she'd asked the question so earnestly that he felt compelled to give her an earnest answer. He told her about Mattie, his housekeeper who'd died of cancer a couple years back, and how she'd made him promise to take care of her troubled granddaughter. He told her how the last thing he'd seen himself doing was being a father, but Zoe's own parents were meth addicts and petty thieves who spent their lives either on the streets or in prisons, so he didn't feel he had a choice. His late wife would be shocked if she knew he'd actually signed custody documents. She probably would have predicted he'd become a cop first.

Tatyana slipped in a few innocuous questions about how he'd met Janet, without it seeming forced at all, and before long he'd told her more about himself than he'd probably told anyone other than Alex and Zoe. There was something so welcoming about Tatyana, as if there was no doubt that she would never in a million years think to use your own past pain and mistakes against you, that everything was heard and understood with a deep kind of sympathy that few people possessed. Even her teasing was never mean. Sharp-edged? Yes. Mean, no.

They shared a bottle of a Willamette Valley Pinot Noir. They ordered meals, her a charbroiled salmon and him a rib-eye steak. He talked until the meals came, and he talked well into the eating of them, until he finally decided it was time for her to do some talking of her own.

"Fair's fair," he said, "now I get to ask a few questions."

"All right."

"When did you come to the United States?"

"Ah," she said, reaching for her wine glass, "that is a complicated question."

"Come on now. Was it before or after you became a doctor?"

Her eyes, already shiny from a bit too much wine, gleamed over the top of her water glass. "Before," she said.

"How much before?"

"I was nineteen."

"Wow, that's young. Did you come with your family or—"

"Alone."

He waited for her to say more. She swirled what was left of her wine, looking down into the red liquid as if trying to divine some meaning there. The tables were full now, the chatter around them loud and full of energy, making the silence at their own table that much more profound. Finally, she put down her glass and sighed.

"All right," she said, "I will tell you something. But you must promise not to laugh."

"You were once in the circus?"

"No. It's ... you have to understand. I really wanted out of Ukraine. I grew up mostly after the breakup of the Soviet Union. It was very poor. Very desperate. Then there was always the conflict. You know of `?"

"Oh yes. Who doesn't?"

"Of course, many people know of it now, after Russia invaded and claimed it for their own. But it was always a very troubled place. In 1991, when the CCCP—ah, what you call the USSR, when it fell, there were those who loved Ukraine and wanted nothing to do with mother Russia. There were also those who thought Ukraine should have stayed with Russia and never went its own way. Even as a little girl, I saw how this would tear us apart and decided I wanted to leave. I also wanted to do something with my life, something more than just marry some poor Ukrainian boy and bear children. But my family was very poor. My father—he made furniture. Do you know how many people buy furniture when they can't even buy bread? Not many."

Gage thought it interesting how her accent had revealed itself even more fully as she'd talked about her past, the R's rolling a bit stronger, the W sounds turning more into V's. *Wanted* became *vanted*. *Was* became *vas*. "How did you get out then?"

"You won't laugh?"

"If I do, I'll hide it well."

"Please. No jokes. This is difficult."

"All right."

"You must also try not to think poorly of me. Please remember how much I wanted to leave."

"Tatyana, come on."

She took another drink of wine, dabbed at her lips with a napkin, and settled both her hands on the tablecloth in front of her as if bracing herself.

"I let myself be ordered," she said.

"What?"

"You know, ordered. From a catalog. "

It finally dawned on Gage what she meant. "You were a mail-order bride?"

"Shh. Not so loud."

"Sorry. It's just—you're a doctor. Obviously really sharp. For someone so smart, I would have thought there would have been another—"

"Smart is one thing," she said. "Having opportunities is another. I thought, if I could get to the United States, I could find a way to do something with my life. I admit, I was very naive. I read magazines about American life and watched American movies and thought if a poor girl from Ukraine could find a way to do something great, it would be in America. At first, I thought I might meet an American working in Ukraine. There were some young men teaching English in Simferopol, but the ones I met seemed so earnest and pure, I could not bring myself to pursue them if I did not think I could love them. And I did not feel it with any of them."

"I imagine you had a lot of suitors," he said.

"Some. Mostly Ukrainian boys." Something changed in her eyes, a darkening, but she blinked a few times and continued. "I needed to get out before I became just another poor Ukrainian woman who spent her days changing diapers and trying to make soup out of whatever was left in the cupboard. And I thought, if I was going to use a man to escape, why not a man who was the sort of person who would order a woman from a catalog? He would think he would be choosing me, but I would be choosing him. I would choose someone kind, who would support me in my goals, but I would make sure I could never love him."

"Ouch," Gage said.

"You said you would try not to think less of me."

"I don't. We all make tough choices in life. I just don't know why you felt you needed to be so hard on yourself."

She touched the CK necklace briefly, then seemed to realize she'd done so and put her hand back on the table. "You must understand, I did not think I deserved love. I think this is why I want to help Miranda so much. I understand her situation very well."

"Oh. You ended up with someone abusive?"

"I ended up with someone very manipulative and controlling."

"And you chose him knowing this?"

She swallowed. "You misunderstand. The man I met through this service, the man I married, he was not controlling at all. He was sweet and kind and generous. He was a chemist for Halton-Hauer, the big drug manufacturer. He was very awkward, especially with women, and not at all good looking, but there was no meanness. I sensed this right away when we started letters. When we were together, I was proved right."

"Then I dont—"

"I'm talking about myself," Tatyana said.

"You?"

"When I say I ended up with someone abusive, I mean me."

Gage shook his head. "I admit I'm a bit confused."

"There are many kinds of abuse," she said, her voice growing hoarse. "Not all abuse is physical. Some is much worse. I let this man believe I was falling in love with him. I ... seduced him to come get me in Ukraine, to marry me and take me back to

Atlanta. I took his last name, Brunner, because I knew having an American-sounding name would be better for me. I made a good home, of course. I took care of his needs. But I controlled him, too. I got him to pay for my schooling at the University of Georgia. Then medical school at Emory University. I told him I wanted to be a smarter wife for him, since he was a chemist. I had power over him and I used it. That is all abuse is, really. Knowing you have power over someone and using it."

Gage wasn't sure what to say to this. She ran a finger down the edge of her water glass, staring at the trail her finger left behind.

"After I graduated," she said, "I decided to tell him the truth. That I did not love him. I told myself I was doing this because it was the right thing to do, but I know that's not true. I did it because I no longer needed him."

"How did he take it?"

Her eyes misted, and she blinked a few times. "He was a sweet man. He deserved better than me. He said he didn't care. He said he could love enough for the both of us."

"Wow."

"Yes. He was trying to convince me to stay, but it only made me feel much worse about what I had done. I told him I would pay back every penny he had spent on me. He would not hear of it. He said I could leave at any time. He only hoped I would return someday."

The waiter refilled their water glasses. Tatyana stared at the tablecloth, not meeting his eyes. Gage thought she was being too hard on herself, but who was he to judge? He was the king of guilt and self-blame. It certainly was not a kind thing she had done, but abuse? Marriages were often full of manipulations and hidden motives, sometimes small and innocuous, other times large and life-changing.

"I don't know why I tell you this," Tatyana said softly. "I have not told anyone before now."

"Is that why you came to Barnacle Bluffs? Because you wanted to get as far away from that past life as possible?"

"Yes."

"Me too."

"Maybe that is why I felt I could tell you," she said. "Maybe I thought you would understand. Or at least, that you would not judge me too harshly."

"My dear, if I judged you too harshly, then how could I have enough judgment left over for myself? Can I ask you something? That necklace you're wearing, did he give it to you?"

Her hand fluttered to the necklace, as if she needed reassurance that it was still there.

"Oh," she said.

"I've noticed you're almost always wearing it."

"Yes. It didn't come from him. It was given ... It is a reminder of life in Ukraine, the life I left behind."

"Have you been back?"

She shook her head. "There is nothing for me there now."

"But the necklace. I would think—"

"I don't wish to talk about it."

"Oh."

She reached for his hand, her fingers cool and moist from holding the water glass. "I apologize. I'm just tired. I have said so much already."

"It's all right. I didn't mean to pry."

"You are not prying. You are being kind. Let's talk of something else for a while. Tell me about Miranda. What are you going to do now? Do you have ideas?"

There wasn't much to tell, but he told her anyway. He told her the few tantalizing glimpses into her past that Miranda had revealed, about the drawing, about how he was certain something else had happened on that boat other than her shooting Marcus Koura. He felt his frustration mounting, and he wished he could talk about something else, but Tatyana, even as she listened attentively, seemed to have retreated into herself and he was hoping that if he talked long enough, she would come back to him. If anything, though, she retreated even more, looking at him but not really seeing him. They finished their meals, and, as she had insisted, split the check.

On the drive back to her place, the night sky was clear enough to see the stars and the highway shined like black glass under the crescent moon. They listened to the rumble of the Volkswagen engine and the whistle of wind against the windows. He was trying to think of something to say when Tatyana beat him to it.

"There is a beach just past the casino," she said. "Do you know it?"

"Starfish Point," he said.

"Yes. Would you like to go there for a few minutes? I think— I think the ocean would be very pretty. It's not often we have nights like this."

"Your wish is my command," he said.

He parked the van in the big lot behind Golden Eagle Casino, the ones mostly full of motor homes and trailers. The lot was well lit, and the path to Starfish Point was marked with a sign. A copse of Douglas firs lined the west side, blocking their view of the ocean, but the persistent murmur of the waves served as a reminder that the vast stretch of water was barely more than a stone's throw away. Already, the air smelled both saltier and brinier, but more invigorating, too. After they'd taken a few steps away from the van, she stopped and looked at him.

"What about your cane?"

"I'm okay."

She raised her eyebrows, but did not object. Perhaps because he had left his cane, she took his arm after a few steps, but he liked to think she would have done so anyway. Even the first part of the path, inside the trees, was lit well enough by the moon and the stars that no flashlight was necessary. Gage feared they would find a bunch of drunken casino goers belting out show tunes around a bonfire, but he was surprised to find an empty beach. Driftwood and kelp littered the rough sand nearest them; down below, where the sand was smooth and dark, the partial moon cast a trail of bone-yellow light on the surf and the darker water leading out to sea. From this vantage point, it looked like a golden path leading right into the moon.

Perhaps he shouldn't have been surprised no one was there. He doubted few gamblers made time to take in the scenery.

Still holding his arm, Tatyana led him to the water's edge. Even the wind, often so strong they wouldn't have been able to hear each other speak, was now only the barest touch on their faces. Around the next bend, beyond their sight, was the beach where Marcus Koura's body had been found. Gage thought about mentioning this but decided that it probably wasn't the sort of thing a man should say to a pretty woman on a night like this.

He turned and looked at her and found she was already staring at him. The breeze picked up, stirring stray blonde hairs across her face. Instinctively, he reached for them, brushing the hair behind her ear, his finger caressing her check. Her skin felt warmer than he expected, almost hot.

She responded by leaning forward and kissing him.

It didn't last long, nothing passionate and lingering, but there was still quite a spark. He caught a taste of the Pinot Noir she'd had with dinner. She leaned back, looking at him with doubt, and that was its own aphrodisiac, her vulnerability, the lowering of the walls.

"Is that all right?" she asked.

"It was wonderful," he said.

"I didn't mean to do that. I don't know what came over me."

"Whatever it was, I hope it comes over you again. Soon."

"What if it happened again right now?"

"Even better."

This time, he kissed her. He cupped his hands around her face and put more of himself into it, making it last long enough that they were both breathless when they finally parted. It was like a magnetic pull, the need to kiss her again. Too fast. He knew it was too fast, that he should slow down, but he didn't care. Did she care? She gave him an answer by reaching for him, slipping her fingers around his neck. Her fingers felt icy against his warm skin, but he didn't care about this either.

His cell phone rang.

The electronic chirp was still so foreign that the sound startled him. It took him a second to realize that it was coming from his jacket pocket—and, with his irritation rising, whatever spell had been cast over them was instantly broken as he fumbled to get the damn thing out of his pocket. He wanted to ignore it, but the ring was too annoying, too invasive to simply pretend it didn't exist. With everything going on, he also couldn't afford to miss a call right now.

By the time Gage finally got the stupid piece of plastic opened, Tatyana was laughing. He barked a hello into the receiver. There was a long pause.

"Hello Mister Gage," a man with a heavy Indian accent said. "I am calling to talk to you about an exciting offer on your cell phone plan. Do you have a few minutes to discuss this exciting offer with me?"

Gage wanted to punch the man in the face. Since he couldn't do that, he did the next best thing. He tossed the cell phone—on a high, looping arc that passed in front of the moon—deep into the ocean.

They watched the cell phone plop into the dark water. It was strangely satisfying, thinking about the infernal device finding its home with the hermit crabs and the sea urchins, wondering if the man from India was still telling him about the benefits of upgrading to an unlimited data plan, whatever that meant, but his satisfaction didn't last long. Already, regret seeped into his thoughts. What would Zoe say? That was two cell phones in less than a week.

"Well," Tatyana said. She was no longer laughing, but there was an unmistakable tone of amusement in her voice.

"It's your fault," Gage said.

"Excuse me?"

"If you weren't such a good kisser, I wouldn't have gotten so angry at being interrupted."

"Hmm. That's what you're going to tell Zoe, then?"

"Ah. You know about her giving me the phone."

"I think she mentioned it, yes. Two phones, actually."

"Maybe we can make up a story about this one. If we both

stick to it, she's more likely to believe it."

She arched her eyebrows. "You mean, you want me to lie for you?"

"That's such a harsh word. I prefer to think of it as embracing an alternate version of reality that's more acceptable to all involved."

She laughed and took his arm again. She wasn't a natural laugher, it was true, but he really liked making her laugh. Every time she laughed, it was as if she cracked open the door a bit more to the person inside her.

"Let's just try to enjoy this for a few minutes," she said. "You will have to face the consequences of what you did soon enough."

"Dire consequences," Gage said.

"Yes. But for now, take a deep breath. The ocean, it can take away your worries. That's why I moved here. I was hoping it would take away my worries."

"Did it?"

"Sometimes. Look at the moon. It is so beautiful. What do they say about the changes? Waxing and … ?"

"Waning," he said.

"Which is it doing now?"

"Waning, I think."

"Getting smaller."

"Yes."

"Soon it will only be a sliver. I know the name for this. It's called a crescent moon, yes? Sometimes, when the crescent moon would fall over Simferopol, I would think it was like a … what? A gateway. A portal. I would think it was closing and there was just enough room for me to escape if I acted quickly. Then, in a few nights, it would be gone, but I always knew it would return again. There would be another chance. One day, I took my chance. I slipped through and escaped."

Side by side, bodies close enough that he felt the warmth of her pressing against him, they gazed at the moon together. He didn't want to say anything, knowing that as soon as he did the moment would end.

A crescent moon … just like Miranda's drawing. Why did she draw a crescent moon? There was nothing distinctive about the drawing. It could have been any of a hundred different ports, a hundred different cities. A crescent moon would fall over all of them.

That's when Gage realized where he needed to go.

"Oh my," he said.

"What?" Tatyana said.

Gage headed back for his van, waving for her to follow. His right knee nearly buckled a few times, but he was too excited to care. She begged him to tell her what was on his mind, but he was afraid if he talked about it, he'd lose it, the connection was so fragile. He opened the driver's side door and fished the old Rand-McNally map of the United States from under the seat, along with a flashlight he kept there for emergencies. He handed Tatyana the flashlight and asked her to shine it on the map, ignoring her questions while he flipped through the dog-eared pages until he came to one picturing the entire state of California.

There it was, a city on the north coast he'd never visited but one he remembered seeing when he was searching for possible ports Marcus may have visited. He pointed it out to Tatyana. She leaned in for a closer look, the breeze billowing her hair across her face.

"Crescent City?" she said.

"That's right."

"And you believe the drawing, because it was a crescent moon …?"

"It's a long shot, I know. But maybe it was her subconscious at work."

"So what are you going to do? Are you going to call—"

"No, I'm done with the phone. I'm going to drive down there. Poke around. Ask questions. You know, the stuff I'm actually good at. It's only about fifty miles from the Oregon border. Maybe five or six hours from here straight down Highway 101. If I leave first thing in the morning, I could be down there early in the afternoon."

Tatyana frowned. "What about Miranda? You are going to leave when she's in jail?"

"There's nothing I can do to change that right now. Besides, it's probably the safest place for her. As long as she's in jail, I don't feel I need to be around to protect her—from Omar, or anybody else."

"Anybody else? Like who?"

"Well, I don't know. That's the point. It's hard to protect her when I don't have all the information." He shrugged. "I'm out of other ideas. Sometimes when that happens, I just take a stab in the dark like this and good things come of it. Bad things sometimes too, but even that's better than the status quo."

Tatyana peered at the map a while longer, as if pondering the merits of the idea, then looked back at Gage.

"I just have one question," she said.

"Yes?"

"Can I go with you?"

Chapter 10

No matter how much he tried to dissuade her, Tatyana was determined to accompany him to Crescent City. She told him she wasn't scheduled for work Sunday or Monday, so there was no reason not to go. A little adventure might do her some good. And didn't he think having her along for the ride, for free, no less, might be of some help? Not only was she a doctor, and could lend some insight on Miranda's mental state from a medical perspective, she was a woman, too, and might be able to think like Miranda a little better than Gage could.

Gage put up a little fight just to show that he wasn't *too* eager, but it didn't take him very long to relent. Truth was, he was mostly thinking about what would happen when they reached the hotel. Would they book one room or two?

They left Sunday morning, Gage driving the van, early enough that the sky was a soupy gray and the sun was not yet visible over the forested hills to the east that made up the beginnings of the coastal range. She brought a compact wheeled suitcase, smaller even than his own duffle bag but with an extremely long extendable handle, the kind of thing that a flight attendant might use. It fit her. Everything about her was neat and tightly contained: the condo, the clothes, the personality. Perhaps it was all *too* contained, like a suitcase that might burst open if someone even fiddled with the latch.

Traffic was light, occasional headlights emerging from the morning fog. The air felt heavy and thick, a humidity that was uncommon on the Oregon coast but not entirely rare. Moisture beaded on the windshield, forcing him to occasionally turn on the wipers. They cracked the windows open, and raised their voices to be heard over the air whistling through the car.

They talked about Miranda, tossing back and forth theories about why the picture she'd drawn might have been Crescent City, California. Perhaps she'd met Marcus there, which was why it was significant to her. If you were hiding from someone, and you wanted a city about as remote and unremarkable as you could get while still offering some of the characteristics of coastal life, Crescent City seemed to fit the bill. A bit grungy, more of a working class town than a tourist destination, it still offered a lot for a person seeking escape and solace from a troubled life. For starters, there were the redwoods. Miranda had made more than few remarks about the beauty of Oregon trees to think that might have been one of the draws for her.

By the time they reached Newport, this line of conversation petered out and they lapsed into long stretches of silence interrupted by occasional comments about the scenery. That was just fine by Gage. He found it to be a comfortable silence, which was definitely another plus in Tatyana's favor. There were lots of people—in fact, most people, in Gage's experience—that felt a growing discomfort the longer a period of silence lasted and eventually succumbed to the need to break it, like a mild form of Tourette's Syndrome. He could already tell that she was one of the few people he could not only tolerate long road trips with, but might actually enjoy the experience.

The fact that he was even considering the idea of taking road trips, something that hadn't even entered his consciousness before he was driving on this highway with Tatyana, could be said to be another point in her favor.

They passed over the big arched bridge that spanned the Yaquina Bay, making good time through Waldport and Yachats. The enjoyed some of the most spectacular scenery along the Oregon coast, sheaths of sunlight breaking through the dense cloud cover along the horizon, before the highway veered far enough to the east that the ocean disappeared behind forests of oaks and firs. They gassed up in Florence, stopping briefly to stretch their legs at one of the many lakes in the area, before continuing south. By this time, the weekend traffic was starting to pick up, but they were so far south of Portland, Salem, and Eugene, which contained the vast bulk of Oregon's population, that a few more cars on the road hardly mattered. They had clam chowder for lunch in Port Orford, listened to a classic rock and roll station until it was out of range, and had a lively discussion about whether today's music even held a candle to stuff produced in the fifties, before they slipped through Gold Beach, Brookings, and into California.

Half an hour later, a little past two o'clock in the afternoon, they rolled into Crescent City.

Unlike in Barnacle Bluffs, where the highway and the city crowded mostly along the coastline, the bulk of Crescent City was situated a few blocks off the ocean. They weaved through town, past the usual assortment of fast food restaurants, gas stations, and a couple of grocery stores, everything fairly drab and unremarkable. It lacked both the touristy charm and tackiness of most of the Oregon coastal cities, a gritty reality pervading the place, reminding him mostly of Newport but much smaller. Verdant forests and green hills bordered the eastern side of the city, giving the place a very isolated feel.

Tatyana said, "When I looked up pictures on the Internet, I didn't see many pictures of the city itself—just the harbor, the beach, the redwoods. Now I see why."

"It's not much to look at, is it?" Gage said.

"It's very strange. They are surrounded by so much beauty. Ancient redwoods just minutes from here. And, look, there's the Battery Point Lighthouse. It really is remarkable. The city just seems so plain."

It may have been plain, but Gage already felt a kinship to the place. He could have relocated here just as easily as Barnacle Bluffs. The combination of gritty realism and natural beauty would have fit him well.

The lighthouse was aptly named, as the little white and red building was located on a tiny rocky islet connected to the shore by a narrow isthmus barely above the water that must have been submerged at high tide. A white picket fence, a bit of grass, and a few lonely wind-blown cypress trees created quite an iconic image, and Gage was willing to bet that pictures of the lighthouse had graced thousands of postcards over the years. The Crescent City Harbor was just beyond it, a big port that was only half full, then a narrow stretch of sandy beach that ended at the base of steeply sloped bluffs and thick forests.

Since it was too early to check into the hotel, they decided to hit the docks first. They parked the van in front of the marina office, an industrial-looking building that also contained a bait and tackle shop, a seafood restaurant, and a boat mechanic. The sun glared high above, marked only by a few jagged white clouds that made Gage think of the stuffing-filled gashes a knife would leave in a blue pillow. Getting out of the van, they were greeted by a warm breeze blowing off the Pacific. He smelled grilling salmon in the air.

Inside, standing behind a counter made from unfinished plywood and looking at a computer that was so grimy it could have been pulled out of the ocean, was a pirate. That was the first word that came to mind. How else to explain the eye patch, the braided black ponytail, and the burlap face partially hidden behind a grizzled beard? His outfit may not have quite fit the part—he wore a red and white plaid shirt rolled up at the sleeves—but otherwise he definitely could have passed as a pirate.

The guy looked up with his one good eye. "Help ya?" he said.

"I hope so," Gage said, though it was all he could do not to ask if the man was a pirate. It was just such an obvious question, someone wearing an eye patch working at a marina, but he doubted the guy would appreciate it. He probably got the pirate question all the time. "Name's Garrison Gage. I'm a private investigator and I'd like to ask you—"

"You the guy called on the phone a day or two ago?"

"Most likely," Gage said.

"You asking about that woman, the one that made the paper."

"You heard about that, huh?"

"Everybody heard about it now." He turned his attention back to the monitor, clicking on a keyboard that was below the counter. "Sorry you came all the way down here. Like I told ya, ain't seen her. That boat neither."

"Are you the only one who works here?"

"Nah, Jerry usually works the weekends. Normally I don't work Sundays, but Jerry had a wedding to go to in Grant's Pass."

"When is he due back?"

"Like I said, the weekends. So next Saturday. You're wasting your time, though. I can tell you right now he hasn't seen nothing."

"You talked about it?"

"Yeah, on the phone."

There was something about the man's demeanor that immediately didn't sit right with Gage, a certain anxiousness in the way he looked away. On the phone, it hadn't been evident in his tone of voice, which made Gage glad he'd decided to come down here. There was a lot that body language could tell him about a person. He *had* heard reluctance on the phone, but he'd assumed it was the same reluctance a busy person felt having to deal with an annoying interruption. This was definitely something else.

Deciding on how best to approach this, Gage leaned his cane against the counter and placed his hands flat on the rough plywood. The man clicked away on his keyboard. Tatyana, hanging back a few steps, observed without saying a word. Outside, a motorboat buzzed out of the marina and a few seagulls cawed far off in the distance.

"I have a picture this time," Gage said. "Maybe that will help."

"I saw her picture in the paper," the man said.

"You've checked your records for the boat?"

"Yeah, man, I checked the records when you called. It wasn't here. Somebody tell you they was here or something?"

"Why, do you know somebody who would say such a thing?"

The man looked at him with his dumfounded grizzled face. "Huh?"

"The way you said that, it makes me think you know somebody who might tell me."

"Man, I don't get you."

"Join the club. What's your name?"

"What's that got to do with anything?"

"You don't even want to give me your name?"

"Look, man—"

"If you don't give me your name, I'm going to call you Pirate Bob."

"What?"

"Maybe you wouldn't mind checking again, Pirate Bob? I have the license number."

He regarded Gage the way he might have regarded a dead trout that someone had dropped on his floor. "What good will that do?"

Gage took the license number written on a paper folded inside his leather jacket and placed it on the counter. "Maybe you made an error."

"An error?"

"You know, a mistake."

"I know what an error is!"

"Good. Then you know they happen all the time, Pirate Bob."

"It's Troy! The name's Troy!"

"Great, now we're getting somewhere. Pirate Troy, if you could just check one more time, I'd appreciate it."

"Just Troy!"

"Fine, Troy. Would you do that for me? Just this once?"

"Why you got to be such an asshole about it?"

"Call it a character flaw, Troy. When I encounter mental stupor, deliberate mendacity, or, worse, both, I usually can't help myself."

Poor Troy, blinking that one eye of his, wasn't quite sure if he'd been insulted or not. Gage thought about clarifying that he *had* been insulted, but Troy must have decided that the fastest way to actually get rid of Gage was to go through the motions of double-checking the license number. That's exactly what he did, go through the motions, his apathy for the task and outright disdain for the person asking him to do it evident in the languid way he went about clicking a few keys, studying Gage's paper for a long time, peering at his screen for a moment, clicking a bit more, staring for an even longer time, repeating this cycle a few more times before finally sighing.

"Nope," he said.

"Huh," Gage said.

"Now, if you'll excuse me, I got work to do."

"I can see that. But what if I told you I have proof they were here?"

There was something in Troy's eye, a split second of fear before it was covered once again by a shade of guardedness, that told Gage everything he needed to know.

"What do you mean, proof?" Troy asked.

"Oh, I didn't say I actually have any," Gage said. "I just wanted to know what you would do if you thought I had some."

Troy shook his head. "I don't have time for this crap. You better leave."

"Oh, I'll leave. But first I want to make sure you understand something. This woman, she doesn't have her memory. She doesn't know who she is. They just arrested her for murder, but we can't prove her innocence if we can't figure out who she really is. If you know something—"

"I don't," Troy said.

"— and you're not telling us," Gage continued, "you may be helping put an innocent woman behind bars. Now, I don't know about you, but I'd have a hard time living with that. Can you live with that, Troy? Can you go to bed at night knowing that you might have put an innocent person behind bars?"

Troy took his time answering, the silence long enough that Gage caught the sound of waves lapping against the pilings outside. For a moment, he thought that he might have gotten to him, that there was a chance he was going to fess up to whatever he knew, but then good old Troy lifted one of his weather-beaten fingers and pointed at the door.

"If you're not out of here in ten seconds," he said, "I'm calling the cops."

"That's how it's going to be, then?"

"Ten ..."

"An innocent person going to jail."

"Nine ..."

Gage would have been happy to play this game all the way down to zero, but Tatyana took his arm and guided him outside. She was so quick about it he almost forgot his cane. They took refuge from the glare of the sun around the corner, under a slight overhang next to a dumpster that smelled of fish. She brushed her hair behind her ears, trying to keep it from blowing in her eyes, but was only modestly successful.

"Does it always go that well for you?" she asked.

"Sometimes even worse."

"I'm a little ... confused about your method."

"I think calling what I do a method would be pretty generous," Gage said, "but getting people off-balance is not always a bad thing—especially somebody who's obviously hiding something."

"And you thought he was hiding something?"

"Most definitely. It could be something unrelated. Maybe he's into some other illegal activity, some drug smuggling maybe, and he just doesn't want the attention. But my gut tells me we just hit the jackpot."

"But if he's seen Miranda before, why wouldn't he tell us? It doesn't make any sense."

"That's the million dollar question. The hours listed on the

144

marina office window show that he closes at six. Maybe we can follow Pirate Troy home. That might tell us a lot more about him than another conversation. In the meantime, let's talk to some folks on the docks. I bet I can piss off a few more people."

He smiled. Tatyana, obviously less enthusiastic about this plan, did not smile back. Early yet in the afternoon, most of the fisherman were still out on the water, but there were still a scattering of people around the docks. They talked to a young man scrubbing the algae off the sides of a thirty-two-foot Catamaran sailboat who said he'd been hiring himself out around the marina for the past six months, but he didn't remember seeing the boat or recognize Miranda's picture. A bum searching the trash around the marina for cans, a man with brown hair and beard so thick he could have doubled for Sasquatch, said he was sure he'd seen Miranda, but when they pressed him for details, it became clear he was willing to say yes to whatever question they asked. An older couple drinking lemonade on the deck of their Sea Ray jet boat said they'd been out at sea for a week and didn't know anything about it.

Nobody acted as suspicious as Pirate Troy, giving Gage no reason to doubt their answers. Around four o'clock, the fisherman started to return, but Gage didn't have any better luck. One of them, an old timer with liver-spotted skin that resembled a checkerboard, said he might have seen Marcus and his boat, but he couldn't be sure. There were just so many ships that passed through and unless there was something remarkable about a boat—a Catalina like Marcus's being one of the most common sailboats there is—it was hard to remember them.

Closing in on six o'clock, they drove the van back to the highway and Gage filled his tank at the Texaco. Traffic had picked up, the weekenders who'd come out for the ocean or the redwoods heading home. A bank of clouds the color of duct tape streaked the horizon, and the air, already cool, had noticeably cooled even more. The plan was to park in front of the little aquarium, where their car could blend in with the others in the lot, and watch the road that led to the marina until they could follow Troy home.

After pumping the gas, he went inside the mini market to pick up a couple bottles of water and some potato chips. On a whim, he showed the pimply young man behind the counter the photo of Miranda. The kid leaned in closer, squinting through his thick glasses. They were alone in the store, the freezers humming, the fluorescent lights buzzing, the traffic outside a dull murmur.

"Huh," he said. "You know, she looks kind of like this lady that always came in real late. I don't know her name, but yeah, it looks like her. She'd grab milk or bread, stuff that always made me wonder why she wasn't going to the Safeway up the road. I mean, we charge way too much for that stuff here. The only time I ever buy stuff here is when—"

"Hold on," Gage said. "You're saying you've seen her?"

"Well ... Not totally sure, but yeah. I mostly work the four to midnight and she'd usually come in about an hour before we closed shop. I mean, not every day. A couple times a week. Usually she was wearing a baseball cap and she kind of kept her head down, you know. Like she was shy or something. I, uh, tried to talk to her a couple times, but she really didn't say much. Who is she?"

"You haven't been reading the news?"

"Nah, man, I don't really follow that stuff. I mostly just work here and play World of Warcraft. I just need a year to save some money before I start school at Humboldt State."

"Did she drive a car?"

"No. She always just walked in. From that way." He pointed south.

"You sure? Not much that way."

"Yeah," the kid said, "I always wondered about that, too. There's the Best Western, the Mill Creek Motel, Los Compadres ..."

"Do you remember about the time she started coming in?"

"Well, I've only been working here about six months, and she was coming in when I started. Haven't seen her in a couple weeks, though. Hey, wait a minute. Something didn't happen to her, did it? I mean, she's not like … dead, right?"

"She's fine. At least, if it's the same woman. She just has a little problem with her memory."

"Wow. Like amnesia?"

"Yes, like amnesia."

"Cool! I mean, not cool. Not cool at all. I just never heard of someone really having amnesia. It happens on TV all the time, but—"

"Can I ask your name?"

"Um, I guess. I'm not in trouble, am I?"

"No, I just might need to follow up with you later."

The kid said his name was Alvin Krafte—like the company but with an "e" at the end. Gage wrote it on the receipt, as well as his cell phone number. He asked him if he knew anything about Troy or any of the other people who worked at the marina. Alvin didn't. Gage showed him a picture of Marcus. The kid didn't recognize him and couldn't say whether he'd been in or not. He had the kind of face—a bit on the doughy side, but a pleasant, beguiling face all the same—that probably wouldn't be able to deceive someone even if his life depended on it. Gage thanked the kid and said he might be in touch.

After parking the van across the street, he told Tatyana what he'd learned. She peered out the window at the couple hotels and restaurants that were all that remained of the city before the highway ascended into the bluffs along the coast. On the west side, beyond the marina, a sandy beach stretched along the full length of the road, a handful of cars parked alongside of it, a few people frolicking in the water.

Tatyana said, "You think she was staying in one of those hotels?"

"I think there's a good chance," Gage said.

"You want to go talk to them?"

"Eventually. I don't want to lose the opportunity to follow Troy back to his pirate ship."

"You think he lives on a ship?"

"No, I'm just making a joke. Obviously it didn't work."

"Oh. Now I feel dumb."

"You shouldn't. It was a lame joke. My specialty, really."

She blinked at him a few times. He was trying to think of something else to say, something that would prove that he actually did have a decent sense of humor, when she leaned across the van and kissed him. It wasn't a long kiss, but there was the same electric charge as the last one, and when she pulled back she was smiling.

"What was that for?" he asked.

"Maybe I like lame jokes," she said.

"Oh. Well, there's more where that came from, I guarantee it."

"Good."

They looked at each other. The way her lips slightly parted was irresistible. He started to learn forward.

"I think we should get two rooms," she said.

"What?"

"Tonight. When we go to the hotel."

"Oh."

That killed the mood in a hurry. She blushed and looked away. On a scale of one to ten, the blush was right there at the top, a full-on pink wildfire spreading from her cheeks down to her neck. He would have found the blush quite endearing if he hadn't been so disappointed.

"You are disappointed," she said quietly.

"No, of course not," he said.

"Liar."

"Okay, I'm lying."

She laughed and it helped break the tension. "I'm sorry. I have just been thinking about it."

"Oh, I haven't been thinking about it at all."

"I *want* to," she said. "It's the first time in a long time that … well, I just … I don't want to move too fast."

"I understand."

She looked at him. "Do you?"

"Sure."

"You're not too disappointed?"

"Oh, I'm *very* disappointed. Crushing disappointment, actually. But I'll get over it."

"Would it help if I kissed you again?"

"It might."

She kissed him again. Perhaps because she was trying to compensate for disappointing him, she really put a lot into it, crossing over into his seat, pressing her warm body into his. All those wonderful, luscious curves, all that soft, pliant flesh—even through her clothes, her physical presence was so overwhelming that it was all he could do to restrain himself.

After she pulled away and climbed back into her seat, there were a few breathless seconds when neither of them seemed to know what to do. In fact, Gage knew *exactly* what to do, but Tatyana had already made it clear she wasn't interested in that yet. The key word being yet. There was a lot of room for negotiation in the word yet.

Finally, she placed her hand out, palm up.

"Give me her picture," she said.

"What?"

"Miranda's picture. Give it to me."

"Why?"

"There's no reason for both of us to follow Troy home. I can show her picture around, see if anybody recognizes her."

"No," Gage said firmly. "I don't want us splitting up."

"We can get more done this way."

"I just don't like it."

"Why? Don't tell me you think Crescent City is a dangerous place. Come on, Garrison. I want to help and this is the best way."

She tapped her open palm with the other hand. He had to admit that there was no logical reason to be hesitant, but there was still something about splitting up that really bothered him, a little voice whispering in his ear that letting her out of his sight was a bad idea. At the time, with his pulse still racing from that lingering kiss, he tried to attribute this reluctance to pent-up sexual desire, but he knew that wasn't quite it. There was something more.

In the moment, though, he could not think of a good reason to say no—and he could tell by the look on her face that if he didn't have a good reason, she was going to be extremely disappointed in him. That was not an emotion he wanted her to experience at the present time. Or any time, really.

He took the photo out of his inside jacket pocket and placed it in her palm.

"Thank you," she said, smiling. That smile was almost enough to get him to forget that nagging feeling—*almost.* "How about we meet at the Apple Peddler down the road in an hour. That long enough?"

"Should be," Gage said.

"Good. It's a date then."

She gave him another quick kiss, then jumped out of the car as if she was afraid he was going to change his mind. At the highway, she waited until there was a break in traffic, then, after a last wave to him over her shoulder, hurried across the road.

He watched her go, thinking maybe he should have been following her instead.

Chapter 11

Gage didn't have long to wait. Five minutes after six o'clock, and three minutes after Tatyana disappeared into the office of the Best Western down the road, Pirate Troy hustled out of the marina office and climbed into a maroon '80s-era Mercury Cougar. It might have been bright red rather than maroon, but enough dust and mud caked the rusting exterior that it was hard for Gage to tell. If that wasn't enough to make it easy to spot, red duct tape had been used to replace the left brake light.

Troy cracked open the driver's side window and lit a cigarette, puffing away as he headed to the highway. When he turned north, Gage let a couple of cars pass before he pulled in behind him.

The sun floated like a bright orange basketball just outside his driver's side window. Gage reached for the sun visor and found it missing, then remembered it had fallen off a few months earlier and he hadn't gotten around to replacing it. It seemed he and Troy had a lot in common when it came to cars. Maybe they were destined to be good buddies. His old Volkswagen van, with its bright mustard color and loud cantankerous engine, was not the ideal vehicle for tailing someone.

But then, Gage seldom did things the ideal way. Somehow, despite this, he still managed to get the job done—at least that's what he told himself.

Staying just far enough back so that he could keep the Mercury Cougar in sight without losing it, Gage followed Troy as he turned left away from Highway 101, following him past the usual signs of suburban life—several small strip malls, fast food restaurants, a Wal-Mart—until he turned right and onto a road that wound through Douglas firs and live oaks. Gage hung back as far as he could, keeping the Cougar's red taillights just within sight. They passed an assortment of older cottages and ramshackle manufactured homes tucked into the trees, a few dolled up with fresh paint and well-tended gardens but the majority hardly more presentable than the moss-ridden woodpiles that sat on most of the properties. They drove a good ten minutes, the houses getting more distant from one another, more recessed into the woods, until Troy turned left onto a gravel drive that was almost invisible from all the pine needles covering it.

Taking it slow, giving Troy time to get away from the road, Gage passed the driveway and noted the address on the rusted green mailbox partially obscured by ferns. Then he drove another couple of minutes, farther than he'd wanted, until he found a good place to park the van—in a muddy turnout for a small power transfer station surrounded by a tall chain link fence topped with barbed wire. He checked his Beretta, then set out for Troy's house.

He left his cane in the van. This was no time to be hindered by the damn thing. Still, after only a dozen wincing steps, he regretted the decision.

The trees loomed tall and dark on either side, the sky a slender silver strip high above that mirrored the road. He was alone, no cars on either side. Wood smoke laced the cool, damp air. He doubted he was more than a mile from the ocean, but it could have been thousands. No hush of ocean waves. No cawing seagulls. He heard sporadic dripping on fallen leaves, and, receding behind him, the faint buzz of the electrical transformer.

Before he reached Troy's driveway, he ducked into the trees. He tromped through the undergrowth until he spotted a silver trailer, then waited until a passing truck covered his sounds to cross the rest of the distance, taking refuge behind a metal shed blanketed in brown needles. He knelt on his good knee, taking stock of the situation.

The Cougar was parked in front, the engine still ticking, a hazy wave of air rising from the hood. Blinds hid all the trailer's windows, a soft yellow light glowing around the edges. He heard faint music inside, rock and roll or at least something with a strong base. An old Chevy pick-up was parked off to the side, partially hidden behind a blue tarp. A large boat trailer sat next to it, and it had obviously been there a while, judging by the weeds growing around the wheels. The boat that went with it would have been nearly as big as the silver trailer where Troy lived. Gage wondered if he'd find that boat tied up down on at the docks.

He got a whiff of gasoline coming from inside the shed, and the stench of wet, rotting wood from the nearby wood pile. A couple cars passed on the road, but nothing else happened. He wasn't sure what he hoped to see, but he figured it wouldn't hurt to just observe for a while.

He hadn't been sitting there more than five minutes when he heard a crash from inside the trailer, like something heavy falling to the floor.

Gage tensed, his hand instinctively going for his Beretta.

He hovered his hand over the holster inside his jacket, but didn't take out the gun. There was nothing for a moment, then another crash, this one the sound of glass breaking, like a bowl or a vase. Unsure of what to do, Gage waited. Two more crashes followed, one that actually shook the trailer. Was Troy going nuts in there by himself, throwing some sort of angry fit? Or was he fighting someone? Gage didn't hear voices over the rock and roll music, and there were no other cars around.

Before Gage committed to even taking a step, a shotgun rang out inside the trailer.

He ducked on instinct, his heart pounding, the hairs on the back of his neck rising, but the shot obviously wasn't aimed at him. There was no mistaking the sound. He'd heard it enough times in his life to know exactly what it was, dating all the way back to his childhood in Montana when he'd gone on hunting trips with his father. He waited a few more beats, but there was nothing else, no other gunshots, no crashing noises, just the music in the background all but muffled except for the steady thump of the drum. It nearly matched the thump of Gage's heartbeat. Had he just heard a man commit suicide?

Gage didn't like this. It was all wrong.

But he couldn't just stand there if a man was bleeding to death inside that trailer.

Still fearing it was some kind of trick, he brought out his Beretta, disengaged the safety, and crept to the trailer's biggest window. His right knee throbbed painfully, but he refused to allow it to hamper his movements. He leaned close to the glass, pressing his face against the cool metal siding, and tried to peer through the crack between the blinds and the window.

No luck. He couldn't see anything at all.

He tried the kitchen window, which was also blocked by blinds, and higher up, too, requiring him to stand painfully on his tiptoes. But the gap was bigger, allowing him a glimpse over a sink filled with dishes into a living room area. He saw a mermaid lamp on the floor, shattered. A leather recliner.

A man was in the recliner, slumped awkwardly to the side, hand draped to the threadbare carpet. A shotgun lay on the carpet, just inches from his open hand.

Gage circled to the front door, where a pair of oars leaned against the crooked wooden steps. He knocked hard, waited a few seconds, then tried the handle.

Unlocked. He stepped to the side, keeping the Beretta high and aimed within, and swung open the door. Garth Brooks was belting something about lonely women and lonely nights. Gage waited a few more seconds, knowing a man's life was at stake but still not trusting the circumstances. He could clearly see Troy, from behind but also the side, a good enough view to see that it was clearly him. He could have been sleeping, or he could have been dead.

There was no blood, though, at least not that Gage could see—not on Troy, the ceiling, the couch.

"Troy?" he said.

No reply. Gage edged into the trailer, stepping over a curling yellow vinyl floor. The place stank of sweat and beer and a faint under layer of something rotten, milk or eggs. There was something else, too, a scent that would have been undetectable if it hadn't been so sharp. A jar of recently opened pickles was the first thing that came to mind, but that wasn't quite it.

He hadn't gone far from the door when someone jabbed something narrow and hard into the small of his back.

"That's far enough," a man said.

His voice had the rough, husky quality of someone who'd probably been smoking since the day he emerged from the womb.

"I'm just here to see Troy," Gage said.

"Uh huh. Give me the piece. Nice and easy now, just hold it by the handle with two fingers in front of you."

"And if I say no?"

"I'll brain you on the head with my Magnum. Or maybe I'll just say to hell with the whole thing and put a couple slugs in your back."

"For some reason," Gage said, "I'm getting the impression you will do that anyway. Especially if you already killed Troy."

"Don't make no assumptions," the man said, coughing a little, definitely a smoker's cough. Gage smelled it on the man's breath. "Troy ain't dead. Now, I'm going to count to three ..."

"All right," Gage said

He didn't have a plan to get out of this yet, didn't even have the glimmerings of one, but he didn't see how getting shot in the back would help. When you didn't have a plan, it was better to stay awake and alive until one came to you. That may not have been in Private Investigation for Dummies as rule number one, but it certainly should have been.

"If I hold it in front of me," Gage said, "how are you going to retrieve it?"

"Shut up and do it."

Gage did it. His question was answered when the music stopped and a second man appeared from the bedroom. He wore a black leather jacket over a black T-shirt and black designer jeans. His hair, just as black, was flat and slicked straight back, as if someone had drawn it on with a marker pen. All that black made what might have been somewhat pale white skin seem alabaster white. He lumbered like a tall man, though he wasn't all that tall, just lean and long-limbed. He pointed his own Magnum .357 at Gage, lumbering over and plucking the Beretta out of the air. When he spoke, his voice was high and nasally.

"You should'na come down here, Gage," he said. "This whole thing is none a your business. You shoulda stayed home."

"Shut up," the man behind him said. "You don't need to tell him nothin'."

"Why?" the man in front of Gage said. "It's not like it's gonna matter."

"Shut up!"

"Fine, fine."

"Took you long enough to do what I says anyways," the man behind Gage said. "What were you doing in here, jerkin' off or something? It took you like forever."

"I was waiting to see if he'd come in on his own, Jake. That's all."

"Don't use my name!"

"Why? In a couple minutes, it's not like—"

"Shut up!"

During this intelligent back and forth, Gage's mind raced as he tried to figure out what this all meant. They knew who he was, which meant they'd expected him. Or, more likely, they'd followed him. All the way from Barnacle Bluffs? It seemed unlikely he wouldn't have noticed a tail, but if they had a rough idea of where he was going anyway, they wouldn't have needed to keep him in sight. In fact, they could have beaten him to Crescent City. But why? Who were they, and why did they care about Troy?

"Hey," Gage said, "I think you guys have the wrong idea. If there's some angle with this amnesia woman, I want in on it. I can be of use to you. There's no need—"

The man behind Gage—who apparently was named Jake—clocked him on the head with the butt of his gun. It wasn't hard enough to knock him out, but it still stung like hell.

"Hey!" Gage cried.

"Keep your mouth shut!" Jake said. "Get over there on that couch. Yeah, the one next to Troy. Come on now! Move!"

"All right, all right," Gage said.

He took the steps slowly, massaging his skull, trying to figure out an angle out of this. Two guys were pointing guns at him, one in front and one behind, and he was unarmed. To listen to them, they might have been idiots, but they weren't amateurs and they likely wouldn't hesitate to shoot him.

There would be an opening. There was always an opening, if he was patient enough.

The problem was, he didn't know how much time he had for patience.

The couch, a hulking battleship-sized thing covered by a big gray blanket with the words *Big Bear Casino* running along the top, was perpendicular to the chair where Troy sat slumped. As Gage neared, he saw the bullet holes in the blanket, white stuffing showing through in a couple of places. So that explained the gunshot. Definitely all a setup to lure Gage inside.

He took his place on the couch, sinking all the way to the springs, an empty beer can sinking into the divotdip with him. He saw right away that Troy wasn't shot at all, just unconscious, a line of drool hanging from the corner of his mouth. He also finally realized what that strange smell was.

Chlorophyll. Or at least something very much like it.

It explained why Troy was so dead to the world, and why he showed no signs of any struggle. They'd obviously surprised him. As Jake, moving along with Gage to the couch, positioned himself behind Gage and out of his line of sight, what these two goons were planning on doing became obvious—and just in time. He had just a few seconds for a couple shallow breaths, trying to take in as much oxygen as possible, before a chlorophyll-soaked rag clamped over his nose and mouth.

This was the opening Gage had been waiting for, and he had just enough advance warning to quell his panic and hold his breath. Jake clamped his other arm across Gage's chest and arms, trying to pin him down, and Gage put on a good show of fighting back. Jerking his legs. Flailing his arms. He bucked his whole body for as long as he could before making himself go suddenly slack, pretending that the chlorophyll had finally kicked in and knocked him out cold.

The real trick, and the hardest part of it all, was to go on holding his breath even when Jake still didn't take the rag away. The seconds ticked by, his lungs buckling under the strain, and it took all of Gage's willpower to remain absolutely motionless. With his eyes closed, the world was a dark coffin shrinking all around him.

Another second.

Just one more second.

Even when the rag thankfully was removed, it took even more willpower to breathe short and shallow through his nose. Easy. Showing even a hint that he was still awake would be the end of him. He didn't dare open his eyes, not even a crack, and the long moment of silence that followed the removal of the rag was one of the longest of his life. What were they doing? Were they watching him, fully aware that he was still conscious? Was one of them pointing a gun at Gage's head?

"He out?" the other guy asked, the one in black. He sounded as if he'd moved in front of Gage.

"Yeah," Jake said, still behind him.

"How you want to do this? Which one shoots first?"

There was a pause. Gage, still concentrating enormous amounts of willpower on keeping his breathing shallow and easy, waited. There was a shotgun on the floor, not far away, but there was still a gun behind him and a gun in front of him. Even if neither of them had their weapons pointed at Gage, the odds were still not good. Better than before—he had the element of surprise now, but still not good. He waited and prayed they chose the better option, and the one that made the most sense.

"Well," Jake said, "we already made it seem like Troy fired first with the shotgun. I guess the private dick should shoot next. A gut shot. Then Troy can get a shot off, maybe get this guy in the face, killing him. Then Troy will bleed out and die. That's the way it will seem, anyway."

"You really going to put the gun in his hand?"

"That's the best way to put his fingerprints on it."

"Okay."

Gage heard rustling behind him, then the metallic click of his Beretta's magazine. Jake murmured something about the gun being loaded and ready to go. It was hard for Gage to believe the world could actually produce two criminals so idiotic they could convince themselves that this harebrained scheme of theirs could actually work, especially in a world where forensic science had advanced so much. Hadn't either of them ever watched *CSI*? Still, their dearth of intelligence was providing him with his best shot of getting out of this mess.

The seconds ticked by. He heard Jake, behind him, breathing heavily through his nose. A faucet dripped somewhere in the house. Outside, a car with a loud muffler roared by on the road. What were they waiting for? Were they changing their minds? Were they exchanging looks, having figured out that Gage was still awake? Perhaps the whole thing was an elaborate ruse on their part. Was his own Beretta pointed to the back of Gage's head right now? A bead of sweat rolled down the small of his back like a cold marble. He fought the urge to open his eyes.

Finally, the Beretta was pressed into his right hand, the metal warm and slightly damp from Jake's grasp.

One big meaty hand clamped over his own, worked his finger over the trigger. Another hand roughly moved his arm, rising it up, aiming. Judging by the man's grasp, Jake stood just to his right. No way to swing the Beretta around and shoot him. No, the better plan was to shoot the man dressed in black first. If he was still where he'd been when he'd spoken last, then he stood just off to the left, maybe ten feet away.

That would still leave Jake in a commanding position, Gage in the chair and Jake behind him.

"All right," Jake said, "gonna aim now. Be ready in case Troy wakes up."

"What you want me to do if he does?"

"I don't know. Just be ready."

Jake's voice was right there, so close to Gage's right ear that he felt the man's breath on his cheek and got a whiff of beer and bar nuts. His finger was pressed tighter over the trigger, the arm steadied, silence pervading the room.

Now or never.

Gage opened his eyes. He was facing Troy, who was still out cold and slumped in his chair, but the man dressed in black stood just to the left looking right at him—and his own eyes flew wide open. The man, lips flapping soundlessly as he tried to voice his surprise, started to raise his gun.

Gage swung his gun arm to the left and squeezed the trigger.

The bullet found its target dead center in the man's chest, the man flailing backwards. The bang rang in Gage's ears, echoing off the walls of the small trailer. A shell casing went flying in a puff of smoke. The man he'd shot stumbled to the floor, out of his sight behind Troy and the easy chair.

"Wha—?" Jake began.

His face was right there, inches to Gage's right, and Gage swung his head hard into the man's face—using the side of his skull to butt Jake on the bridge of his nose.

It hurt like hell, but it hurt Jake a heck of a lot more. The man cried out in agony, but unfortunately he did not do the one thing Gage had been hoping he'd do—let go of Gage's arm. Instead, he clamped over Gage's gun hand even tighter and pulled Gage backwards halfway out of the couch.

He was a big man, stronger than Gage had first estimated,

and even as he moaned in pain he was doing his best to yank Gage's arm right out of its socket. Gage got a quick glimpse of Troy—who was blinking rapidly, waking to this chaos—before he swiveled his body around, using his weight and Jake's grasp on the Beretta to pull Jake forward.

Jake may have been standing, but behind the couch and leaning over it put him in a much more awkward stance. It didn't take that much to topple him over the couch.

Gage had hoped that Jake would release his grasp on the Beretta in the process, but no such luck. The big man rolled right on top of Gage, a big sweaty mass of muscle and fat, and the two of them grappled for control of the weapon.

He heard moaning not far away. Troy or the other goon? It was impossible to tell. If it was the other man and he recovered, Gage's chance would be lost.

Jake may have been bigger and stronger, but Gage had one distinct advantage: it was *his* hand that held the Beretta. They rolled over one another on the floor, clutching and clawing, the two of them locked in a deadly arm wrestle for control of the gun. He got a flash of the man's bloodied face, red streaks from his nose. The gun fired, blasting a hole in the ceiling. It fired again and a picture of a sailboat on the wall shattered. The ringing in Gage's ear drowned out all other noise. Jake managed to get on top of Gage, bearing down on him with his full weight.

He got both hands on the Beretta. He started to turn it, angling it for the underside of Gage's chin. It was close. Gage, barely able to breathe, turned his head, trying to keep out of the line of fire. He had his other hand on the Beretta now, but pushing up was a lot harder than pushing down, even if their strength had been equal.

He was going to lose.

There was only one thing to do—take away the Beretta's power. When the gun was still pointed just to his right, barely keeping him out of the range of fire, he squeezed the trigger. Not just once, but again and again, emptying the cartridge into the threadbare carpet and the bottom of the couch. He kept going

until there was nothing but empty clicking. This seemed to surprise Jake, and it was that flutter of surprise that was all Gage
needed because, for just a second, no more than a blink of an eye,
Jake slightly relaxed his grip.

Now emptied of bullets, the gun was nothing more than a
hunk of metal. Gage, having intended this, was quicker to take
advantage.

With great fury, he used both his hands to slam the butt of
the Beretta into Jake's face.

He aimed straight for the bloodied nose. Hindered by Jake's
grasp, the gun didn't hit with quite the force Gage had hoped,
but there was still a sickening crunch, a *thwap* like a wet towel
slapping against a concrete floor.

Jake screamed, his face a mask of red. In his fury, he scrambled off Gage, on his feet now, reaching behind him. His own
Glock was suddenly out and pointing. Coming down. Aiming.
Out of bullets, on his back on the floor, there wasn't much Gage
could do.

Then, just when it seemed the crimson-faced Jake was going
to unload his Glock into Gage's face, a shotgun blasted Jake in
the chest.

He went flying like some kind of carnival piñata, spinning
backwards, blood everywhere. When he hit the floor, it shook
the entire trailer.

Gage rolled onto his stomach and got himself onto his hands
and knees. He saw Troy, still looking dazed, rising from his recliner with the shotgun in hand. He was teetering, blinking
rapidly, but somehow still having the sense that danger lurked
behind him because he started to turn.

He never even got halfway around before three shots rang
out, two taking him in the chest and one slicing him across the
throat.

Troy, too, fell hard to the floor. This put the shotgun within
Gage's reach. Just as he saw the man dressed in black rising from
the floor, brandishing his own gun, Gage dove for it.

Two more shots rang out, one of them whizzing right by his

ear and puncturing the couch behind him. The man had been holding his right shoulder with his bloodied left hand and his arm had wobbled, his aim unsteady.

Gage slammed to the floor, grasped the shotgun and fumbled it around until he was aiming it in the direction of his assailant. The recliner blocked his view. Troy lay moaning next to him. Gage expected to see the man dressed in black spring around the chair and unload his Glock, and he clenched his teeth and waited for it, his heart pounding, sweat in his eyes … any moment now. Any moment and the guy would start firing.

Then he heard footsteps. The front door banged open, followed by a thudding run on the dirt outside. Gage waited until the footsteps outside silenced, then waited some more, five seconds, ten, his heart gonging away in his ears and pulsing behind his eyelids. He tasted blood in his mouth. His right knee felt as if it had been snapped in half, the agony was so crushing.

It was only when Troy moaned that Gage snapped out of his reverie. Still with his eye on the door, still aiming the shotgun, he crawled to his knees. Troy's neck was a bloody mess, but there was still Jake to contend with. One glance in that direction, though, confirmed what Gage had suspected when Jake had been blasted with the shotgun.

The guy lay curled on his side in a pool of his own blood, his eyes open, unblinking.

Gage had seen those eyes on enough bodies over the years— far too many bodies, far too much death—to know that good old Jake wasn't going to be bothering anyone ever again. There might have been someone out there who actually liked this guy, maybe even loved him, but if the scales of his encounters with people over the years were weighed fairly, Gage had no doubt that few would mourn his loss.

Troy, on the other hand, seemed more like a two-bit criminal who'd gotten mixed up with the wrong crowd. That was the sense that he hoped to confirm, but when he crawled on his aching knee to Troy and got a good look at the shredded flesh his neck had become and the voluminous amounts of blood pooling on the balding brown carpet, he knew that the old trailer pirate was going to be joining Jake in the afterlife momentarily.

For the moment, though, Troy was alive and flapping his lips like a trout dropped onto the deck of a boat. Blood filled his mouth, too, enough of it that he choked and gagged. So much blood. His red plaid shirt was soaked in it.

"It's going to be all right," Gage lied.

More lip flapping, lots of rapid blinking, his one good eye splashed with a watery veil—Troy was definitely on his way out. Gage grabbed the gray casino blanket from the couch and pressed it hard against the man's neck, trying to staunch the bleeding. The man reached for the blanket himself, but his arms seemed to have lost most of their strength; he barely managed to raise them off the floor.

"Where's your phone?" Gage asked.

Troy sputtered out some blood, tried to speak but ended up coughing. Instead, he pointed feebly toward the kitchen. Gage took the man's hand and clamped it over the blanket, which was already soaked. He started to rise, intent on calling 911 no matter how hopeless Troy's situation seemed, but then the man clutched at Gage's arm.

"Didn't—didn't have—" he managed.

"Save it," Gage said. "Let me get some help first."

"Didn't have—have a choice," Troy said. "Had to help them. Jessica … They said—they said they'd hurt Jessica."

"Who's Jessica?"

"Daughter. In Ashland. They took my wallet. Saw her picture. Tell her … tell her …"

"What did they make you do?"

"Tell her I'm sorry. For not being there."

"Troy, what did they make you do?"

"Didn't know …"

"Troy …"

It was too late. He clenched down hard on Gage's arm. His body spasmed, his back arching. This lasted a few pulsating seconds, then Troy's pupils dilated until they filled his eye sockets like shiny black marbles. The shine didn't last long. The life faded, the gaze turning distant and unseeing, all that energy coursing through the man's body shutting off like someone cutting a wire.

He slumped, lifeless, to the floor.

Gone.

Chapter 12

The mess Gage had made at Troy Langford's house—which turned out to be the man's full name—took three hours of explanations, arguments, and a half-dozen phone calls, including a long one back to Chief Quinn in Barnacle Bluffs, before the fine folks who worked in law enforcement in Crescent City finally decided to believe him. Or if not believe him, they at least were less sure he was a murderer. By then, Gage had drank far too much bad coffee and spent far too much time repeating his story to one officer after another to maintain any sort of professional composure. His throat became hoarse from all the shouting. If it hadn't been for his concern for Tatyana, he surely would have punched someone.

The thug who'd died, Jake, turned out to be Jake Sheffield out of New York according to the driver's license in his pocket. He had a rap sheet a mile long, mostly petty stuff when he was younger, and he was more of a freelancer than someone associated with one of the crime families. The police back east were going to do some checking, but nobody thought it would lead anywhere. Apparently almost all of Sheffield's work came from a go-between that had been on their radar for years and had been impossible to pin down.

Still, New York. Maybe it meant something.

Gage managed to arouse the sympathy of a young female cop, who fetched Tatyana from the Apple Peddler. After Gage was finally told he could go, he found Tatyana waiting for him in the reception area, paging through a wrinkled copy of *Time* magazine. When she saw him, she sprang out of the chair, reaching for his face before self-consciously pulling her hand back.

"I was so worried," she said.

"Sorry," he said. "Somebody decided to throw me a surprise party."

"I heard. And one got away?"

"Yep, he's still out there. Not in good shape, though. That guy doesn't get medical attention, he's not going to make it. They've got police watching all the hospitals and clinics for a hundred miles. Come on, let's get out of here."

His van was waiting in the back. The night sky stretched over the little parking lot devoid of stars but wavy with different shades of black and indigo; it was like looking up at the surface of a pond while standing on the bottom. He smelled the ocean on the breeze. The police station was in the heart of the city surrounded by modest houses, a Methodist church across the street and an assortment of one- and two-story buildings, almost all of them dark. Gage, thinking about the goon who was still out there, touched his gun holster through his jacket.

Would the guy come after him? He didn't think so, but then the two thugs had not exactly proven to be candidates for Mensa.

Getting into the van, Gage saw two men sitting in an unmarked navy blue Chevy Tahoe parked in the corner. The police chief, a guy so gruff he made Percy Quinn seem almost charming, had insisted on providing Gage with protection. Gage had equally insisted that it wasn't needed. The fact that the chief had gone ahead and given him protection anyway was irritating even if it wasn't surprising. This wasn't just about protection, after all. This was about finding out what he was going to do.

When he informed Tatyana about their escort, she appraised them for a while.

"I'm not sure I feel any safer," she said. "Are you sure they are going to follow us?"

"Oh yes."

"What do you want to do?"

"Curl into a ball and whimper for a few hours," Gage said. "But since whimpering probably won't impress you, maybe I'll just lie down. First, though, tell me if you discovered anything on your end."

Tatyana shrugged. "Not much. I talked to people at three different motels. I also talked to the manager at the Mexican restaurant. Nobody knew who she was. But the man at the Mill Creek Motel, he did act a little ... strange."

"Strange? How?"

"He just seemed a little distracted. As soon as I showed him Miranda's picture, he changed. He seemed to want me out of there. Maybe it was nothing."

"Or maybe this clerk has something to hide."

She pulled a card out of her jacket pocket and handed it to Gage. "These were on the desk. It looks like he's actually the owner."

"Bob Martin," Gage said, reading the card. "How do you know this was him and he's not just a clerk?"

"I asked him."

"Well look at you. You're like a real detective and everything."

"You want to talk to him?"

"Oh yes."

"Right now?"

"Yep. Besides, we need a couple rooms anyway. Why not stay at the Mill Creek Motel? I'm sure it's a fine establishment."

He started the van. Just as he expected, the blue Tahoe followed them out of the lot and back to Highway 101. He told Tatyana about Troy's comments about his daughter.

"So he was forced to help them," Tatyana said.

"Looks like it. The problem is, he died before he could tell me exactly what they made him do. I have a few ideas, though."

"Such as?"

"Well, let me ask you. Troy works at a marina. It was also pretty clear that he has a boat at that marina. That boat trailer at his place obviously goes to something. We don't know for sure, of course, but let's assume Marcus Koura stopped in Crescent City. Either Miranda was already with him or he met her here and took her with him. What do you think those two idiots wanted with Troy?"

"His boat?"

"Or *a* boat. Why?"

"Hmm. To go after Marcus?"

"That's what I'm thinking," Gage said. "Why else would they want Troy to keep quiet? If they'd just showed up asking questions, they wouldn't have needed to strong arm him so much. No, I'm figuring that Troy took them on his boat to find Marcus. Maybe he was told to call them when he saw Marcus leaving the harbor. Maybe they're even the ones who killed him."

"But why?"

"Don't know yet. Probably has something to do with eTransWorld, though. We know that Marcus and Omar had a falling out. Maybe Marcus was intent on doing something to bring his brother down. "

"If Miranda was on the boat," Tatyana said, "why would they leave her alive?"

"Don't know that yet either. It doesn't look good, though."

"You think she was part of it?"

Gage tapped his steering wheel. "I really don't know. I hope not. Maybe they didn't know she was on the boat? And if that was the case, then maybe she hid below, maybe in one of the storage compartments. If they had no reason to think someone else was on the boat, then maybe they didn't have reason to search."

"I like that theory better."

"I do, too," Gage said. "I don't think either us wants to think that Miranda could be an accessory to murder. It also might explain why she lost her memory—the shock of what she witnessed."

"Did you tell any of this to the police?"

"Heavens, no! If there's one thing I've learned in all my years of being a private investigator, it's that the less I tell the police, the better. Otherwise they just muck things up."

The Mill Creek Motel was past the marina and across from the beach. The motel was U-shaped, two stories, with redwood log siding so prominent it bordered on parody. Only eight of the maybe twenty rooms were lit, with half that many cars in the lot. A neon-green vacancy sign lit up the office window. Gage saw a bald, heavyset man sitting behind the counter, peering through reading glasses that seemed far too small for his pale round face. He looked all the more pale because of his black T-shirt.

"That's the guy," Tatyana said.

When Gage pulled into the parking spot in front of the office, he watched his rearview mirror. The blue Tahoe drove past, heading south on the highway. Tatyana, following his gaze, noted this as well.

"Maybe they weren't following us at all," she said.

"Oh no. Just watch."

A minute later, the Tahoe returned heading north, and when it reached the motel it slowed and turned left, not into the motel parking lot but onto the strip of sand that bordered the beach and served as parking. Gage raised his eyebrows at Tatyana, as if to say *I told you so,* and she smirked in response.

They walked into the office. Gage, in no condition to suffer the pain in his knee, took his cane. The counter, the chairs, even the paneling were made from redwood, all stained a warm brown. From the outside, and seeing only the man's head, Gage got a sense that Bob Martin was heavy, but it wasn't until he saw the man's massive, pear-shaped body that he realized just how overweight he really was. His cascading folds of flesh completely swallowed the chair, making it seem like Martin was sitting suspended in mid-air. His pasty head sat upon his shoulders like a giant snowball, no neck visible, as if the whole thing might roll off if someone pushed hard enough. He did have more hair than Gage had thought, but it was so blond and spread so thinly across his shiny scalp that it was practically invisible. Even his eyebrows, atop his fleshy drooping brow, looked as if they had been drawn on his skin with colored pencils.

Gage always felt a piercing sympathy for people so obese. He'd been a little pudgy himself until he'd hit puberty. His sympathy quickly faded, however, when Martin did not so much as glance up at them. Ten seconds passed. Then ten seconds more. Martin was writing something in a ledger book with great care, the scratching of the pen as loud as a dagger against concrete in the tiny office.

"Hi," Gage said. "We'd like a room for the night."

"We're full," Martin said, still not making eye contact.

"Excuse me?"

"Someone just called and reserved the last couple open rooms. I was just about to get up and turn off the vacancy sign."

"You're kidding," Gage said.

This finally got Martin to put down his pen, clasp his hands, and place what little chin he had on his fingers. There was an air of superiority about him, a smugness, that immediately made Gage want to rap the man across the side of the head. What good would come from that? He might even break his cane, the man's skull was so thick. Martin knew he was the king of his own little domain, but smugness wasn't the only emotion on the man's face. Dew-sized droplets of sweat beaded his forehead like a crystal headband.

"I'm sorry, sir," Martin said, clearly not sorry at all. "I'd suggest the Best Western down the street."

"We have our hearts set on staying here. I love the smell of redwood in the morning. And I see you have complimentary coffee in those carafes over there. A real plus."

"Sir—"

"Besides, we both know you're not really full. Let's cut to the chase, shall we?"

Martin tried to maintain his smug facade, but his loud swallow gave him away. "Excuse me?"

"There's only one reason you don't want us here. It's because you didn't like the questions my associate was asking you earlier."

Blinking rapidly, Martin did his best to appear nonchalant as he glanced at Tatyana, but it was all too forced and hurried.

"Oh, I didn't recognize you until now," he said. "Did you find that woman you were looking for? I'm sorry I couldn't be of more help."

"Didn't *want* to be of more help, you mean," Gage said.

"What? I don't know what you're talking about. I simply didn't know who this woman was."

"Bullshit."

"Excuse me, sir! I'm afraid I will have to ask you to—"

"You can ask whatever you want, but I'm not leaving."

"Well now!"

Gage leaned over the counter so that he was only inches away, a short enough distance that he got a good whiff of the musky scent emanating from the man's body. "Bob—can I call you Bob? Sure I can. I've had a long day, Bob. A very long day. We drove six hours to get here. Then someone tried to knock me unconscious with chlorophyll. If that wasn't bad enough, he would have killed me if I hadn't head-butted him. Still have a hell of a headache from that one. Oh, and I shot somebody and watched as two others got shot and died. I'm sure it will be all over the news tomorrow. You can read about it then. So maybe you can excuse me if I don't have a lot of patience. I know you're lying."

Bob's pasty white countenance bulged and darkened like a marshmallow over a fire. He opened and closed his mouth a couple of times, but nothing came out but a faint gasp of air.

"Here's the thing, Bob," Gage said. "I'm a private investigator from Barnacle Bluffs. My hunch is you might already know that. You've probably already heard all about the woman we're calling Miranda. You saw her picture and recognized her. You know she can't remember who she is."

"I really—I really dont—" Bob began.

"Sure you do," Gage said. "I don't know what you got mixed up in here, but there's some very bad people involved in this. One of the men who tried to kill me is still at large, and I'm sure he has friends. Now, if you look across the street there, over by the beach, you'll see a blue Tahoe. That's my police protection. I'd be happy to tell them to extend their services to watching over you if you cooperate. If you don't, and we walk out that door, they're going to go with us. Which means nobody watching over you when we're gone."

Bob stared past Gage out the window. With the darkness outside, it was hard to see more than their own reflections, but the shape of the Tahoe was still evident.

"So how about it, Bob?" Gage asked. "We already have someone nearby who identified her, and what this person said leads us to believe she was either working or staying down on this end of town. I'm guessing it was here. Am I right?"

Bob remained silent a long time, but all the smugness was gone. The highway was still. Suddenly the phone rang and Bob flinched, a double chirp that must have been an internal call from one of the rooms, but he made no move to answer it. He sat there until it stopped ringing, then sat there some more. Finally, he looked down at his hands.

"She worked here," he said.

"All right," Gage said, "now we're getting somewhere."

"It was—it was all under the table. She said she'd clean rooms if I just gave her a place to stay and a little money for food. She told me she couldn't sign anything or have it be official in any way. That's the only reason I didn't want to say. I didn't know what she was mixed up in. I didn't really know anything about her. She just seemed like she—like she needed some help. I thought I'd help her out."

"And fact that she was a very pretty woman didn't have anything to do with it, huh? Did she give you a name?"

"Mary. Didn't give me a last name. I don't—I don't think that was her real name, though."

"Why is that?"

"Because a couple times early on, when I called her by that name, she didn't really respond right away."

"How long did she work here?"

"I don't know."

"Bob."

"A few weeks. Maybe a month. I guess it was about a month. Must have—must have been about a month. Yeah, it was right after most kids are on spring break, because we had a lot of families heading home. A lot of rooms to clean. I'd just had one housekeeper quit on me, so I needed the help. Listen, you don't need to tell the police any of this, do you?"

Gage drummed his fingers on the counter. "Well, that depends."

"Depends?" Bob said.

"It depends on whether I feel you're holding out on me. When was her last day?"

"I don't know. A couple weeks ago."

"Bob, I need you to be more specific."

"Okay. Okay, hold on."

Bob opened a black ledger book and flipped through the pages, each of them filled with handwritten entries. The man's trembling fingers left sweat marks. While Bob's attention was fixated on his book, Gage glanced at Tatyana, who smiled furtively but he could see the concern in her eyes. He knew what she was feeling. What he'd said to Bob wasn't a lie—there really was somebody out there in the city who'd tried to kill him—and the danger was real. He wondered if he was making a mistake, having her stay in Crescent City. He shouldn't have brought her at all. He was always doing this, putting the people he cared about at risk. And for what? Because he wanted company? His selfishness knew no bounds.

"M-M-March 24," Bob said, stuttering over the words. "No, wait. Wait. March 22. Yeah. That would have been the last day I saw her."

"You don't put all this in a computer?"

"I do. I do. I just, I transfer it later. I don't trust the computer. We have lots of power outages."

Gage nodded. The same was true in Barnacle Bluffs. With

the high winds so common on the north coast, most locals developed a healthy skepticism that electricity was a dependable fact of life. "Why do you know that was the last day?"

"Because—because she was ... well, she was staying in room 214, on the back side. She didn't show up to work one Wednesday. When she didn't show up the next day either, I checked her room. All her stuff was gone. I mean, she didn't have very much, just one suitcase, but it was gone. I ... uh, I cleaned out her room that night. We were real busy and I figured I might as well rent the room. It was real annoying, though. Sonya had to work round the clock until I hired more help."

"Sonya was your other housekeeper?"

"Yes."

"Does she stay here, too?"

"No. No, she lives in that trailer park not far from here. Misty Village, I think it's called."

"Why did Miranda—I mean, Mary—leave?"

"I don't know. Like I said, she just didn't show up."

"Bob, come on. Tell me the truth.

"I am, I am!"

Gage had gotten to be a pretty good judge of whether someone was giving it to him straight, but he didn't need keen powers of observation to know that Bob Martin was hiding something. The sheen of sweat coating his face was so thick he'd just emerged from a dunk tank. Ugly red splotches dotted his forehead and cheeks. To top it off, his left eyelid twitched regularly, as if in time to a silent beat.

Sometimes, when facing someone so wound up about whatever secret they kept buried inside them, the best move was simply to wait—which was what Gage did. An engine with some loose gears would rattle apart if left alone. He stared at Bob, letting the moment stretch out uncomfortably, the tension grow. Most people couldn't stand being confronted by someone who offered them only silence, even a few seconds of it, and would usually blurt out something far more helpful than if Gage kept pressing. Bob turned out to be no exception.

"She quit, okay?"

"She quit?"

"Yeah."

"Why did she quit?"

"I don't know."

"Bob."

"What do you want from me? I didn't really know her at all! Nothing I tell you can help her. I read about it, her amnesia. If I knew about her past, I'd say something, I swear. But I don't. I don't know anything."

"You don't know anything," Gage said. "Fine. So if I talk to Sonya, you think she'll give me the same story?"

Bob's eyelid twitched even faster. The beat of the twitching had moved from a waltz to ragtime.

"See," Gage said, "it really is hard to spin a lie for long. Eventually it will catch up to you. So here's how it is. You can either tell us the truth now and save us a lot of trouble, or I can go find Sonya and get the truth from her. In the meantime, my police protection will come with me. What's it going to be?"

"You have to understand something," Bob said in a strained voice, as if someone had just tightened a noose around his neck. "There was—there was an accusation made. It was not true at all, but it did not—I understand the accusation. I understand how it looked. But it wasn't true."

"Tell me," Gage said.

"It—it sounds bad."

"Bob, out with it."

Bob glanced at Tatyana, swallowed hard, then leaned forward in a conspiratorial manner. Since Gage was quite a distance above him, the gesture seemed absurd, but he played along anyway and leaned in himself.

"It's like this," Bob said. "She thought I was, um, spying on her."

"What?"

"I guess she found a hole in her wall. It was in the middle of a painting, and—and it led all the way to the other side, to the room. You couldn't, um, see it unless you took off the painting. There's a storeroom on the other side, so someone could stand there and see into her room. But I didn't do it! That's where she was wrong. I agree that *someone* put it there, but it wasn't me. That hole has probably been there forever. I've only owned this place for nine years. It was probably the previous owner or manager or whatever."

"And yet," Gage said, "you're the one who gave her that room when you agreed to hire her?"

"It wasn't because of that hole!"

"And that's what Sonya would say?"

"She just got the wrong idea! She saw me in the storeroom one day and thought I was—I was looking through the hole. But I was just getting new hand towels for one of the rooms. They both had the wrong idea, that's all. I'm not that kind of person. I'm *not.*"

Gage let this admission stand for awhile without saying anything. Good old Bob was obviously living with enough guilt about the whole thing that offering him nothing but a wall of silence, no kind of absolution at all, was probably the worst kind of punishment. The question was whether Gage could get the man to admit a little bit more, because while finding out that Bob was a pervert was certainly disturbing, all they had really accomplished so far was confirm what they already suspected: Miranda, or Mary, had spent some time in this town. What they didn't know yet was how and why she had ended up on that boat with Marcus.

"Okay, Bob," Gage said, "here's what we're going to do. I could do a whole song and dance with you about this story you've cooked up. I believe on some level, you even believe this crap yourself. Nobody wants to think of themselves as a peeping Tom."

"I'm not—" Bob began.

"Hear me out. I really don't give a rat's ass. I may find your personal behavior disgusting, but focusing on that is not going to help me with the main purpose I'm in your city. I need to find out who Miranda is and how she came to be on Marcus Koura's boat."

"I told you—"

"I know what you told me, but I don't think I'm getting the whole story."

"I don't know her real name! I swear!"

"Do you know how she ended up on that boat?"

"No!"

"I want the truth."

"It is, it is!"

"The whole truth?"

"Yes!"

Bob blurted his reply without hesitation, but there was still something in his eyes, a cloud of doubt or guilt or something else that gave him away. He was like a pressure valve that needed to vent or the whole thing would blow. The water cooler in the corner, which had been silent this whole time, suddenly gurgled and bubbled, as if it, too, was buckling under the strain. Gage didn't want the man to completely crack. A man who cracked was much more unpredictable. He needed Bob to stay focused on the moment, on seeing the clear benefit of cooperating. Leverage. Gage needed a different kind of leverage to get this pathetic little small-town motel owner to tell Gage what he needed to know—and it was in the motel part of the man's identity that Gage saw his opening.

He picked up the man's card from the tray on the counter, holding it between his thumb and forefinger as if examining a specimen in a lab. "Owner. That's true, right? You are the owner of this fine establishment?"

Bob nodded.

"And as the owner," Gage continued, "you undoubtedly care quite a bit about the reputation of the Mill Creek Motel, correct?"

"Yes."

"See, Bob, I'm not the most technologically savvy guy in the world. Hell, I can't even manage to keep a cell phone for long without finding a way to destroy it. But I do try to stay up on things. I know how important reputation is to hotels these days. I know about Yelp, Trip Advisor, and the like. These things matter, right?" He turned to Tatyana. "Wouldn't you agree? Some bad customer reviews can really hurt a business, especially in a small-town motel like this one."

"I agree," Tatyana said.

"So let's do a little thought experiment," Gage said. "Let's say someone—oh, why be coy—let's say that someone is me, and I tell the news media all about this little hole in the storeroom wall and how it connects to this fascinating amnesia story. They won't be able to resist. Maybe we bring in Sonya, too. This won't just make the local paper. It'll go national. How long do you think your motel will survive once it's known there are holes in the walls that let the owner watch while you're undressing? It'll be much worse than a bad review on Yelp. So, you see, the truth doesn't really matter, does it? It just matters that it will *seem* true to people."

Bob, who listened to all of this with a grave expression, slowly bowed his head. When he finally mustered up a reply, he sounded defeated.

"You'd do that to me?" he said.

"You did it to yourself. Besides, those cops across the street are probably wondering why we're spending so much time talking to a motel clerk. We don't move this along quickly, I won't have to do anything. You're going to have lots of other people asking questions. But, Bob, it doesn't have to be that way. Your little secret can stay between the three of us if you tell me what you know. Oh, and Sonya, too, but I imagine she's probably afraid of being deported or something if she comes forward. Am I right?"

Bob nodded, still avoiding eye contact. "I don't know all that much."

"Tell me."

"I don't know her real name. I didn't know the guy's name, either, but it is the guy from the paper. Marcus. I think they met when he came to shore. I know Mary—Miranda, whatever, she liked to sit on the docks and watch the boats. Oh, and she liked to draw. When she wasn't working, I often saw her with that sketch pad under her arm and she'd go down there and draw the seagulls and stuff."

"What else?"

"I actually don't know much else. When they were in here, in the motel, they actually didn't talk a lot. They spent their time, um, doing other things."

"Which I'm sure you thoroughly enjoyed watching," Gage said.

Bob swallowed.

"Sorry," Gage said, "that was punching low. What else do you know?"

"Not much. She really didn't talk about herself. She didn't talk much at all, really. I just got the sense she was on the run. Then we had … we had our misunderstanding. She came into the office screaming at me. She wouldn't even hear my side of it! Next day, she was gone."

"Did you see her leave?"

"No."

"Did she say anything about going with Marcus?"

"I'm telling you, she didn't say anything to me at all!"

"And your housekeeper, Sonya, she'll confirm your story?"

"I don't know what she knows. I don't really think they were close or anything."

"How about you give me her phone number?"

Bob hesitated.

"So," Gage said, "you *aren't* telling me everything?"

"No, no, it's not that. It's just—you meant what you said, right? If I cooperate, you're not going to make trouble for me, are you? Sonya's been a good employee."

"Ah," Gage said, "you're also worried about her being de-ported."

"Well, good help is hard to find."

"I wonder if you even realize the irony in you saying that."

"Sorry?"

"Forget it. Just give me her number. If everything you said checks out, I think I can look past whether she has a green card or not."

Bob nodded glumly, then fumbled around on his desk until he found a black spiral notebook. He flipped through it until he found the page he was looking for, scribbled a number on a yellow sticky note, and handed it to Gage. He struggled to maintain eye contact with Gage. "And the other thing? The, um, talking to the press thing?"

"Depends on how it goes," Gage said.

"Okay."

"But I'll tell you one thing. No matter what Sonya says, I'm going to check back with her from time to time. She better tell me that one, she has a job with you unless she chooses not to have it. And two, that the little hole in the storeroom was patched over never to be used again."

"Already done," Bob said.

"Good."

"Is that it?"

"No, there's one other thing." The trepidation on Bob's face made Gage want to wait as long as possible before continuing, but he was too banged up to enjoy watching the man squirm for long. "We'd like to book two rooms for the night, please."

Chapter 13

Relieved that his torture appeared to be at an end, Bob wanted to give them the rooms compliments of the house, but Gage insisted on paying. No way he would allow himself to feel even the slightest bit of indebtedness to such a pathetic slimeball. Tatyana also further insisted on paying for her own room. Gage wished she'd insisted on only staying in *one* room, then felt like a bit of a slimeball himself.

He liked to think there was a wide gulf between someone like him and Bob Martin, but perhaps the gap wasn't so big after all.

The rooms were spartan, spacious, and decorated with the same over-the-top redwood, the furniture airlifted straight form the '70s. A faint dank smell pervaded both rooms, which may have been why the windows were cracked open. They were sparkling clean, though, no doubt a testament to Sonya's housecleaning abilities, and the beds were large and firm enough to do the job. A big bed, a built-in desk, a couple of chairs—Gage didn't need much else. They brought in their bags, refreshed for a few minutes, then got together in Gage's room to call Sonya from the room phone.

It didn't take long. Her spoken English was a bit disjointed, but she understood him perfectly well—especially when Gage made it clear he understood all about Bob Martin's dirty little secret. Her English also seemed to improve when he explained that he was going to do everything he could to leave her, Bob Martin, and the Mill Creek Motel out of this so long as she cooperated and told him everything she knew about the housekeeper she knew as Mary.

"I don't know her much," Sonya said, raising her voice to speak over a baby crying in the background. "She clean rooms. Then she meet a man and leave."

"After she had her little blow-up with your boss," Gage said.

"Yes," Sonya said. "But I think maybe she leave anyway. She was scared."

"Scared of what?"

"Of someone finding her. She say only one time, when we talk about how rude some boys were who stay there to surf beach, she say, 'I was with a man much worse.' And I ask her who, but she not tell me. I think this man look for her."

"Do you have any idea where she was from?" Gage asked.

"No," Sonya said.

"Or anything else that might help me figure out who she is?"

"No. I wish I help more. Oh, *creo que ella era rica …* I mean, I think she very rich before."

"What makes you say that?"

"Because she very bad at cleaning. *Muy mal.* Like she never have to even clean one toilet in her life. She did not know what a toilet brush is. But I show her and she learn fast. She get good. So she not dumb. She just not know."

Gage didn't get the sense that she was holding anything back. He thanked her for her help, told her he might call again but only if it was really necessary, and hung up. Mostly it was because his eyes felt like they were coated in lead. The little digital clock next to the bed showed that it was just past eleven, but it felt much later, another day, another week. A lifetime had passed since they'd left Barnacle Bluffs that morning.

Tatyana, who'd been standing at the window, turned to

face him. Far from the bedside lamp that lit the room, she stood partly in shadow, the walkway lights outside casting her blonde curls with an amber hue. Something about her shape, the way the jeans hugged tight to the curve of her hips, was alluring. The little denim jacket, which actually hid most of her curves, still managed to offer a tantalizing promise of what lie beneath. He marveled at himself. Even after everything that had happened, even as tired as he was, he couldn't help but be attracted to her. He caught the glint of the CK necklace and wondered, again, who had given it to her. Tatyana. Tatyana Brunner. So many layers. Such a complicated woman.

Sitting as he was on the bed, the two of them alone in the room, the mood changed. He could sense it. When Tatyana spoke, her voice had a slightly husky quality.

"Learn anything?" she asked.

"Excuse me?"

"From Sonya."

"Oh right." Gage relayed Sonya's half of the conversation, then said, "Unfortunately, it's not enough to prove that she didn't kill Marcus."

"She doesn't seem to have a motive."

"Not an obvious one, that's for sure. Why would she kill a man she had just met, a man who was taking her away from all of this? If we can catch the other guy who tried to kill me, maybe the police can offer to cut him a deal for testifying against whoever is behind this. My bet is on Omar Koura. He must have wanted Marcus killed."

"Why?"

"I'm sure it has something to do with eTransWorld."

"But I thought you said Marcus had already sold his half of the business."

"Well, that's the official story," Gage said. "Who knows what was really going on between them. This is a pretty shady financial company dealing with pretty shady people, after all."

"And if we can't find this other man? Or if he will not turn against Omar?"

Gage shrugged. "I admit, we don't have much else to go on yet. There might be enough already to create reasonable doubt in a jury's mind that Miranda is guilty, but I'd hate to pin our hopes on that. Any ideas?"

Tatyana fell silent. He couldn't tell if her eyes were closed or open. He liked looking at her, hoping she would just go on standing there. He knew she'd said nothing was going to happen between them tonight, but as long as she was in his room, he could pretend.

"Maybe we're digging into the wrong person's past," she said.

"What do you mean?"

"You've been trying to figure out who Miranda is because of the amnesia. But maybe we should be trying to figure out a little more about what Marcus was up to before he set sail. Instead of proving Miranda is innocent, maybe we should be trying to prove that someone else is guilty."

"Hmm. I'm trying to avoid a trip to San Jose, but I suppose I'll go down there if need be."

"You might start by talking to his ex-girlfriend. There might be things she would tell you that she will not tell the police."

"Actually," Gage said, remembering what Quinn had said back in the hospital a few days earlier, "I think the police got their information from Omar. I don't know if anyone has talked to her directly at all. Would be pretty easy to check to see if Miranda was his girlfriend down there, so I doubt Omar would lie about that. But she might have something to say that he didn't want us to hear. Hey, you're a pretty smart cookie, you know?"

"Well, I do have a medical degree," Tatyana said. "I guess that means I'm not a complete dummy."

"My dear," Gage said, "I can think of many words to describe you, but dummy is not one of them."

"Oh? And what words might those be?"

"I better not say. They might give you the wrong idea."

"And what idea would that be?"

"Oh, I think you know."

"Pretend I don't."

Her tone was coy, playful. He couldn't see her face well enough to read her expression. What was she doing? She'd already drawn the line between them they weren't going to cross. He didn't want to be presumptuous, take the chance on offending her.

"Well," he said, "I could give you a long list of adjectives that are much more fitting than the word dummy, but under the circumstances I think you would question the sincerity of my motives. Let's say we call it a night, okay? This bed is just begging me to use it, and I think eight hours of sleep will do me a world of good."

"Yes, I think rest is a good idea." Her playful tone was gone. "I should go back to my room. Maybe you will have a brilliant insight while you sleep and figure out everything in the morning. Then this will all be over."

"Don't count on it. I can barely think straight even when I'm conscious. We'll head back to Barnacle Bluffs first thing, okay?"

"All right. Good night then?"

"Yes, good night."

She put her hand on the door knob, but didn't not turn it. She stood like that for a while, then bowed her head.

"Tatyana?" he said.

"I hate to admit this," she said, "but I am a little afraid to go back to my room."

"Oh."

"I hate seeming so weak."

"You're not weak. You're human. We do have police protection, you know? And the chances of that guy trying to do something, after everything that's happened, are pretty slim."

"I know." She looked at him, hand still on the door knob. "But maybe I could sleep in here? I mean, on the floor?"

"Honestly, you're probably better off in your own room. In the slim chance that somebody came after me, at least you wouldn't be in the line of fire."

"Oh. I guess that's true."

The way she nodded, it was as if she was trying to convince

herself, but she didn't move. It was obvious to Gage, as it should have been from the beginning, that logic and reason weren't going to assuage her fears. He felt like a heel for even trying.

"What am I saying?" he said. "Of course you can stay in here. But you take the bed and I'll take the floor."

"Absolutely not."

"Tatyana—"

"No, no, no," she said. "I'm the one imposing. I will definitely take the floor, no matter how much it hurts your pride. I will just go get a pillow and bedding from my room, okay? Just make it a bit more comfortable."

"All right," he said.

"All right?"

"Yes."

She nodded, then turned back to the door, hand still on the knob. But she didn't turn it. A truck passed on the highway. The pop machine across the parking lot rattled out a can for someone. The seconds ticked away.

"Do you want me to go with you?" Gage asked.

"No."

"What then?"

She sighed. "I don't want to sleep on the floor."

"Well, like I said, I'm more than willing—"

"I don't want *you* to sleep on the floor either."

"Oh. Well …"

He trailed off. Was she really saying what he thought she was saying? She locked the door, and the click of the deadbolt was answer enough. When she turned around, slowly, with purpose, it was even more clear what her intentions were. Gage was no womanizer, at least not by his own standards, but he'd been with enough women over the years to recognize the steady look in Tatyana's eyes—a mixture of appraisal and hunger, of desire and trepidation.

"But I thought you said—" Gage began.

"I changed my mind," she said.

"Are you sure? I don't want you to do anything you regret."

"I won't regret it."

"It's probably just your nerves. When people are frightened—"

"Garrison, it's not that either."

"You say that, but I don't want to take advantage of you. You just said you were scared to be alone."

"Yes."

She took off her denim jacket and laid it on the back of the chair near the door. She slipped off her shoes, her socks. Then, while looking at him, a bit of rabbit fear in her eyes, she started to unbutton her shirt.

"Tatyana ..." Gage began.

"Shh. I know myself. I *am* scared to be alone tonight, but that's not the only reason I want to be here with you. That's what I just realized. I realized if I was lying on the floor, I would just be thinking all night about being held by you. Something has changed, changed inside of me. I don't want to wait anymore. I was more afraid of being with a man again than being alone. I was never afraid of being alone before. I wanted to be alone. So this is a very different feeling. It's not just because of the danger."

While she spoke, she worked her way down all the buttons, then slipped off the shirt and laid it, too, on the back of chair. She did this with such deliberate care that it was actually more tantalizing to Gage than if she had been trying to do a more traditional striptease. He was only slightly surprised to find that her blue bra perfectly matched the color of her shirt. He was even less surprised to find that the shape of the body beneath the shirt exceeded what he had imagined, and he had imagined the body of some kind of goddess.

This *was* a goddess. It was only more so when she slid off her tight designer jeans, folded them neatly, and placed them on the seat of the chair. Blue lace panties, blue silk bra, and her CK necklace—that's all that stood between him and her naked body. It was not that everything about her was perfect. In isolation, her shoulder blades might have been a little too pronounced, her breasts just a tiny bit lopsided, her stomach not quite as flat as some kind of ideal, but like all goddesses, Tatyana wove these imperfections into a perfect whole.

She took a tentative step, bare feet silent on the thin carpet. The swish of her blonde hair, and the way it fell over her bare shoulders, mesmerized him.

"I'm a little nervous," she said.

"You don't have to do this."

"If you say that again, I think I will yell at you."

"Okay."

"Just promise you won't laugh. If I do something wrong."

"Tatyana, I could never laugh at you. You're beautiful in every way."

Her eyes started to mist before she shook her head, a vigorous, forceful shake, the way she might have tried to shake water out of her hair. She unbuttoned her bra and slipped off her panties, and these she simply let fall to the floor. Here was the goddess, naked and pure, standing before him with wide-eyed expectation. He felt as he always did when a woman chose to give herself to him in this way: unworthy. Grateful, yes, he felt that, too, gratitude in abundance, but the unworthiness was like something cold clenching over his heart.

This passed. It had to pass, if only because eventually masculine desire always swamped all other feelings. The world had suddenly gone quiet, Gage's heartbeat loud in his ears. There were no tan lines, but the flesh around her breasts and thighs was slightly more pale, all of it as smooth and white as milk. He had the feeling that if he touched her, her skin would ripple like the surface of a pond. Perhaps she was like a reflection in that pond, and if he touched her, it would all go away.

"I want you to see me," she said.

"Oh, I see you."

"Do you? Nobody ever really sees me. I want *you* to see me. Call me beautiful again."

"You're beautiful."

"Call me good. Call me a good person."

"You're a good person."

"I don't believe you."

"Tatyana—"

"Shh. It's all right. Garrison?"

"Yes?"

"What are you waiting for?"

Since Gage couldn't think of a good answer to that question, he stopped waiting and reached for her.

Chapter 14

If Tatyana's lovemaking skills were rusty, the rustiness certainly did not last long. Her first tentative touches suddenly gave way to ravenous grasping and clutching. In the span of a few seconds, she went from gingerly stroking Gage's cheek, in a way someone might touch a crystal figurine, to grabbing and ripping at his belt buckle. What he had presumed would be a slow and sensual affair, with lots of false starts and tender give and take, turned into something much more frenetic.

It bordered on violence, the way she acted, her fingers scratching across his back like claws, her touches more akin to punches and shoves. He expected this mood to burn out quickly, that it was the result of a lot of pent-up hormones, but whatever rocket fuel she had stored inside her seemed to be in endless supply. It went on this way for hours, testing his stamina, each time leaving them both sweaty and spent, and yet within minutes she was on him again, yearning for more, always more.

At some point, no matter how much he wanted to will himself to stay with her, the deep fatigue of the long day and his injuries must have finally caught up with him, because suddenly he was opening his eyes to darkness. Tatyana lay pressed against him, naked flesh against naked flesh, her head on his chest. He saw a vertical bar of light between the closed curtains, a red glowing dot on the ceiling where the fire alarm was, a green glow off to his left where the digital clock sat on the nightstand.

His own breathing stirred her hair, and he breathed in the smell of her, of cooled sweat and sex, of some honey scent of her shampoo tinged with remnants of the ocean breeze. He felt a tangle of sheets around his ankles, but otherwise they lay completely exposed. He might have been cold except that she had tried to press every bit of her body against his own. One of her hands pressed against his chest, as if she had been feeling his heartbeat.

"Awake?" he whispered.

"Mmm hmm."

"I must have fallen asleep."

"Yes. In the middle of it."

"Oh."

"I don't think I have ever had that happen before."

"Sorry."

"Don't be. If it had been the first time, maybe. But I think it was … the fifth."

"Fifth? I didn't even know I was capable of four."

"Mmm. You will do better next time. I'm a doctor, so I know what the male body is capable of. We will get you in better shape soon enough."

The comment, mortifying him, hung in the air with all of its implications until he realized she was laughing. It wasn't the sound, because he'd managed to stifle any noise deep in her throat, but the vibrations of her diaphragm pressed against his body. He laughed with her and held her close, as if he could *be* any closer, as if it was even possible after what they'd done during the night. He felt that CK necklace falling on his chest, the coolness of the chain, and he wished he could ask her about it, but this was not the time.

They slept, and in the morning they showered together. She saw him looking at the necklace and blushed. Still, he did not ask. They did not talk much, even as they dressed and packed, but it was a comforting and lovely silence, the kind of silence that was like a spell that both of them were afraid to break. They paid their bill—Bob Martin was conspicuously absent, a young woman worked the counter—and had breakfast at the Apple Peddler. A morning mist hung over the city, the headlights of passing cars yellow bubbles in the fog. Over coffee and pancakes, they talked not about Miranda's situation, but about Crescent City and what it might be like to live there. What they were really talking about, Gage knew, was what it would be like to live there *together*.

Tatyana, who'd never seen the redwoods and sequoias that made this part of California so famous, asked if they could stop briefly at the Jedediah State Park before they headed north. It was only fifteen minutes east of the city on US-199, and Gage was happy to oblige. Who was he kidding? If it had been an hour away, or even ten, he would have been happy to oblige.

There was something stirring inside him, something both exhilarating and terrifying. He hadn't expected to feel this way. He liked her, of course, really liked her, but this was something else altogether. He wasn't ready. It wasn't the right time. But, of course, love refused to be dictated by other people's schedules.

Was it really love, though? He was probably confused, so relieved that such a spectacular woman had come along to spare him from his loneliness.

They had taken their time both at the motel and at breakfast, so it was already eleven in the morning by the time Gage parked the van in the paved parking lot of Stout Memorial Grove. The fog, which had partially burned away by then, still clung to the tops of the towering trees. His van was so loud in the serene stillness that he felt like a man charging into a library with a roaring chainsaw. Judging by the disgusted look a young couple gave him as they crossed the lot, both of them decked out head to foot in REI gear, this feeling was very well justified.

Other than that couple, though, they were alone, and they strolled along a paved path into the heart of towering old-growth redwoods, a thick carpet of ferns on either side. Shafts of sunlight sliced through the mist in the canopy high above, a cathedral ceiling that bested anything created by a human being. The trees were so much larger than life that it was only when Tatyana stood by one of the trunks that it became clear just how massive they really were. The young couple he'd irritated disappeared along a side trail, leaving them completely alone with the moisture dripping on the ferns and the silent, slow movement of the occasional yellow banana slug.

While the path was paved, the big roots still created hidden bumps and unevenness, so he took his cane even though he was having one of his better knee days, hardly even a twinge. After their night together, Gage was self-conscious about it, but Tatyana was so entranced by her surroundings that she barely noticed him. He kept stealing glances at her, trying to assess her mental state. She seemed sad. Why was she sad? Was she pulling away from him? Even when they'd playfully talked about moving to Crescent City during breakfast, he'd sensed her pulling away, battening up the hatches, reverting back to her preferred buttoned-up state of being. He knew there was a part of her that was totally closed off from him, an important part. It gnawed at him, this scar from her past. He was a man of a scarred past himself. He knew how deep the scars could run.

"You know," he said, "you really can talk to me about anything. People tell me I'm a pretty good listener."

She didn't look at him, but he saw a faint smile cross her face. "Oh? They tell you this?"

"Some people, anyway."

"I see."

"So if there's something that bothers you, I want you to know ... you can talk to me. Even if it's something that happened a long time ago."

She nodded, but said nothing. He thought he heard the faint whisper of Smith River through the forest, though it may have been a breeze high in the treetops. They walked until they'd rounded the grove, reaching the entrance once again. There she turned to face him, squarely. Whatever sadness had taken hold of her moments before had disappeared, her eyes steady.

"I need to say something," she said.

"Okay."

"I'm *not* broken," she said. "I don't need to be fixed. I don't need to be rescued. Yes, I may have come from a broken place, but *I* am not broken."

"Ah," Gage said, "somebody's been talking to you."

"Don't be mad. I think I would have said this even if your friend had not told me about your ... tendencies."

"Some friend."

"Garrison—"

"No, no, it's all right. I feel like some kind of psychiatric case study, but, hey, there are worse things in life, I suppose."

"He cares about you, Garrison. That's all."

"Well, if he actually cared about me, he'd butt out of my—"

"No, listen. Please. This is important." She reached for him. He tried to pull away, but she was too determined to be denied, grabbing his right hand with both of hers. Even the touch of her cool fingers was enough to spike his heart rate. "Just listen for a moment. I like you. I'm so glad we finally met."

"Me too," Gage said. "I wish we'd met sooner."

"But, see, that is exactly my point. We are who we are in this moment, the people who want to be with each other, exactly because we did *not* meet before. Our past makes us who we are."

"You're saying you have no regrets? I seem to remember—"

"Oh no, I have regrets. I told you about one of my big ones. But just because I regret it does not mean I wish I could change it. It makes me who I am."

"So if you could go back in time, you're saying—"

"But we can't go back in time, Garrison. That's what I'm saying. And since we can't go back, we can only go forward. Everything that has happened to me has brought me to this point. It brought me right here, standing in this forest, holding your hand. Who is to say that another path would bring me here? It might be a better path. It might not. It doesn't matter, because this is the only path I could have ever been on, because this is the path that life offered me. Does this make any sense at all?"

"I guess," Gage said. "But if you take that philosophy too far, doesn't that mean there's no point in helping anyone? Why should I even help Miranda, then? After all, all her suffering today will just make her who she is tomorrow."

"But that's the difference."

"Sorry?"

"Today. Tomorrow. But not yesterday."

Gage sighed. "Now you've really lost me."

"Miranda needs help *now*. Who she becomes tomorrow is not certain. If someone needs help today, of course it is a good thing to help them. But that is different than always trying to fix them. I can't speak for everyone. I could be wrong. But for me, I don't want you to fix me. I want you to *understand* me. To know me, to really see me. Do you see me?" She placed his hand on the center of her chest. "Do you feel me? Do you know me as I am? That is enough. Does that make sense?"

"I think so," Gage said.

"Really?"

"No. Probably not."

"Oh."

"But I really like having my hand on your chest. That counts for something, right?"

That got her to laugh. She was still laughing when they walked back to the van. Gage may not have totally agreed with her philosophy about the past, but he did like making her laugh. When he'd met her, she'd barely even smiled. Now he had her smiling and laughing. That was a change. Call it a fix or not, it was definitely a change.

It was good, this change. It was the kind of good that gave him purpose, and he wasn't about to let go of that purpose no matter what anyone said.

Chapter 15

They reached Barnacle Bluffs shortly after sunset Monday night. Gage, quite aware that one of the men who'd attacked him was still on the loose, stayed vigilant, but he'd seen no signs of being followed. He almost wished someone *would* come after him, since that might help him figure out who they were. As it stood, he felt frustrated at how little progress he'd made. Yes, Miranda had come to Crescent City, probably on the run from a powerful man, and yes, she'd likely met Marcus there and fled with him on his boat, but that's as far as he'd gotten.

Who were the men who'd come after him and why? Did they kill Marcus, and if so, why didn't they kill Miranda?

It was all a big mess.

The sky was a shade of indigo bordering on black, a surprising amount of stars visible through the fine strands of clouds that stretched overhead like a cotton ball pulled apart until only the tiniest threads held it together. The wind rustled the tops of the firs surrounding Tatyana's apartment complex, and he heard the lonely whine of a single jet ski on the lake beyond their sight. There was a chaste kiss at Tatyana's door, a promise to talk after she got off work tomorrow, and then he was on his way home.

He was still thinking about the chasteness of that kiss and

what it meant, when he pulled up his gravel driveway and saw the silver pickup parked in front of his house, a ten-year old Toyota Tacoma with nobody inside the cab.

He felt a blast of iciness through his veins. Was the truck owned by the guy who'd come after him? It had Oregon plates. Then he saw that Zoe's white Corolla was parked in front of the Tacoma, as if the truck had tried to block her in, and the ice in Gage's veins only intensified.

It didn't take him more than a few seconds to burst into the house, the Beretta in his hand, the cane left behind. The house was dark. He heard a loud thump from the back of the house—Zoe's room. He almost called her name, then decided, no, if the man had her, he wanted the element of surprise.

His mouth dry, his heart booming in his ears, he ran down the hall and flung open Zoe's door.

Only a red heart-shaped nightlight in the corner cut through the darkness, but it was enough that he saw the shape of a man pinning Zoe to the bed.

"Get off her!" Gage cried.

It was only then that Gage realized his mistake. The man's bare back was the first clue, bare all the way down to the naked bottom. The equally naked young woman beneath him, her legs wrapped around the young man's waist, was the second clue. All the other clues, the ones he missed, fell into horrifying place in Gage's mind. Jazzy music played faintly from her stereo. A candle on her desk burned low. He got a glimpse of Zoe's astonished face, and Zachary's too, before Gage ripped himself away from the spectacle. There was yelling and shouting, a flurry of movement, but Gage was already staggering back to the front of the house.

There were things in his mind now that could never be removed, images, even smells, that could never be purged from his memory. Sweat and sex. The slow movement of glistening flesh. He didn't know what to do with himself and found himself pacing in the kitchen in the dark, the Beretta clutched in his hand. What had he done?

An hour later—it may have only been a few minutes—Zachary stumbled out in jeans and a half-tucked-in white T-shirt. He wore sneakers but no socks. As he neared the oven light, Gage saw that the kid's face was red and sweaty, wearing the kind of terrified expression of a child who'd finally come face to face with the monster in the dark he'd always feared was there. He saw the Beretta in Gage's hand and his knees buckled a little before he caught himself.

"I'm—I'm sorry," Zachary said.

Gage didn't say anything. He didn't know what to say. He looked at the gun, looked at the kid, and by then, Zachary was already fleeing the scene in abject terror. Gage watched him go, only barely aware of Zoe bolting out of the house after him. By then, the Tacoma was kicking up gravel and roaring down the driveway.

Seconds later, Zoe burst back into the house, yelling at him before the door had even slammed behind her.

"What were you *thinking?*"

He didn't look at her. He didn't *want* to look at her. He was vaguely aware of her standing at the edge of his vision, glaring, short of breath, all disheveled in sweatpants and a loose T-shirt. The faint buzz of the oven light. The low hum of the refrigerator. The way the shadows weaved across the ceiling. He was willing to focus his attention on just about anything else but her.

"You have a gun in your hand," she said finally. Her tone had changed. It was less accusatory, more concerned.

"Yeah," he said.

"Why?"

"Something happened in Crescent City. Some men came after me."

"Okay ... you think, I don't know, maybe you can put the gun down now?"

"Yeah."

He engaged the safety and put the Beretta on the kitchen counter, pointed toward the wall.

"So," she said, "you were worried about me."

He nodded, then realized she might not be able to see his face in the near darkness, so he said, "That's right."

"Okay. Okay, that makes sense. I'm not mad anymore. It's fine. I forgive you."

"Thank you."

"Not a problem."

The conversation sounded so pedestrian to his ears, they could have been talking about how he'd used her favorite mug by mistake. He glanced at her, caught a glimpse of her staring at the floor through the tangled mess of her hair, and that image of her in bed with Zachary leapt back into his mind. He forced it away. Deep down. Buried it.

"Listen—" she began.

"It's all right," he said.

"No, no, we should talk about this. I don't want it to be weird and awkward. I just … I guess I got it in my head you were coming back tomorrow."

"It's fine, really. You're a grown woman now. You can … you can do what you want."

"He's really nice, you know."

"Okay."

"I just didn't want you to think … I don't know, he's just not like a normal cop. He's really sweet. I like that. I didn't know I liked that, but I do. I mean, with him. I just haven't been able to stop thinking about him, you know?"

"It really is fine."

"I just wanted you to know."

"Okay."

"It's not just, you know, about … *that*. About what was going on in there. It's more than that. I think it's more than that. I think it's really something special. I hope it is."

"Zoe—"

"So, we're good then."

"Yeah," Gage said. "I'm sorry."

"No, no, don't be. You were worried. I get it. But, um, it's okay?"

"What's okay?"

"If he's around."

"Oh. Well, you don't need my permission. Like I said, you're a grown woman. I'm—I'm happy for you."

"Really?"

"Sure. Sure, I want you to be happy. If he makes you happy, that's—that's, um, good. Are you happy?"

"I think so."

"Great!"

"So we're good?"

"Yeah, good. Very good."

"Good."

"I think I'll, um, go take a shower."

"Good. Great. You, uh, want me to make some dinner for us?"

"I already ate."

"Okay."

"Thank you, though."

"No problem."

They both stood there, a couple nodding fools, then at some point she wandered down the hall. He remained in the kitchen, unsure of what to do, until he heard the bathroom door close, then the shower start. He holstered the Beretta and headed to the front door, where he paused, debated about yelling out where he was going, then reconsidered and returned to the kitchen. He scribbled a note on the pad affixed to the refrigerator, *Gone to see Alex.* He thought something was missing, but he couldn't figure out what, exactly, so he wrote *See you later.*

EVE AND ALEX were doing dishes when he showed up at the Turret House, having enjoyed a big salad of mixed greens, boiled eggs, and cranberries, but there was plenty left over and Eve insisted that Gage sit and eat. He knew better than to protest, and he was plenty hungry. He was more of a steak and potatoes kind of guy, but if Eve cooked it, he would gladly eat it. The three of them chatted about the trip, about how he'd been attacked, and when they had been assured that both he and Tatyana were okay, Eve drifted away to do some bookkeeping and Alex and Gage retired up to the turret.

All the blinds were up, but the windows were so dark Gage couldn't make out the ocean. Alex turned on the beaded lamp, hardly casting off more light than a single candle—which suited the room just fine. While Alex fixed himself a brandy and Gage a bourbon on the rocks, Gage settled into one of the leather recliners. They said nothing until both of them were seated, drinks in hand, the first sip already warming their faces.

"I assume there's a reason you wanted me to bring my cell phone and laptop up here," Alex said.

"There is," Gage said.

"All right. But before you tell me your reason, I have a little bit of news for you. Miranda hired a lawyer."

"She *what?* With what money?"

"That's just the thing. It's D.D. Conroy. He offered to do it pro bono. He's the lawyer who—"

"Oh God, that guy?" Gage said. "The one from Alabama who looks like Colonel Sanders?"

"Mississippi, actually. The same."

"The one who was involved in all that business in Minneapolis, with that white girl who was killed by a black police officer? And all those other cases over the years where he can get himself in front of a television camera?"

"Yep. And, according to Miranda, he called up and offered his services pro bono."

"So long as he gets to represent her in a civil suit later, in which he will take his massive cut? And he also co-writes a book with her?"

"That's his usual procedure," Alex said.

Gage took a sip of the bourbon, then, thinking of Conroy working his tricks on Miranda, took another. "Has he met her yet?"

"No. He stopped by here today and said she insisted you or I be there when they meet tomorrow morning for the first time." Alex shook his head. "Man, that guy is quite a character. The accent alone will leave your head spinning. And the rumors are true. He drinks whiskey out of a little metal flask and smells like it. I went down to see her to try to talk her out of it, but the police wouldn't let me see her. They said D.D. had stopped by to ensure that he was present for any visitor meetings. I tried to explain that he's not her lawyer yet, but I think they're a little intimidated of him."

"I don't like this at all," Gage said. "We already have Buzz Burgin. We don't really need another slimy character sticking his nose in this."

"Maybe two slimy characters will cancel each other out. So what do you want with the phone?"

"I need to call Marcus's girlfriend," Gage said.

"And you think I can somehow magically find her number for you?"

"I thought maybe you could look it up on that computer thingy of yours."

"Sure," Alex said, "I'll just type in 'Marcus Koura's girlfriend' in Google and I'm sure her name will come right up."

"Actually, it might, considering that the media in San Jose has probably already done a story on his death. But, if not, Quinn told me that she was a long-term girlfriend, and that usually means cohabitation. Find out his address the last couple years, search for an address with that time frame, and … *voila.*"

"*Voila?*"

"I've been practicing my French," Gage said. "Thought it might come in handy because of the huge Francophone population in Barnacle Bluffs."

"If I didn't know you better, I might say you were being sarcastic."

Gage took another sip of the bourbon, closed his eyes and allowed that warm feeling to cart him away. "But you do know me better, so you know that I am always deadly serious. If Google doesn't work, you can always ring up your friends in the FBI again."

"Yeah, about that," Alex said, "that's something I need to tell you. Those channels have suddenly dried up."

This news brought Gage back to the present moment in a hurry, stealing away the cozy feeling he'd been doing his best to embrace. He opened his eyes and looked at Alex, whose face was now glowing blue from the laptop screen. "What do you mean, dried up?"

Alex clicked away on his keyboard. "My connections have all suddenly stopped responding to me. That, and what little direct access I had to information in the database all vanished. Everything about the eTransWorld operation has suddenly been locked down and you need very high level access to get to it. Far beyond the access of a mostly retired former academy instructor, I'll tell you that."

"You were a lot more than a former academy instructor," Gage said.

"Sure, but when that was true, most of the people in the FBI were in diapers. Now I'm just that strange retired guy in Oregon who does oddball consulting now and then on the cases nobody else wants to work on." He squinted at the screen. "Looks like we lucked out anyway. Nothing about her in the media that I can find, but you were right about searching by the address. There's a woman named Claire Brandt who lived at the same address as him for two years."

"Got a phone number?"

"Working on it … well, no home phone number. Looks like she's an OB-GYN, though, and there's a work number here. New Springs Mother and Baby Clinic."

"I bet there's an emergency line," Gage said. "Give me your cell phone and I'll work my magic."

"I'll do you one better," Alex said. "I bought you a little gift."

"Oh no."

Sure enough, Alex didn't produce his own cell phone from his pocket; he produced a different one—small, black, and of the same model as the first two Gage had briefly owned. Alex placed it on the end table between them, and both of them stared at it as if it was a bird that settled there and would fly away at any moment.

"What is it with all of you?" Gage said.

"My friend, we've all pretty much given up on bringing you into the twenty-first century, but we are determined to at least bring you into the twentieth. Well, are you going to use it or not?"

"I'm thinking about it."

"Well, while you're thinking about it, I'll refresh our drinks. Go ahead now. Third time's the charm. The phone number's right there on the computer."

It was no use arguing, since there was a call to make, so Gage snatched up the phone, made note of the number, then dialed the clinic. It rang twice and he listened to an automated, after-hours message until he heard that he could push nine if it was urgent. He pushed nine and a woman answered whose rough voice made him think she was between smoke breaks.

"New Springs hotline," she said. "What is the nature of your emergency?"

Gage took a deep breath, then fired it all out in one big rapid-fire burst: "It's my wife she's gone into labor call the doctor quick."

"Slow down, sir. What is your wife's—"

"Beth. Beth Anderson. We're in the car and I think the baby's gonna come any second. Call her now!"

"Sir, I'm not finding a patient with that name in our—"

"Doctor's name is Grant or Lance or something."

"Brandt?"

"Yes, that's it! Claire Brandt. I'm on a friend's cell. Can you have her call me?" He told her the number and heard the click of her keyboard.

"Sir," she said, "I'm going to need a little more—"

"Oh God! It's happening! Hurry!"

He hung up. Alex, returning with their drinks, shook his head at Gage.

"You know," he said, "have you ever considered just telling people the truth? I actually found it worked wonders when I was doing field work."

"And miss my chance to sharpen my thespian skills? *Certainement pas!*"

"There's that French again."

They had perhaps thirty seconds to enjoy their drinks before Gage's new cell phone rang. He answered it.

"This is Dr. Brandt," a woman said, who had one of those smooth voices that made her sound both young and old at the same time. "I'm afraid I don't have a Beth Anderson—"

"Actually," Gage said, "there is no Beth Anderson."

"Excuse me?"

"Name's Garrison Gage. I'm a private investigator in Barnacle Bluffs, Oregon, and it was urgent that I talk to you. Sorry for the ruse, but under the circumstances it was the best way to get in touch with you quickly."

She didn't answer. In the background, Gage thought he heard the clink of glasses and the dull murmur of conversation.

"Ma'am?" Gage said.

"This really isn't a good time," Brandt said. "I'm out with friends and—"

"Do you know why I'm calling?"

"I—I have a pretty good idea." She dropped her voice to just above a whisper. "I have already told the authorities everything I know. There isn't anything else."

"Are you sure? There's a woman behind bars up here who could really use your—"

"I know her situation," Dr. Brandt said coolly. "Now, I'm afraid this conversation is over. Please don't call this line again, Mr. Gage. It really is for medical emergencies."

"Dr. Brandt—"

But she was already gone. Gage, perplexed, stared at the phone.

"I think there's something wrong with this thing," he said. "It lost the connection."

"Somehow I don't think it was the phone," Alex said. "Didn't sound like she was happy to talk to you."

"Nope," Gage said, "which makes me all the more inclined to talk to *her*. What's that emergency number again?"

He dialed the emergency number again, told the dispatcher he and the doctor had been disconnected, and she paged Dr. Brandt again. Less than a minute later, his phone rang.

"Don't hang up on me," Gage said.

"I knew it would be you!" Brandt shot back. "I thought I made myself abundantly clear. I have nothing more—"

"Shut up," Gage said.

"Excuse me?"

"Just shut up for a second, will you? Are you someplace you can talk now?"

"I told you, I'm not going to—"

"Yes. You will."

"Mr. Gage, I don't appreciate being spoken to in this—"

"Listen, we can do this now over the phone, or I can catch the next flight down to San Jose and we can do it in person. Trust me, I'm a lot less pleasant in person. I'm also a lot tougher to get rid of. The more you refuse to talk to me, the more I think you have something to hide, and the more I think I better start sniffing around your life to figure out what it is."

"I have nothing to hide!"

"Good. Then let's start over. I need five minutes of your time. Don't you think your dinner companions can survive five minutes without you?"

There was a pause. Gage did hear something in the background, the same noises as before, but it sounded much more distant, much more hollow, and he guessed she'd moved to some kind of hall.

"If I give you five minutes," Dr. Brandt said, "can you promise to leave me alone?"

"Nope."

"Well then! How do you expect—"

"But I can promise that the more forthright you are with me, the less I'm going to think you're some kind of accomplice in the murder of Marcus Koura."

"Accomplice! That's ridiculous!"

"Is it? I heard you broke up a few weeks before he left on his boat. Did you break up with him, or did he break up with you?"

"I told the police! It was mutual. We just grew apart."

"Dr. Brandt, I have this sense you're not telling me everything. What is it you're holding back?"

"I'm not holding *anything* back! After he sold out to his brother, he changed. He became withdrawn. He bought a sailboat and spent most of his time on it. He told me he was going to sail around the world in it. But he didn't seem committed. Months passed. I kept hoping it was a phase. I kept hoping he'd come back to me. Then one day he called and said he was leaving the next day to start his journey. It was very abrupt, not at all like Marcus. We both agreed it was better to part ways then to drag it out."

"You both agreed?"

"Yes!"

"Do you know why he sold out to his brother?"

"No! He was not an emotionally open man. I had a hard enough time getting him to tell me when he was hungry, let alone something that actually required him to think more deeply about his feelings. I would say it was his Egyptian heritage, but I have known Egyptian men who were not emotionally stunted." She sighed. "Mr. Gage—"

"Please call me Garrison."

"I'd rather keep this more formal," she said icily. "I've told you what I know. I agree it isn't much, but I don't know much. Even when Marcus still owned half of eTransWorld, he never talked about the business. He withdrew from me, we broke up, he left."

"When I mentioned the woman up here," Gage said, "the woman we're calling Miranda because she can't remember who she is, you seemed … irritated."

"I don't know what you're talking about."

"Oh, I think you do. What, were you jealous?"

"Don't be ridiculous! I told you that we broke up and it was mutual. You can ask my close friends if you want. They'll tell you that I was thinking about breaking up with Marcus for months. I don't care who he was with after he left. Now, can I go back to my dinner or do you want to badger me some more to no purpose? My food is getting cold."

Gage thought about it. He didn't get the sense Dr. Brandt was withholding anything big, but there was something there. What could it be? She sounded like somebody who thought of herself highly and would expect the person she was with to think highly of her as well. Then it came to him.

"Did you think he was cheating on you?" he asked.

"What?"

"It might explain your reaction when I mentioned Miranda."

"That's absurd."

"Is it?"

"Of course it is! I have never been with a man who cheated with me. I never gave any of them a reason to do so. I would have *known* if that was the case. I am not an easy woman to fool, Mr. Gage."

Now Gage knew he was onto something. It was all about her pride. "I imagine not," he said. "Your past boyfriends … I'm guessing *you* were the one who usually broke up with *them*."

"What does that have to do with anything?"

"Am I right?"

"It's irrelevant."

"Was it *really* a mutual breakup with you and Marcus?"

"Yes!"

Gage sighed. "Why don't you just come clean with me here, Dr. Brandt? There's obviously something that you didn't tell the police. It really will make things easier for both of us."

"I've told you everything I know!" she protested. "There's nothing more. Now, I'm afraid my patience—"

"All right, I'll fly down there tomorrow. If you're not helpful, I'll talk to some of your friends. Your colleagues. Your patients. I'm sure I can dig up whatever it is you're not telling me. It may not be fun having me poke around your life, Dr. Brandt, but there's a woman's life at stake here. You'll have to forgive me if your patience is the least of my concerns."

He heard her breathing into the receiver, then, distantly, hollow laughter as if coming from a television. They were separated by nearly a thousand miles, but he imagined he could see her right in front of him, closing her eyes and bowing her head. He thought he could smell the wine on her breath. When she spoke, it was too quiet to make out the words.

"What was that?" he asked.

"I said, it was just a feeling," she said.

"What kind of feeling?"

"I don't know if it was another woman." Her voice was so low that he had to press the cell phone tight against his right ear. "I really don't. I just ... If it was someone else, it wasn't someone in San Jose."

"How do you know?"

"Because I ... I watched him."

"You what?"

"I'm embarrassed to say this. But when he started getting distant, started pulling away ... Well, I'd never had that happen to me with a man before. I didn't understand. I started ... I started parking outside his condo. Just now and then. A few times. I, um, followed him, too. There wasn't anyone else. His life was very mundane. He went to his boat alone. He went home. But ..."

"Yes?"

"This is very embarrassing."

"Please. This could be very helpful. If I can, I promise this will stay completely between us."

"Do you mean that?"

"Dr. Brandt, I admit I am far from a perfect man. But if I give someone my word, I mean it."

"All right. I just ... It's very embarrassing. You see, I started snooping around his condo when he was at his boat. I still had a key then. I just wanted some sign, you know, that I wasn't crazy.

There really wasn't much there. He was a very tidy man. It wasn't possible to get on his computer, either, since he was fastidious about keeping everything password protected. I didn't find any signs of another woman. Except …"

"Yes?"

"I found a receipt in his nightstand. It was to a restaurant in Manhattan. That wasn't all that surprising, I guess, since he used to go to New York all the time when he was still heavily involved in eTransWorld. It was fairly recent, though, only a month earlier. I didn't think he'd been traveling at all the past six months. It was also obvious the receipt was for two people—two meals, two glasses of wine. Only one dessert, though, a chocolate mousse. Do you know when you buy only one dessert, Mr. Gage? You buy it when you're sharing it with someone. Otherwise hardly anyone would buy a desert for themselves just to have the other person watch them eat."

"Probably true," Gage said.

"Even then, I wasn't convinced. It wasn't until I turned the receipt over and saw the drawing on the other side. It was just a sketch done with a pen, but it was obviously a likeness of Marcus. It wasn't just that it was a sketch, either. It was very … loving. He had quite a glow to him, a warmth in his eyes. He used to look at me like that."

Gage, knowing Miranda's artistic talent wasn't public knowledge, mulled over what it meant. There was also Miranda's memory about working on a puzzle that seemed to indicate she was from a big city. Why not New York? If Marcus was doing business there, that might have been where he met Miranda. Perhaps they had some kind of love affair and made plans to run off together. But why the rendezvous in Crescent City? Perhaps because they were afraid of someone finding out about them, someone powerful? Miranda had obviously gone to great pains to live anonymously.

It was a lot of supposition based on a drawing, one he hadn't even seen. But the pieces were starting to come together.

"Why didn't you tell any of this to the police?" he asked.

"And tell them I was skulking around, spying on him? This thing has already gotten so much news. I have my practice to think about, my reputation. It didn't make me look good at all. And then there was the receipt. I destroyed it."

"You did what?"

"It's humiliating to even think about. And he must have realized it was gone right away, because he broke up with me within days. Never said why, and I never said anything about the drawing. That's not even the worst part, the part I can barely even think about. I don't know why I'm even telling you this. What difference does it make? I could just tell you I flushed the receipt down the toilet. You wouldn't know the difference."

"What did you do, Dr. Brandt?"

She sighed. "I ate it."

"You what?"

"It was … impulsive. I was crying. I couldn't stand looking at that drawing. So I crumpled it into a ball and ate it."

"What did it taste like?"

"Excuse me?

"Never mind. Is there anything else?"

There wasn't. He probed for a few more minutes, Dr. Brandt getting increasingly more exasperated, then let her go. He tried to hand the phone back to Alex, who shook his head, so Gage grudgingly put it in his own jacket pocket. He relayed everything he had learned, then the two of them sipped their drinks in silence. Often the wind blew on the windows, a constant whistle, but tonight the air was still enough that Gage could hear the swish of the waves on the beach. He felt the alcohol warming his bones, trying to tease his mind away, and he fought the impulse.

"So," Alex said finally, "it's probably safe to say that Miranda meeting Marcus in Crescent City was not an accident. The two had plans to escape together. Those idiots who tried to take you out were probably the ones who caught up with Marcus and killed him. And left Miranda alive for some reason."

"Maybe they didn't even know she was there."

"What do you mean?"

Gage put down his empty glass and folded his hands under his chin. "It's something I thought of before, and seems more likely now. If they didn't even know she was on that boat, then they would have no reason to look for her."

"Hiding while he was murdered," Alex said, "then having to survive that terrible storm—it would explain a lot about her current mental state."

"Yes. There's another possibility, though. Miranda killed Marcus, and Troy and his pal never caught up with Marcus's boat at all. She just got unlucky because she ended up in the middle of a storm. They just came back to kill Troy because they didn't want anything pointing to them at all."

"You really think she's capable of it?"

"I don't know anymore. I'm just wondering if this whole thing about running from someone was completely made up. It all came from her—the thing she said on the beach, seeing that man at the outlet mall."

"She would have to be an incredibly good actress. I mean, why not just run? She's had plenty of opportunities before Quinn arrested her."

"Has she?" Gage said. "Maybe she thought she had a little more time to get herself together. If Marcus's body never washed up on the beach, Quinn probably wouldn't have charged her. There's also the possibility that she really does have amnesia *and* she's the one who killed Marcus."

"Seems far-fetched," Alex said.

"My friend, this whole thing is far-fetched. I feel like a fly who's buzzed his way onto a circus train and is just waiting for the train to get to its next stop."

"Well, what are you going to do?"

Gage, feeling the drowsiness brought on by the long day, his aching body, and the bourbon really starting to take hold, rose to his feet. "I'm going home. If I don't do it now, I'm going to fall asleep in his chair."

"And tomorrow?"

"Tomorrow, I guess I'll go see Miranda with her newfound

lawyer and try to get her to fire him. Maybe see if I can rattle her a bit with what I know and shake something loose. Then Omar. He's still around, right?"

"Yes. I heard he tried to see Miranda yesterday too and was also rebuffed."

"Good," Gage said. "As long as she's in that jail, she's safe."

"Or we're safe from her?"

"Could be. Could be Omar really is just a distraught brother. Maybe she'll confess and this will all be over tomorrow."

"And maybe she'll strangle D.D. Conroy while she's at it."

"Don't get your hopes up," Gage said. "By the way, I don't really appreciate you playing Dr. Freud with the women who enter my life. I'd like to at least pretend I have a clean slate before all the skeletons get dragged out of my closet."

Alex smiled. "Tatyana."

"Tatyana, yes."

"I do admit to a tiny bit of meddling."

"You don't say?"

"Just a tiny bit. I had to in this case."

"Oh, you did? Why is that?"

Alex stood. The wan light accentuated every crease and crevice in his face. Most of the time, Gage forgot that the two of them were nearly a generation apart, but now Alex looked even older than his years, like some kind of wise oracle who possessed all the secrets of the human soul. He patted Gage on the shoulder.

"My friend," he said, "this one's a keeper. I'm just trying to prevent you from screwing it up until you figure that out for yourself."

Chapter 16

D.D. Conroy was waiting for Gage on the concrete bench outside the Barnacle Bluffs Police Department. It was just before nine o'clock on Tuesday morning, still early enough that the morning mist clinging to the tops of the Douglas firs hadn't yet cleared, but true to form, Conroy already had a metal flask in his hand. Seeing Gage approaching, he lifted it in a salute.

"Never too early for whiskey, is it?" Gage said.

Conroy chuckled, a good-old-boy chuckle that was slow and good-natured. He was everything Gage had anticipated and more, like a character out of a Tennessee Williams play. His white doubled-breasted suit barely contained his enormous girth. His thick white hair and full beard were nearly the same color as his suit, with just a hint of yellow. He had a big round head that seemed all the rounder because of the tiny gold-rimmed glasses perched at the edge of his nose. He wore a gold pocket watch on a chain, which he took out and examined.

"Well, would you look at that," he said, in that smooth Southern drawl that had made him an easy target for late-night comics to mock. "It's just as I thought. Today happens to be a day that ends in Y—just like the word whiskey. I've always seen that as our Lord Maker's way of sayin' it's always whiskey time."

He peered at Gage over the top of his glasses, his eyes gleaming. There was something about him that made him difficult to dislike. Even Gage, an Olympic champion of detesting people, had to resist the urge to smile. The man had so much charisma, it was impossible not to look at him. It exuded from him like a gravitational force.

"That's an interesting philosophy," Gage said. His bad knee was acting up that morning, and he leaned on his cane to take the weight off. "It would seem to guarantee that you spend every day that ends in Y in a state of drunken stupor."

"Not a bad state to be in, my boy," Conroy said. "Not a bad state at all, if I do say so myself. Really does make it easy to get through life without tying yourself in knots." He leaned forward, dropping his voice. "Can I let you in on a little secret, though? You just got to promise not to tell nobody."

"What's that?"

Conroy held up his flask. "Go ahead, take a whiff."

"That's all right, I'm well aware of the smell of whiskey."

"Just humor me some, boy. Take a whiff."

Gage leaned forward and put his nose over the flask. Bracing himself, he inhaled slowly. He didn't smell anything. When he gave Conroy a quizzical look, the man chuckled again.

"The reason you don't smell nothin' is cause there nothin' to smell."

"Water?" Gage said.

"Mississippi spring water, in fact. Never leave home without it."

"Why the flask then?"

"Why not? It's good for my image, ain't it? People think I'm just some drunk old coot, they're more likely to drop their guard around me."

"I have a hard time believing anybody drops their guard around you anymore, Mr. Conroy."

"Well, that's probably true. I do admit, Mr. Gage, that in my younger years this flask was often full of something other than water. But the point still stands, don't you think? You as a private investigator —of some distinguished merit, I might add—should well know that things are not always what they appear to be."

"And sometimes they are," Gage said. "For example, a famous lawyer who only shows up when the cameras are rolling is probably just looking to see his face on the evening news."

"Nobody watches the evening news anymore, Mr. Gage. We've got this thing called the Internet. It's all about getting your name on Twitter and your face on Instagram. Besides, you see any cameras around these parts right now?"

"Oh, they'll be here soon enough. And I'd be willing to bet there's probably some photographer taking a picture of us right now."

"Maybe so, maybe so. But let's just say, for the sake of argument, that your observation about my motives is basically sound. What does it matter, if the lawyer in question is still able to prevent a miscarriage of justice and help a young lady taste the sweet freedom she so deserves?"

"You're telling me nobody hired you?" Gage said, still suspecting that Omar or somebody else might be trying to get Miranda out of jail just to kill her. "You're telling me you're here completely of your own accord?"

Conroy got to his feet, an act of such flair and panache that it was a performance all by itself. "As God is my witness," he said.

"I'm not sure that witness is all that reliable."

"Ah! I do like a man with wit. Not a believer, are you?"

"I think of myself more like an undecided voter."

"Well, I'll try not to hold it against you, son. I may have parted ways with my friend, Mr. Whiskey, but I don't know if I could make it in life without the good book. But anyway, I'm sure we both got better things to do than to stand here on this wonderful mornin' discussing the finer points of religion. By the way, you may have noticed I have not extended my hand in the more formal manner of one gentleman greeting another. I always feel the need to tell people that this is no intentional slight, but only a byproduct of my fairly recent aversion to germs. These days, a cold seems to set me down for a month rather than week, and something worse might set me down altogether."

"I'll try not to take any offense."

"Good. Shall we go in and see the woman in question?"

"We shall," Gage said. "But first, you should know that I'm going to do everything I can to convince Miranda not to hire you."

"Oh! That's not a great way to start things off. But I understand. You see me as an unwanted interloper, someone out only for his own fame and glory, and I won't deny that my own interests do play at least a small part in me being here."

"A small part."

Conroy slipped the flask inside his jacket pocket. "Yes. But all I ask is that you allow me to have a fair hearing with the lady. After all, she did request that I be here."

"I might quibble with the word 'request,' but you'll get a chance to make your case."

"All I ask! And, son, looks like we should get to it. The cavalry has already arrived."

He motioned to the Portland news van rolling up the street, but Gage had seen it. He'd also seen the purple Pontiac Safari approaching from the other direction, Buzz Burgin already aiming a camera with a long lens right at them.

They turned to the door. Conroy was in front, but he stopped and looked at Gage.

"Would you mind getting it, son?" he said. "Germs, you know."

Gage, with some reluctance, opened the door for him. He couldn't help but feel that even getting Gage to open the door was a small power play itself, as if this was Conroy's way of making him feel like he was the man's servant.

It only took a few minutes inside the police station for it to become apparent that not everyone felt the same distaste for D.D. Conroy's celebrity presence. In fact, Gage was stunned to find, it was quite the opposite. With a few notable exceptions—Quinn seemed a bit wary— most of the officers and administrative staff buzzed around Conroy in a happy smiling dance of sycophancy, as if just by being near him some of his star power might rub off on them. Even Brisbane and Trenton, usually with fixed stares of grumpiness and anger, were seen laughing at the old man's ribald jokes. Trenton didn't even take offense when Conroy wouldn't shake his hand, accepting the old man's explanation about his frail health and susceptibility to local viruses without a frown.

They were led into the meeting room just off the jail section of the building, a small windowless box with a metal table bolted to the floor, four folding chairs around it. Gage and Conroy sat on one side, Conroy humming a ditty, Gage staring at the way the caged fluorescent lights formed warped patterns in the dented metal table. The air smelled dusty and stale.

A woman from the front poked her head in and asked if they needed anything. They said no. Someone else asked if they wanted coffee. They said no to this, too. Fortunately, it was only a minute later that Quinn emerged with Miranda, sparing Gage the need to endure any more pleasantries.

She wore prison orange, her red hair pulled back in a ponytail, her eyes bright and fearful even as her face seemed pale and gaunt. She started toward Gage, to hug him, and was stopped by handcuffs. Her eyes welled up.

"Come now," Conroy said to Quinn. "Surely this pretty lady is no risk to any of us. Those skinny arms of hers, I doubt she could even lift a pile of wet laundry."

"It's standard procedure," Quinn said. It may have been Gage's imagination, but those big bags under his eyes seemed even darker than usual, a good match for those dark eyebrows. "It's really nothing personal."

"*Everything's* personal, son, when you get down to it. Can't we just extend this minor bit of kindness to her for a few minutes?"

After some hesitation, Quinn shrugged and removed her handcuffs. She embraced Gage, and there was fierceness to it, like the clutch of a person trying to prevent themselves from falling. Conroy introduced himself and again had to kindly rebuff her offer of a hug, explaining his poor health in a way that strangely seemed to make people like him more rather than less. The three of them seated themselves at the table. Quinn remained standing.

Conroy raised his white eyebrows at the chief. "As I understand the law, there are certain attorney-client privileges that suggest that law enforcement should excuse themselves."

Quinn said, "Well, as I understand the situation, she hasn't agreed to hire you yet."

"A mere formality, sir."

"A formality that matters in my jurisdiction, I'm afraid."

"Ah. Well, I mean no offense. I suppose the good lady could settle this by making my presence here an official capacity. What do you say, Miranda?"

They looked at her, and even the weight of their gazes seemed to shrink her in her seat. She was the shy child in class who'd been called on unexpectedly. Regardless of his doubts, Gage felt sorry for her. Strange lawyers, grumpy police officers, rabid journalists—it must have felt like the whole world was crashing down on her slim shoulders. She looked at Gage for guidance and he shook his head.

"Maybe—maybe not yet," she said.

"Are you certain, darling?" Conroy said. "It would make things a lot easier. We could have a bit more privacy."

"I don't need privacy," she said. "I have nothing to hide. At least, I don't think I do."

"So no memories yet?" Gage asked.

She shook her head.

"It's not about having anything to hide," Conroy said. "It's about preparing the best possible defense."

"But I didn't do anything!" she protested.

"That you know of," Quinn said. He looked at Gage. "You going to tell her what happened to you down in Crescent City?"

There was something in her eyes, a flicker, at the mention of Crescent City. Gage saw it. Quinn saw it, too, and it was a good bet he'd said it precisely because he wanted to see if he could get her to react. Score one for the chief.

"You—you went to Crescent City?" she asked.

"You remember being there?" Gage said.

"No. I mean, I don't know. But the name … it does sound familiar."

"Well, you were there a couple weeks ago."

"I was?"

"Yep. So was Marcus Koura, apparently."

He had everyone's attention now. Miranda watched him as if expecting the worst, but he still couldn't get a good read on whether she was lying or not. Gage had been forced to tell the police in California about why he was there, and to get them to let him go he'd had to rope Chief Quinn into the mess as well. They didn't know what he'd learned about her staying at the Mill Creek Motel, but he didn't see what advantage there was in withholding this information.

Perhaps overwhelming her with information, rather than withholding it, might change the status quo.

So Gage told her everything. He told her about the kid at the market who'd seen her, how she'd worked at the Mill Creek Motel for a month, and the observations of her fellow housekeeper—her coming from money and being on the run from a terrible man. He told her how the evidence seemed to suggest she'd fled with Marcus on his boat, how Troy at the marina had taken some men after her, and even how Marcus's former girlfriend in San Jose suspected he'd been seeing a woman from New York, one who'd demonstrated artistic ability by drawing his portrait on the back of a receipt.

As Gage talked, he watched her wilt under the barrage. So far the tears hadn't come, but Gage knew they couldn't be far behind.

"I don't know what you want me to say," she said.

"Do you remember going by the name Mary?"

"No."

"Well, you did. Apparently it wasn't your real name either,

and you were paid under the table."

"I've got some information, too," Quinn said. "The second guy who tried to take Gage out, the one who got away, his name was Aaron Flores. They found him dead about an hour ago, parked behind an out-of-business grocery store in Eureka. Bled to death. He had some loose connections to the Italian mafia in New York, but like Jake Sheffield, he was pretty much a mercenary. Seems interesting, him being from New York, huh? What do you think the connection is there, Miranda?"

Before Miranda could answer, Conroy said, "You don't have to answer any of these questions. Just invoke your Fifth Amendment rights and we can stop this right now. Your arraignment is tomorrow. We'll get you out on bail, then we'll work on clearing you of this preposterous murder charge."

"Murder," she said. "I have a … have a hard time even saying that word."

Quinn said, "Somebody shot Marcus Koura. If not you, then who? And if it was these boys who went after Gage in Crescent City, then why did they leave you alone?"

"I don't know."

"Even now," Quinn said, "you're going to claim you don't remember anything?"

"I … I …"

"Come on now. Be straight with us."

"There is something," she said. "I don't know. Something. I can't—it's so hard. I want to remember. Maybe I will."

"Maybe?" Quinn said. "You're running out of time, sister."

"I need—I need to think."

The dam that had been holding back her tears finally crumbled. It was not a slow crumble, but a quick and violent collapse. Gage had been expecting an outburst of some sort, but nothing like this. She wailed like a small child, balling up her fists and covering her eyes, her whole body shaking. The display shocked all of them enough that none of them moved for a long time until Quinn finally muttered something about getting a box of tissues and disappeared from the room. He was back in a few seconds, and by then at least her convulsive sobbing had been slowed to something less hysterical, a lot of sniffling and swallowing as she tried to pull herself together.

It took half a box of tissues, a crumpled white mess that littered the table, but she finally managed to get enough control of herself that speech was again possible. Even so, when she spoke, it came out in a jumbled, jagged mess with lots of stuttering and false starts.

"You have to—you have to understand," she said. "What it's like. What it's like for me. I try to remember. I do. I think and think and think all day. It's all dark. It's like looking into a pit. Into a giant—a giant hole. Like I'm trying to see the bottom. Like there's things down there, I know there are, and if only I look hard enough—I'm trying. I want to see. And—and—and every now and then, there's a little bit of light. Like I remember being scared. I remember being in something, something small, something like a coffin. There was the ocean. There was the sound of—of sails. In the wind. And there were terrible noises. But what is it? If I tell you more than that, if I tell you I know what it means, I'm lying. I don't know."

Gage said, "You're telling me you were hiding on the boat?"

"I don't know. Maybe."

"You've got to give us *something*, Miranda."

"I'm trying!" she cried. "Marcus, New York, Crescent City—maybe, maybe there's something there. I'm looking into the dark. I want to see. I told you all! I know there's somebody coming for me. I know there is. I know he's a terrible man. I know he's—he's capable of terrible things. I'm looking into the dark. I'm trying to see his face. It scares me. Do you know how much it scares? But I'm looking. I'm looking."

A silence settled over them. Conroy took out his metal flask, brushed off the top with a handkerchief, and held out the bottle to Miranda.

"Take a drink, girl," he said. "I'm sure your throat is parched now. It will make you feel better."

"Oh," she said. "Oh, I don't—I don't drink alcohol. I don't

remember much, but I remember that for some reason."

"It's nothing of the sort," Conroy said. "This is Mississippi spring water."

"I can get her a glass of water of her own," Quinn said.

"Not like this," Conroy said. "This water is from my home state, a kind of secret elixir like none other. You take a drink of this, then drink the chief's water, and you tell me if they're the same thing."

"It's really not booze?" she said.

"Not even a drop, darling. Ask Garrison here. I let him on my secret, too. Must be getting soft in my old age."

She looked at Gage, who nodded. She took the flask and drank, a tentative sip at first, then a couple of huge gulps. She handed it back to Conroy with a guilty look on her face, but he told her not to worry about it, there was plenty more where that came from. She wiped her lips with the back of her orange sleeve.

"It's sweet," she said. "I mean, it's water, but it's kind of sweet."

"The magic of Mississippi," Conroy said. "You feel better?"

She nodded. And it was true. Gage could hardly believe how much calmer she already seemed, how much more relaxed and at peace. Maybe he'd have to get some of that water himself.

"Good," Conroy said. "Now look. You need to get yourself together. You don't have to make a decision right this second, you can hear out what these two gentleman have to say, but I'd like to talk to you later today, just the two of us. If that's all right with you? And the chief, of course."

He glanced at Quinn, who offered back a curt nod. Miranda looked at Gage, as if for approval, but as much as he didn't like or trust Conroy, he decided it was no longer his place to weigh in on this matter, so he shrugged. She nodded at Conroy.

"All right, darling," Conroy said. "Collect your thoughts, get some rest, and I'll see you in the afternoon."

He headed for the door, walking deliberately, pensively, as if he was an actor on a stage who knew the spotlight was shining on him. Even for Gage, it was impossible not to stare. He stopped at the door, glanced at the doorknob, and raised his big white eyebrows at Quinn. The chief undoubtedly knew exactly what the man from Mississippi wanted, but he decided to play dumb, leaning against the wall with his arms crossed and glaring coldly. The standoff lasted a few seconds, until Quinn sighed and opened the door for Conroy.

After the lawyer had gone, Quinn slammed the door behind him hard enough that Miranda flinched.

"Not a fan, huh?" Gage said.

"What makes you think that?" Quinn said.

Miranda buried her face in her hands. "I don't know what I'm doing. I know—I know hiring him is a bad idea."

"You do what you have to do," Gage said. "Forget what I think. Forget what the chief thinks. None of us is in your situation. You've got to make up your own mind."

"I don't know. He's—he's just here for the publicity."

"Doesn't mean he can't help you."

"He probably doesn't even believe me."

"The kind of lawyer he is, the truth is the least important thing to him."

She groaned and lowered her forehead to the table. Gage glanced at Quinn, who shrugged. In the stillness of the room, he heard the dull murmur of voices outside, the ring of a phone. Finally, she leaned back slowly, languidly, and stared at them with a pale face and glassy eyes.

"I'm tired," she said.

"Understandably," Gage said.

"Do *you* believe me?" she asked.

Gage had been expecting the question, or at least some form of it, but he still didn't have a good answer. She looked so beaten down, shoulders sagging under the weight of her troubles, eyelids drooping as if it took all of her will just to keep them open, and he didn't want to take away what little hope she had left. But what could he say?

"I want to believe you," he said.

"Well, that's something at least."

"You've got to give me a reason, Miranda. You've got to give me something more."

"I'm tired. I'm so tired."

"Why did you run to Crescent City?"

"I don't know."

"You met up with Marcus Koura there. Why?"

"I don't know."

"Did you know him in New York?"

"I …"

"Give me something. Anything."

"Tired," she said.

"Miranda, I do want to help you. You've got to help *me*. Otherwise, there's nothing I can do."

She nodded, but it was a bare tip of the chin. Her eyes were reduced to slits. She crossed her arms on the table and sank her head into them.

"It's dark," she murmured. "It's all … dark."

She said something else, but Gage couldn't make it out. Then she lay still. They both watched her, Gage unsure of what to do, Quinn fidgeting with his shirt. Gage felt an odd, incompatible mix of sympathy and frustration; he wanted to tell her everything was going to be all right while at the same time slap her face to see if he could knock the truth out of her.

Then something changed. He felt a cold prickle along his neck and he knew this wasn't right, this whole thing wasn't right.

"Miranda?" he said.

She didn't answer. The cold prickle turned into an icy fear shooting through his veins. He shot a glance at Quinn and saw the same alarm mirrored in the chief's face. There was a second, maybe less, while the world froze on its axis and the two of them did nothing, a moment that seemed to stretch forever, and would later become an infinite memory caught in its own unending loop. All the guilt, all the harsh and well-deserved blame, all the embarrassment that they could have been so easily fooled—it would live on in that moment.

Gage understood, with perfect clarity, what had just happened. The beguiling lawyer who was not what he seemed. The harmless drink from a flask that had not been so harmless after all.

The moment passed and the two of them sprang into motion. Gage jumped to his feet, chair upending, and dodged around the table. At the same time, Quinn yanked open the door and started shouting, yelling for help, yelling to call 911, yelling to get that bastard Conroy before he got away. Gage felt for a pulse on her neck. There were people in the room, a crowd of them surrounding her, and they had her on the floor. A woman from dispatch had a first-aid kit. Another man tried CPR. There were sirens. There were medics in the room. Miranda's eyes were open. Miranda's eyes were open and unseeing.

She was gone.

Chapter 17

After all the life-saving measures had been taken, after Miranda was whisked away to the hospital in an ambulance, Gage riding along only to watch Tatyana declare her dead mere minutes after they reached the emergency room—after Zoe brought him back to the station where everyone was caught up in a whirlwind manhunt that included every officer on the street and every desk jockey scrutinizing the security footage for any clue where D.D. Conroy might have gone, after all this, only then did Gage finally look inside his van.

The metal flask was there, on the seat.

Rather than bring it himself, he had Brisbane do it, wearing gloves and holding it by the edges in the hopes of preserving any fingerprints. Gage doubted there would be any. The flask was whisked away to the lab for testing, though Gage didn't see how identifying the exact poison was going to help them catch the man who had given it to Miranda. If her killer was shrewd enough and bold enough to waltz into the Barnacle Bluffs police station and poison a prisoner in custody, then he certainly wasn't dumb enough to use a poison that would easily lead back to him.

"I'm probably stating the obvious," Quinn said, "but that

wasn't D.D. Conroy."

The two of them were alone in Quinn's office, a moment of reprieve from the frenzied activity. Raised voices, ringing phones, the sound of many footsteps—it was all just beyond the door. Gage even heard laughter. It was so out of place that he felt a flash of anger. Who would laugh at a time like this? The blinds covering the windows were closed. Except for the glare of sunlight rimming the outside window, Quinn's computer monitor provided most of the light.

"I gathered as much," Gage said. He still felt numb, trying to process the fact that Miranda was gone. "Where's the real D.D. Conroy?"

"Soaking up the sun on a beach outside his condo in Miami. Trenton got him on the horn a few minutes ago. He also got the local PD to send an officer to make sure the man wasn't playing us. He was there."

"And pretty surprised to hear what someone did dressed as him, I imagine."

Quinn drummed his fingers on a stack of paper. "Nobody told him yet. I'm trying to keep a lid on this just a little while longer. You know what kind of shit storm it's going to be when the world finds out? I hate being played the fool!"

"You weren't alone. He played me too. Even that flask. He was sitting outside the station with the cap off, as if he'd just taken a drink. But I never saw him actually drink it. The bastard even had me smell it."

"And all that crap about not wanting to shake hands or touch doorknobs. He just didn't want to leave behind any fingerprints."

"He knew she didn't drink alcohol either. That's why he did that whole bit about it only being water. He knew that was the only way he could get her to drink it."

"Jesus."

"If this was like one of those TV shows," Gage said, "your crack team of crime scene investigators would find a stray hair, identify the man's DNA, and we'd have him in custody before the next commercial break."

"I've got a tech in the investigation room right now," Quinn said, seemingly missing the sarcasm, "but I wouldn't hold my breath he'll find anything useful. Do you know how many people come in and out of that room every day? And it's not like we sterilize the place. I'm just as likely to find a hair from some wife-beater who was sitting in that chair a year ago as I am the man who just carried out the most daring murder this town has ever seen." He pounded his fist on the desk. "I can't believe this!"

Gage, slumping in his chair, couldn't believe it either. It just seemed too impossible to be real. Even in his shock, though, even as he tried to grapple with the guilt that he had let Miranda down in such a profound way, he had to grudgingly admit that the man who had carried out this plan had guile and smarts Gage had rarely seen. It might appear at first to be extremely foolhardy to chose one of the most famous lawyers on the planet as a disguise, but the more Gage thought about it, the more brilliant it seemed. Conroy's beard, heavy frame, and outlandish appearance easily hid the real man underneath. When someone looked so distinctive, who would even notice that the nose might be a little bigger, the eyes tiny bit wider, the cheekbones a little more pronounced? It was as if the man had come dressed as a clown. Would anybody recognize a clown out of costume? Unlikely.

Even Conroy's fame had worked to the murderer's advantage. If he had come dressed as some random person, he might have received a lot more suspicion. But because Conroy was so famous, the scrutiny had not been about whether he was who he said he was, but on his motives. He had used Conroy's showboating reputation as just another way to hide his true intentions.

"Who the fuck is this guy?" Quinn asked. "I want you to tell me everything you know right now. No secrets, Gage. I swear, if you hold back from me like you usually do, I will spend the rest of my days making your life a living hell."

"I haven't held anything back," Gage said.

"Bullshit."

"You really want to do this? I can walk out of here right now."

"And I can charge you as an accessory to murder."

"What the hell are you talking about? I was right here with you!"

"Sure, good cover," Quinn said. "Maybe you were working with this guy. Best alibi in the world, sitting next to him while he poisons this poor girl. It's only water, you told her. Sure it was. Maybe you knew all along."

"Come on."

"What do you know?"

"I told you—"

"You've got to know something!"

"There isn't anything else," Gage insisted. "Just a lot of guesses."

"Give me guesses, then!"

Gage sighed. "Fine, let me think out loud here. We know Marcus and Omar had some kind of falling out over eTransWorld, which was why Marcus sold out to his brother. Marcus was meeting with Miranda in New York, or at least that's the best guess. Maybe these things are connected, maybe not. Miranda was with a powerful man and somehow she and Marcus met, fell for each other, decided to run away together—the old story. They meet in Crescent City but this powerful guy sends some people after them, kills Marcus. Miranda survives somehow, maybe by hiding ..." He shook his head. "It doesn't add up, does it?"

"Why?"

"Well, if this powerful guy sent some people after them because he was jealous, then they would have found her on the boat. No way she could have hidden. So maybe it wasn't Marcus who sent the guys. Maybe it was Omar."

"Because of their falling out over eTransWorld?"

"Maybe. Maybe something bigger. Omar was trying to take out Marcus. He might not have even known about Miranda until you called to tell him about his brother's boat turning up here with amnesia girl on board."

"So his anger is all an act?" Quinn asked.

"Makes sense, doesn't it?" Gage replied. "I mean, what else is he going to do? He may have thought she was just some random woman Marcus picked up on his journey until he saw her in person. Maybe then he knew she was fake Conroy's girl, maybe not. Depends on whether Omar and fake Conroy are really connected and how much they knew about each other. Maybe Omar and this guy had cooked up some kind of scheme and Miranda got wind of it. She told Marcus and he found a way to stop it."

"That's a lot of maybes."

"I told you all I had were a lot of guesses. Remember the rumors are that eTransWorld was working with certain terrorist organizations. Maybe Marcus and Miranda were trying to steal it for themselves. We don't know. We do know that the FBI was working on Marcus, but he wouldn't betray his brother. Maybe he wasn't willing to send Omar to jail, but he still wanted to stop whatever eTransWorld was up to."

Quinn chewed at his bottom lip. "Okay. I believe at least one thing now. You're not holding anything back. It's all a mess. So back to our D.D. Conroy double. If he didn't come here to kill Miranda for revenge, then he did it to, what, prevent her from eventually remembering him?"

"Probably for both reasons," Gage said. "He risked a hell of a lot killing her this way. My best guess is that he was tying up loose ends. If we couldn't identify her when she was alive, then we're going to have an even harder time identifying her now that she's gone."

"Well, then mission accomplished. The person to talk to now is Omar. Maybe we can get him to … to …"

Quinn trailed off. They both looked at each other suddenly, and Gage knew they were undoubtedly thinking the same thing.

Omar was another loose end.

THEY ROARED over Highway 101 in Quinn's patrol car, sirens blaring. It wasn't necessary to voice their suspicions. They would know soon enough whether what both of them was thinking was true.

With the traffic parting before them, it took less than two

minutes to reach the Inn at Sapphire Head. They screeched to a stop under the covered front entrance, another patrol car pulling in behind them, and soon all were barreling through the gusts of wind into the plush lobby. A gaping clerk directed them to Room 317 and Quinn barked at him to come along with the key. Rather than wait for the elevator, they clambered up the stairs, Gage holding his cane and biting his lip at the knife jabs of pain in his knee.

Quinn, reaching the door before everyone else, pounded on it.

"Police!" he shouted. "Omar, you in there?"

There was no answer. He knocked even harder, but still there was nothing.

Quinn nodded at the clerk and the kid fumbled the key card through the reader. Quinn pulled out his Glock and the two cops with them took it as their cue to do the same. A cleaning woman down the hall emerged from one of the rooms with a cart, saw what they were doing, and ducked back inside.

Standing to the right of the door, Quinn pushed slowly on the lever.

The door swung open. Peering over shoulders and between heads, Gage saw tan carpet and off-white walls, a framed picture of two sea lions, and a white sheen billowing in front of a partially open patio door. He heard and smelled the ocean … and then something else, too, something more foul. Putrid, like a sewer. Everyone recoiled from the odor, one of the cops pressing his nose into the sleeve of his uniform, the clerk lunging away down the hall.

"Omar?" Quinn called.

Again, nothing. His Glock leading the way, Quinn entered the room. The cops followed, Gage behind. Quinn checked the bathroom, saw nothing, proceeded into the main room. He was the first one to get a clear view of the bed.

"Well, crap," he said.

Gage, following the uniformed cops, saw Omar on the edge of the bed, his feet on the floor. He wore socks but no shoes, an untucked white dress shirt, charcoal gray pants. His eyes were closed and his mouth partly open, as if he was merely sleeping, but his face bore a sickly gray pallor. There was an empty glass in his right hand, tipped to the side as if it might have spilled on the bedspread and yet there was no wet spot. There was, however, a darkening around his groin, no doubt the source of the foul odor.

Quinn checked the man's hand for a pulse. They all waited until he shook his head. He told one of the cops to call it in, and the kid, covering his mouth, was more than happy to duck out of the room to use his radio.

"Cold as hell," Quinn said. "Been dead awhile."

"Probably poison again," Gage said. "He probably took care of him last night before coming to see Miranda this morning. No signs of struggle. Omar knew who he was, let him in, they had drinks."

"Bastard never knew what was happening."

"Nope."

"We were played again, Gage."

"Yep."

"I'm feeling like this case is slipping away. He just tied up another loose end."

"Yep."

Quinn sighed. "You were supposed to disagree with me. Use that brilliant detective mind of yours to see something we're all missing."

Gage tried to think of a sarcastic retort, but there was nothing. The cloud of despair that had settled over him was so dark it overwhelmed all over thoughts. Gage crossed the room to the open window, where the ocean breeze rippled the sheen. He thought about pushing aside the curtain, but he could not even summon this much effort. It was hard enough to simply stand there and let the sheen press up against his face like a veil. He saw the ocean, tinted brown through the material, and the sky above it a dull shade of gold, the whole thing like an alien landscape on some distant planet where nobody lived and nobody died.

A cell phone rang. The sound made him flinch, and he turned to face the room, seeing Quinn and the others staring at him, before he realized the cell phone was his. He groped for it in his pocket, finally getting it out and clicking it open. He forgot to say hello, but the man on the other end didn't wait for Gage to speak.

"Hello Garrison," the man said, "I imagine you're feeling a little blue about now."

It was the same Mississippi drawl Gage had heard a few hours earlier. He tightened his grip on the phone. "Calling to rub it in, huh? You can knock off the phony accent. We know you're not Conroy. How did you get this number?"

"I'm a resourceful person," the man said. "I'm sure you've figured that out by now. And I think I'll stick with Conroy's wonderful delivery, on the off chance that somehow this gets recorded. Tell your friend the chief that there's no need to try to trace this call either. It's just a burner phone I picked up today, and I reckon I'll dispose of it soon enough."

"What do you want?"

"Want? Oh, dear boy, I don't want anything from y'all. I just thought you should know that the poison used in both cases was quite rare, quite untraceable. It's amazing what modern science can create these days that was not possible even five years ago. You just have to know people, the right people."

"You're calling to help us with our toxicology reports?"

The man chuckled. "I'm calling, dear boy, because I could not resist the temptation of hearing the sound of utter defeat in your voice."

"Well, why don't you come down here, then? I'm sure it will sound much better to you in person."

"Oh, as appealing as that is, I'm afraid that would be tempting fate one too many times. No, I'll settle for this call, then be on my way. But I do so look forward to reading what you say to the media. The great Garrison Gage! Some of the things I've read about you in the papers have made you out to be like some kind of mythical figure. This should cut you down to size."

"Trust me, I'll find out who you are. If you read about me, you know the one thing I don't do is quit."

"That's the spirit, my boy! I'm afraid it won't do you a lot of good in this case, but I do like to think of you spending the rest of your days chasing my shadow. You have no idea how outside the system someone like me is. And what a stroke of luck, having the woman you call Miranda forget everything about me! That was such a wonderful name, by the way. I do so like that play. I see myself like Prospero, using my powers to fool you all, taking my revenge for past misdeeds."

"Miranda was Prospero's daughter. He loved her dearly."

"I loved her, too, but she had to be punished. Even if you somehow discover who she really is, there won't be any hard evidence against me. And Omar, as tenuous as his link was to me, he's now gone too. The curtains will close, and I will take my bow."

"They must have stolen a lot of money from you," Gage said, "for you to go to so much trouble."

The man made a *tsk tsk* sound. "Ah, there you go, fishing for clues in the most sloppy manner. I'd like to think you'd have a bit more respect for me, Gage, after the demonstration of my abilities you just witnessed."

"I'm afraid I don't have much respect for murderers."

"Well, that's too bad. Some of the most brilliant men in the world are killers. I'm not talking about freak shows that shoot up schools and movie theaters. Some of the folks I'm thinking of end up as presidents and prime ministers. You just have to expand your definition of killer a little bit."

"If you don't tell me who you are, your name can never live in infamy."

The man sighed. "Now you're just boring me, dear boy. And with that, I think I shall take my leave. Just remember, if I could get to Miranda, I could get to others. I'm sure you're not worried about yourself, but what about Zoe? What about Alex?"

"Threats?" Gage said. "Now who's the one who's getting sloppy?"

There was a long moment of silence. Gage strained to hear something in the background, some clue as to where the guy was calling from, but he heard nothing.

"Goodbye Gage," the man said.

"Wait—" Gage said.

But it was too late. The phone went dead.

Chapter 18

The man who'd masqueraded as D.D. Conroy was right about one thing. The press, once they got wind of what happened, made them all out to be fools.

In fact, as much as it burned Gage, the man turned out to be right about pretty much everything.

With so much media interest, Chief Quinn couldn't hold back the truth for long—and it turned out he couldn't even hold it back an hour. Somebody in the police department must have blabbed, because by the time they got back to the station, the hordes of journalists lined up outside were yelling questions about who they thought the Conroy imposter was and why he had been so determined to kill the woman with amnesia. Buzz Burgin, he of the doughy face and the purple presentation, shoved a microphone in Gage's face and asked him what it felt like to get so close to the killer only to have him slip away.

It was only the presence of two network television cameras behind Burgin that prevented Gage from giving in to his worst impulses. If he couldn't get his hands around the killer's throat, Burgin's would have been the next best thing.

Inside the station, once they'd gotten past the throngs of detectives and officers and safely into the confines of the chief's office, Quinn said, "God, I hate that guy."

"Burgin?" Gage said. "Join the club."

"I haven't said a word to him, but he's still spewing stuff all over his blog like he's got an inside track. And next day, whether the stuff he says is true or not, all the other reporters are picking it up and running with it."

"Isn't there some kind of exception in the law for violence against lowlifes like him?"

"Afraid not. But enough about that creep. Tell me how we're going to catch our killer."

"Right now, I've got nothing."

"Nothing? Come on, man! I've got thousands of cops across the state on high alert, ready to pounce on this guy, but I can't even tell them what he looks like! He could be stepping onto a plane in the next few minutes in Eugene or Portland and there's nothing we can do to stop him."

"Nope."

"Damn it, Gage!"

"Well, what do you want me to say? He won this round, no doubt about it. I'll still get him eventually."

"*We* will get him eventually. We, Gage, we."

"Of course."

Quinn aimed his index finger at him as if it was the barrel of a gun. "You better not be planning to do something on your own here. If you've got some kind of idea who this guy is, or at least a lead on something that will point us in the right direction, you better tell me right now."

"I have no idea who he is," Gage insisted.

"If you're lying to me—"

"I'm not lying."

Quinn searched Gage's face as if looking for any sign of deception, until finally shaking his head. He turned his intense gaze to the stacks of paper on his desk. A vein pulsed on his temple, and Gage sensed the anger coiling inside of Quinn, growing tighter, the pressure mounting. The room was very still even as the department outside was a hurricane of activity.

Then Quinn let loose with a primal roar and swept everything off his desk in one violent motion.

IT WAS TRUE. Gage wasn't lying, not about knowing who the killer was. He still had no idea.

What he *hadn't* said was that a plan to entice the killer to reveal himself on his own—not even a plan, but only the faintest shadow of a plan—had started to appear in his mind. The police, if they were involved, would only screw it up. He knew that much at least.

Quinn's comment about Buzz Burgin was what got Gage thinking. The man was certainly annoying, no doubt about it, but maybe there was a way to use Burgin's nosiness and over-eagerness to be in the middle of things to Gage's advantage.

Leaving the station, stepping into a stiff breeze and a bright afternoon sun, he said nothing to Burgin or any of the other journalists who shouted questions at him. He climbed into the van and headed across town, driving slow enough that Burgin and a few of the others who'd decided to follow him rather than remain at the station could safely keep up. For once, he didn't mind. The shadow of a plan was becoming more substantial by the minute. After he parked in front of the Turret House, he waited until Burgin's purple Pontiac Safari parked behind him before getting out of the van.

He approached the Pontiac with a friendly wave, but Burgin, in full panic mode, still lunged to lock the door. He twirled the ends of his handlebar mustache and peered out through his windshield with fidgety ferret eyes.

"Now is that any way to treat a friend?" Gage said. He tapped on the glass. "Come on, roll it down. I'll be nice."

Burgin sank further into his seat.

"If you want a scoop," Gage said, "you're going to have to take a chance. Come on, the other guys are getting out of their cars. You've got maybe five seconds."

The word scoop seemed to motivate Burgin, because he lowered the window enough that they could talk without going so far that Gage could potentially reach inside. The crew from the Portland news van was quickly approaching—a woman in a gray pantsuit and a stocky guy lugging a camera.

"Yes?" Buzz said.

"Give me your card."

"What?"

"Your card, your card! I might have some news for you later. I need to know how to get in touch with you."

It took Burgin a few seconds to realize that Gage was actually serious, but he did eventually fish around in his jacket pocket until he found a business card, which, no surprise, was a shade of lavender. Gage snapped it away, said he'd be in touch, and headed into the Turret House.

Home as usual on a Tuesday, Alex waited for Gage in the entryway. Perched on the edge of the credenza, his hands clasped under his chin, he had the look of someone who had been waiting a long time.

"You heard?" Gage said.

Alex's eyes were bleary and red. "Everybody's heard. It's all over the news. I'm so sorry."

"I don't think she was lying. She really didn't know who she was."

"Tragic," Alex said, shaking his head. His breath smelled of wine. "It must have been terrible, dying like that. So confused, so alone."

"You've been drinking."

"Of course I've been drinking! You should be drinking, too. This is horrible."

"Where's Eve? She here?"

"Yeah. She's... she's lying down."

"And Zoe? She at the store?"

"I told her she could close, but she said it was better to work."

"Good," Gage said. "I like knowing where she is. I'll need to talk to her, too.

"About what?"

The skin around Alex's eyes was puffy and threaded with thin red lines. The man had once been such a rock, his emotions in his FBI days fortified by the usual tough guy act, but the years had made him soft. It wasn't a bad thing. Gage took him by the arm and led him into the kitchen, away from any curious ears outside. The late afternoon sun slanted through the high windows, placing yellow rectangles on the countertops and illuminating the flecks of black and gold in the green marble. A bottle of Oregon Pinot Noir and two wine glasses sat next to box of crackers that looked like they hadn't been opened.

"We've got to catch this guy," Gage said.

"Well, that's stating the obvious."

"No, I mean we have to catch him now. He leaves town, we'll probably never get him."

Alex picked up the wine bottle. In a shaft of sunlight, the glass was a vibrant green and obviously empty. He sighed and put it back on the counter.

"I assume it's going to be something you do by yourself," he said. "Because, you know, you wouldn't take the help even if it was offered. I also assume, like usual, it will put your life in danger in the most stupid and crazy way possible."

"You think I should risk everybody's life?"

"I think maybe you should use the police—for once."

Gage took out Buzz Burgin's card and slapped it on the counter. "Maybe I can tell you my plan before you piss all over it, okay?"

"That card really is a nice shade of purple," Alex said.

"Be serious."

"All right. I *seriously* think that's a nice shade of purple."

"Alex …"

"Tell me your damn plan, then."

Gage leaned against the counter. "It's like this," he said. "What do we know about our killer? Nothing definite, but we have a lot of bits and pieces. From what Miranda said, he's a man of huge ego who's prone to fits of violent anger. We also know he took an enormous risk to cover his tracks. From what we learned from the FBI, eTransWorld might have been moving money for certain terrorist organizations. This man, our killer, was probably either working for them or stealing from them. Omar was working with him on this. Miranda and Marcus screwed up their plans somehow. Either way, these people he works for are not going to be happy if their money is gone. It would explain why Omar sent people after Marcus, his own brother. He was scared out of his mind that the truth was going to get out. Maybe eTransWorld let them remain mostly anonymous, but Marcus and Miranda definitely knew who they were."

"This all sounds plausible," Alex said. "But what reason does our killer have to show himself now?"

"Exactly," Gage said. "We need to give him a reason. That's where my friend Buzz Burgin comes into play. As much as I dislike the guy, he's got some influence. He puts something on his blog, it gets picked up everywhere. Maybe we can use that to our advantage."

The thought seemed to breathe a little life into Alex, not a lot, but enough to get him to straighten his back. "All right. I'm seeing where you're going. But what do you tell him? Even if all the stuff you just said is true, I'm not sure there's anything there that you could tell Burgin that would flush out our killer. He must know that at least that much of the truth is going to come out."

"That's just it," Gage said. "I'm not going to tell Burgin the truth. Not completely, anyway. In this day and age, rumors can do more damage than the truth."

"Okay, now you've piqued my interest."

"Good. I'm glad the wine is finally wearing off. Here's the deal. I've got to make this guy angry enough that he wants to come after me right now. How do I do that? By making him seem like an idiot and a coward. Later today, when I'm sure that everybody I care about is safe, I'm going to call Buzz Burgin. I'll tell him that when I talked to our killer, he obviously sounded scared of me. Then I'll tell him that I'm working on some leads that indicate our killer was a kind of patsy that was played by Omar and Marcus, an idiot who was working for a terrorist organization. I'll just tease Burgin with this stuff, tell him I want to meet him tomorrow morning for a much bigger scoop. I'll hint that our killer said some pretty nasty things about these terrorists he works for, especially about the stupidity of Islam. I'll say I've got all kinds of proof."

Alex nodded. "All right. You're putting a big chunk of bait out there. You really think this guy won't see right through it?"

"I don't think it will matter. He'll know that I know it's not true, but he'll hate that other people might *think* it's true. And he might be a bit nervous that his terrorist friends will be pissed off enough about his insults to come after him. I'm really hoping he's so angry that he'll want to take me out to send a message."

"What, you're just going to hole up at your house?"

"That's exactly what I'm going to do."

"Garrison—"

"I know what you're going to say, and don't bother."

"I'm not going to let you do this alone."

"No," Gage said, "you're not. What I need you to do is protect all the people I care about. You still have your Glock?"

"And my Remington. And my Winchester. I'm well-stocked, you don't have to worry about that. But, Garrison—"

"No, no, don't argue with me. This is a crazy last-ditch effort and I know it, but this guy needs to feel he has a clear shot at me. I'll also call Quinn, ask him to put someone parked here in an unmarked car."

"Won't the chief want to know why?"

"I'll just tell him I have reason to believe the killer might come after you. He doesn't need to know more than that."

"He won't believe that's all it is."

"Nope, probably not. But he'll still make sure you're all safe."

"Hey," Alex said, "I may be a bit rusty, but I can protect us."

"I know you can. I just want to make sure we catch this guy, too. You have to promise me you won't come over to my house to help. I'm counting on you."

"Oh, don't worry about that. If it's a choice between helping you or protecting my beautiful wife, it's no contest, pal. There are still two big reasons why this plan of yours isn't going to work, though."

"What's that?"

"Zoe and Tatyana. Convincing them to hole up here while you go through with this harebrained scheme of yours is going to be a lot tougher than convincing me. And without them safe, I know you won't do it."

ALEX WAS RIGHT. There was no way Gage would put any of his friends at risk—not any more than they already were just being in his life. Violence had always followed Gage, in one form or another, and anybody who spent any time in his orbit eventually found themselves caught up in it. After Janet's death, he'd decided that he was just one of those people who should not be allowed to love or be loved. Only he could bear the responsibility for the darkness that surrounded his life and, never being one for whom suicide was ever an option mostly because suicide would release him from the guilt he felt he deserved to suffer, he'd moved from New York to Oregon to live out his days alone.

Yet, over the past six years, people had found him. Connections had been made. As much as he'd resisted, he'd found himself loving and being loved back. The violence came, too, as he knew it would.

It had finally dawned on Gage that he needed *both* in his life to feel whole. Love and violence didn't find him by accident. As much as he found this truth about himself despicable, he sought them out. He may have clothed his need for violence in some kind of self-righteous crusade to help those in need, but he knew the real reason he kept putting himself in harm's way. It was a selfish addiction, made all the worse by his inability to insulate himself from others so they wouldn't be affected by it too.

But what of it? It was what it was. All he could do was never put those he cared about at risk if there was something he could do to protect them.

The green-glowing electric clock on Alex's stove read a quarter past three in the afternoon, meaning time was already growing short if he wanted to put his plan into motion tonight. He called Zoe first. He abhorred having the conversation over the phone, but the hungry press parked outside the Turret House would not be easy to lose on the way to Books and Oddities, and he didn't want them—or the killer—getting any kind of sense of what he was doing.

He got right to the point, which was actually easier because it allowed him to skip past any awkwardness that might exist between them after the incident on Monday night, and told her his plan. She protested, of course, but he silenced her by asking if she thought Miranda might deserve a little justice. She reluctantly agreed to come straight to the Turret House after the bookstore closed, and he got her to promise, even more reluctantly, not to even think of coming to their house in some misguided effort to help him.

He called Tatyana's cell and she didn't answer. He called her at the hospital, and after five minutes on hold, the unit clerk returned to tell him that Dr. Brunner was busy with a patient and would have to call him later. When he told the clerk it was urgent and that he was willing to wait, he spent another ten minutes on hold drumming his fingers on the marble counter before Tatyana finally came to the phone.

"What is it?" she said.

"Sorry to call you at work," he said. "I need to talk to you about something important."

"Right now? It's crazy here."

"When do you get off?"

"Usually at three, but I'm going to be here until at least four, I think."

"Can I meet you at your place at 4:30?"

There was a pause, and when she spoke again, her voice was

softer. "Garrison, I think maybe we need a little break. Things happened very fast. And after Miranda … Well, I'm not sure we should—"

"Fine," Gage said curtly. "Whatever. But this isn't about us. It's important."

"What is it about?"

"Can you be at your place at 4:30 or not?"

"All right."

He called Quinn next, and as expected, the chief did not take too kindly to being asked to provide undercover police protection for the Turret House without a little more information, but after some heated back and forth, he finally relented—on the condition that Gage wasn't withholding the identity of the killer. This Gage could promise with a clear conscience.

After checking in one last time with Alex, he drove to Tatyana's condo. While he'd been inside, a bank of gray clouds had moved in from the west, approaching the beach. They did not look like rain clouds to Gage's eyes, but solid gray, like a wool blanket being tucked over a bed. Without the sun warming his face, the air felt cooler. The headlights of the approaching cars burned brighter in the deepening gloom. Those who kept track of the weather may have designated a specific time for sunset, but in Gage's experience, it was more of a moving target on the Oregon coast. The sun went down when it felt like going down.

As he'd anticipated, Buzz Burgin and some of his journalist friends tried to tail him, and this time he was in no mood for an escort. Knowing the town much better than them, he darted through some side streets on either side of Highway 101, finally losing them by parking in a state campground on Big Dipper Lake and waiting until they passed.

When he knocked on Tatyana's door, she answered even though it was only a quarter past four. She still wore blue hospital scrubs. Seeing her, he felt his pulse quicken, an immediate reminder of how intensely he already felt for her. But there was something in her eyes that had not been there when they'd last seen each other, as if she was trying to see him through a thick sheet of bulletproof glass. She ushered him inside without a word.

"So what was so urgent?" she asked; if she was trying to play it cool with him, her voice sounded strained with worry.

Gage looked around her condo, not at all surprised that everything was new and perfect and in its place—a leather couch, *Architectural Digest* on the end table, dried flowers on a gray granite breakfast bar.

"How long will it take you to pack a bag?" Gage asked.

"What?"

"I booked a place in Newport for you. Just for the night."

She sighed and rubbed a hand against her forehead. Her fingers looked particularly white and pale, as if they'd been bleached. "Garrison—"

"It's not for us. It's just for you."

"Excuse me?"

"It's a nice place, right on the ocean. It's called the Sylvia Beach Hotel and every room is themed after an author. Won't it be nice to wake up and look at the ocean? Come on, I'll help you pack your bag. I was going to have you stay with Alex, but I think this will be better. Nobody will even know where you are."

"Garrison, what is going on?"

He told her. Like Alex and Zoe, she did not respond positively to his plan. She said he was being an idiot. She said he had some bizarre need to do everything on his own when there were plenty of people who would help him. Her voice, cool at first, quickly became heated. The wall she'd erected between them fell away and suddenly she was more emotional than he'd ever seen her, voice strained, a high pink flush riding up her face. Unlike with Zoe, asking her if Miranda deserved some justice didn't change her mind, and in fact, only made her more angry.

She told him to get out. He refused. She picked up the vase with the dried flowers in it and threw it at his face. He ducked. The vase smashed against the wall, breaking into pieces, which only seemed to enrage her further. She came after him with her fists and he grabbed her and held her, even as she pummeled his chest. He embraced her more tightly until the storm passed and she was crying. They stood like that for awhile, in the middle of the living room, him holding her until her body stopped shaking and they were both silent. It was quiet enough that he heard the wind blowing through the firs.

"I did not want this to happen right now," she said, sniffling. She spoke into his chest, and he felt her words as much as he heard them. "I've been acting stupid. I was not in control of myself."

"I like you when you're stupid," he said.

"Don't joke."

"I'm not. I mean, I like it when you lose some of that control."

"I don't ... I don't know who I am when I'm not in control. It was a fantasy, our time in Crescent City. I realize it now. It was not real. I was pretending to be someone else, but now that I'm here, I have to be the real me again. I'm a doctor. That's all I am. There is no room for anything else."

"Don't say that."

She shook her head against his chest and didn't answer.

"Right now," he said, "I just need to know you're safe. After what happened with Miranda, I can't take any chances."

"I'm not going."

"Tatyana—"

"No."

"You have to."

She sighed. "Why? Why should I do anything you say?"

"Because I love you."

He'd said the words without thinking, but once he'd said them, he knew they were true. He knew it without any doubt whatsoever. Her body stiffened, and it took her a long time to pull away and look up at him. The bulletproof glass in her eyes was gone. She searched his face, a fragile thing, a woman exposed.

"You are just saying this to convince me," she said.

"No."

"You don't know. It's too soon."

"I know."

"Garrison—"

"I love you, Tatyana. I want you to be safe. I need you to be safe. Will you do this for me?"

She stared into his eyes for a long time, as if trying to tease out any hint of deception, then finally nodded and headed for the bedroom. The same compact suitcase she'd used to go to Crescent City, the one with the long handle, was sitting by the door. She set it on the pastel blue bedspread and popped it open. It was still full of clothes. He leaned against the doorframe and watched her pack, taking out a few things, putting in others. He took out the paper on which he'd written the name of the hotel and the address, placing it next to the suitcase.

Five minutes later, she was ready to go, and he walked her to her car, a Honda Accord that was the same blue as her bedspread. Of course it would be that way. Of course it would, and he loved her even more for it. He scanned the parking lot but saw no dangers. He didn't see any reason for danger now, before his plan had been set in motion, but he felt apprehensive nonetheless. The canopy of fir trees blocked what little sunlight had made it through the graying sky, and the street lamps glowed a faint amber.

Once in the car, she rolled the window down and looked up at him. He wanted to tell her many things in that moment. He wanted to tell her he loved her. He'd said it before, but he wanted to find some other way to say it so she would really believe it.

"You will call me when it's over?" she asked.

He nodded. She put the car in gear and drove away. He watched her go, watched her taillights disappear into the trees, stood there in the chill air long after he could no longer hear the sound of her car's engine.

It was only then, as he started back to the van, that he realized she hadn't been wearing the CK necklace.

Chapter 19

An hour later, after first calling Alex to make sure Zoe was indeed at the Turret House and police protection was outside, Gage set his plan in motion.

Sitting in his recliner, dialing Buzz Burgin's number on his cell phone, the house was completely dark. With the thick clouds smothering the moon and the stars, it could hardly be darker. He wanted it dark. Though he could not see well, his memory of his own house filled in the rest of the details and that gave him the advantage. He felt the cold weight of his Beretta in his hand, resting in his lap.

Burgin answered on the second ring, already breathless.

"Garrison?" he said.

"Yeah," Gage said, and as he continued, he tried to make his voice sound slurred. "Listen. This is—this is very important."

"Are you still in the bar? I went in there and didn't see you."

The phone already felt hot against his ear, and Gage adjusted it. He'd parked his van at Tsunami's and walked home, just in the off chance that some of the press would see fit to come to his house. Now he was glad he'd done so. The last thing he needed was Buzz Burgin getting in the line of fire.

"I went home with a friend to his place," Gage explained.

255

"Had—had a bit too much to drink. Listen, I went to tell you something. I got a scoop for you, pal. You can tell your blog readers I got a scoop for you."

"Yes? Yes? You're such a great detective, I'm not surprised. I knew you'd crack the case."

"I can't tell you everything now. My head's a little too fuzzy. But I can give you a hint. A little … tease. You want to write this down? I don't want you to miss it. I know your readers will soak up every little detail."

"I'm typing as we speak!"

Gage gave him the whole spiel. He insulted the killer at every turn, called him a patsy for terrorists who were using eTransWorld to funnel money to their causes, a coward who hid behind disguises, a minor player in a scheme concocted by Omar. He'd been played by Marcus and Miranda, a woman who'd been with him in New York and told him that her lover had suffered a debilitating impotence that had twisted his mind. He told Buzz there was more, much more, but he'd tell him in the rest in the morning. How about eight o'clock at the Turret House?

Buzz, his voice humming with barely controlled glee, pressed for more details, but Gage told him it was tomorrow at the Turret House or nothing. Then he hung up.

And waited.

In this kind of darkness, the eyes deceived, conjuring up red and orange afterimages, hints of things that might have been there but probably weren't. He sat motionless for so long that the recliner began to feel like part of his body. He lost the sense that his feet were touching the floor. The handle of the Beretta was slicked with sweat.

Time passed, maybe an hour, maybe two. How late was it? It must have been drawing on midnight, but he had no sense of time. Maybe he'd slept without realizing it. Maybe a whole other day had passed and he'd come to a new night. Maybe this whole exercise was a complete waste of time. Why did he think the killer was so stupid? He was never going to fall for such an obvious ploy.

He heard a noise.

It was a creak from the back of the house, one of the bedrooms maybe, a wall or floorboard, loud enough that he doubted it could just be the shifting and settling of old wood. A chill ran up his spine. Was the killer already in the house? He checked his gun one last time, making sure the safety was off, and started to rise.

That's when the cell phone rang.

The creak from the back of the house was nothing like the piercing chirp of the phone in how it penetrated the stillness and set Gage's heart racing. Settling back into the recliner, he opened the phone and saw Tatyana's name and number. He punched the answer button.

"Tatyana," he said, "I thought I told you—"

"Hello, Garrison," a man said.

He spoke in a raspy whisper, in a voice that was not at all like the D.D. Conroy imposter, but Gage had no doubt it was the same man. It only took a split second for the shock of hearing the man calling from Tatyana's number to be replaced by an overwhelming fear of what the killer had done. He swallowed hard, his mouth suddenly dry.

"Where is she?" he asked.

"Preparing for a cruise to Hawaii," the man said with a laugh. "Actually, she is totally safe. Totally safe—at least for now."

"I swear, if you hurt her—"

"You'll what? You don't even know where she is. Barnacle Bluffs is quite the tourist town, isn't it? How many hotel rooms do you think there are? Twenty thousand? Forty? You think you can find this needle in a haystack? You haven't even heard the worst part."

"We can make a deal," Gage said. "We can come to a—"

He was in the middle of the sentence when he heard a rattle, then a creak—the front door opening.

Gage aimed the Beretta. The door swung open slowly. He'd left his porch lights off, and his house was isolated from the houses around it by tall hedges of arbor vitae, junipers, and laurel bushes, but there was still enough ambient light that Gage saw a tall lean figure in the doorway. He felt a cold draft blow into the room, one that smelled of the dust and gravel from his driveway.

"I know you're there," the man said, no longer bothering to speak in a whisper. He had a smooth voice, a confident voice, the voice of a man who liked to dip his words in honey not for the sake of others but for himself. "I also know what you're thinking. You're thinking you could shoot me right now. And it's true. You could. But then you would not be able to save Tatyana. You'd better think twice before pulling that trigger."

Gage, lowering the phone to his lap, didn't answer. He didn't want to give away his location.

The man said, "I'm coming in. I'm also going to turn on the light. This is your best chance to shoot me—if you decide that killing me is more important than saving the woman you love. Oh yes, I heard you say that to her outside her place. Very nicely put, very stirring. But know this: I don't plan to shoot you, Garrison. I had a hundred opportunities to do that in the past few days. No, I have something else in store."

Gage said nothing. Should he take his chance now? The killer may have been bold, but Gage doubted he was stupid enough to leave any obvious clues as to where Tatyana was on his person—no hotel receipt in a wallet, no room key in his pocket.

"You won't find her if you kill me," the man said, as if reading his mind. "I know what you're thinking, too. You're thinking you could just wound me or maybe disarm me, then beat the truth out of me. I believe you are capable of it, too. But that won't work either, and after I turn on the light, you'll find out why."

When the man flicked the switch nearest him, the light over the entryway still made Gage wince.

It was not much of a light, a soft glow in a small bulb, but it let them see each other well enough. Based on the voice, Miranda's reaction to the man she had seen at the outlet mall, and his own assumptions, Gage expected a young man dressed in a fine suit. The man *was* on the young side, early thirties maybe, but he was not dressed in a suit. His face was partly shadowed by the brim of his black Portland Blazers cap. He wore a slick green jacket over an Oregon coast sweatshirt, denim pants that were a little worn at the knees, and white tennis shoes with sand stuck to the soles. Except for the Ruger in his right hand, a suppressor attached to the barrel, it was the sort of outfit that could have been worn by any of the thousands of tourists who frequented Barnacle Bluffs every day.

In other words, it was the perfect disguise if you wanted to blend into the background.

He expected a powerful man with broad shoulders and big hands. This man, who could not have been more than five feet nine, was lean to the point of being slight. His hands seemed small, childlike even, and he held the Ruger as lightly as he might have held a cigarette.

When he moved, however, stepping out of the foyer into the living area, he did so with the smoothness and assuredness of a panther. No energy was wasted. The Ruger was not held lightly because he was lazy. The Ruger was held lightly because the man expended exactly the right amount of energy to accomplish a task and no more.

He stopped a good ten paces away. Closer now, and out from under the light, Gage got his first real glimpse of the man's face—strong chin, hard cheekbones, a handsome face, even if there was still something a little soft about it. Except for the eyes. He'd remembered Conroy's eyes being a bright blue, but those must have been contact lenses. These eyes were a dirty, lifeless gray, like puddles of still water that had caught every bit of dirt and flotsam that floated their way.

"Engage the safety on the gun," the man said. "Then put it on the floor and kick it over to me."

"Why should I?" Gage said.

The man smiled. It was not the smile Gage was intended to see, but the tiny blue capsule held between his perfect white teeth. He quickly sucked the pill into his mouth.

"I'll spare you the technical name for the poison," he said, "but suffice it to say, it will kill me very quickly if I swallow it."

"You're lying," Gage said.

"It's certainly possible. I mean, what kind of man would come up with such a crazy scheme? I suppose the same man who's played the edges all his life, who thrives on those edges and has made millions doing it. As I said, I could have killed you many times without you being able to do a thing to stop it. But why? Then I wouldn't enjoy it. Now, do as I say with your lovely Beretta or I'll just shoot you anyway. Not as much fun, but you'll have forced the issue. If you want to hear what you have to do to save Tatyana, you better do it now."

"I'll kill you, then find her myself."

"I concede you might find her in a day or two, but she'll be long dead by then. And not just because she's bound and gagged. You see, Garrison, less than twenty minutes ago, I injected her with a poison similar to the one in my mouth. This poison does not even have a name, it is so new. Developed by North Korean chemists who are not, um, inhibited by some misguided sense of ethics. Much slower acting, and she'll be quite fine if we can get her the antidote in the next twenty minutes, but longer that, well ..."

Gage hadn't heard a car. It could have been parked at the gas station or someplace nearby, but it could have also meant the man had walked. If he walked, that probably meant she was in a nearby hotel. Still, that only limited the list to a few hundred places.

"Thinking, thinking," the man said. "Do as I say, and there's a chance she lives. It's all up to you. You will make the choice. I don't kill innocent people. I kill people only out of necessity. It's up to you, Garrison, whether you make that a necessity or not. Right now she is merely a tool."

"A tool for what?"

"Tick, tock, the poison does its work."

"All right, all right," Gage said.

He engaged the safety on the Beretta and put it on the floor. He kicked it with his foot and slid it across the rug, halfway to the killer. The man, moving with precision, plucked it off the floor and slipped it into one of his jacket pockets. He nodded curtly, then stepped over to the kitchen counter. Keeping his Ruger fixed on Gage, he searched the cabinets until he found a bottle of bourbon. He winked at Gage, then found a shot glass. He poured the brown liquid into the glass until it was about a third full.

"You're going to have a drink?" Gage said. "Now?"

"No. But I think you will want to drink this in a moment. I know you're quite a fan."

"I'm not thirsty, thanks."

"Thirst has nothing to do with it. And, honestly, you never drank bourbon because you were thirsty, did you?"

The man reached into his other jacket pocket and brought out a tiny vial, one containing a white powder. He took off the cork and poured the powder into the glass. He opened the drawers until he found a spoon.

"You see," the man said, while stirring the powder until it dissolved, "I am perfectly willing to admit that I have a number of weaknesses. My ego is the biggest one. My anger is another. When my ego is threatened, I sometimes choose to give into my anger. You were counting on this by telling that journalist your ridiculous collection of lies. But what you did not know is that whether I give into my anger or not is always a choice. I never do so blindly."

"Whatever you've done to Tatyana," Gage said, "stop it now. You want revenge on me? You can have it. Just leave her out. She's innocent, like you said."

"Ah," the man said, setting down the spoon and picking up the drink, "how well you play the part of the gallant hero! But, you see, we now come to *your* weaknesses, which are far more of a liability than mine are to me. First, you're smart. A dumb man, either unable to think rationally or incapable of seeing all the consequences of his decisions, would have just shot me. But you, you calculate the odds, look for your chance. I know you played poker when you were younger, and I was counting on this."

"I'll play poker with you right now if you save Tatyana."

The man approached with the drink. "And you'd win, I'm sure! That is not my game, and I only play games I know I can win. You see, we have not yet gotten to your primary weakness, Garrison. You are not willing to sacrifice those you love to obtain your goals. I am. I also loved a woman, you see. But when it was necessary to sacrifice her, I did not hesitate. Now, take this."

He held out the bourbon.

"What's in it?" Gage asked.

"Take it, and I'll explain. I'm offering you a simple choice, and the clock is ticking. I doubt your girlfriend has more than fifteen minutes before the effects of the poison are irreversible."

Gage took the drink, their fingers brushing. The man's skin was almost as cold as the glass. Rather than hold it, Gage set the drink on the stack of magazines. He couldn't see the powder in the bourbon, but he knew it was there.

"You put poison in it?" he asked.

"Of course. Different than the one I gave Tatyana, much swifter, and with no time for an antidote even if I had one."

"And you want me to drink it?"

"If you want her to live, yes."

"So I die, then you give her the antidote?"

"Now you've got it. I want you to know, as you die, how your weakness killed you."

"Why should I believe you'll actually save her?"

"I told you. Because I don't kill innocent people. And with you dead, she's no longer useful as a tool."

"She could identify you."

"No, she can't. I took steps to ensure it."

"I have no reason to believe anything you say."

"No, you don't. But what difference does it make? If you value her life, you have to believe me. It is the only chance she has. Now, I'm going to count to three. On three, if you have not drank that bourbon, I am going to shoot you. I suppose, knowing how terrible that poison is in your glass, it will be a faster, less painful way to go, but then Tatyana will die. In order for my threat to be credible, I have to carry out what I promised. And believe me, I will do exactly that. A deal is a deal, and I always see a deal through to the end."

The man stepped back, five paces away, then ten, his Ruger still pointed at Gage. He was too far away to make a play. He'd get off three shots before Gage had hardly gotten out of the recliner. What else could he do? The cell phone was still in his lap, but there was no way to call for help.

"One," the man said.

"Wait ..." Gage began.

"Two," the man said.

Gage looked at the glass. Was he willing to do it? This was not at all the game he had wanted to play, and all the warnings from Quinn, Alex, and others about the dangers of going it alone came back to haunt him. Now he was being forced to make a choice. He either sacrificed himself willingly, or Tatyana died.

"Three," the man said.

Gage, seeing the man edge his finger back on the trigger, reached for the glass.

It was in that moment that he heard a bellowing cry from the corner of the room—and a blur of motion at the edge of his vision.

If the killer was surprised, the surprise did not last more than a nanosecond, because he whirled his gun in that direction and got off two shots before the blur even took shape. *Thump, thump,* the Ruger sounded no louder than a hammer hitting a nail. It was only after the bullets hit their target, one slicing through a leather jacket and into a shoulder, the other blasting through blue jeans and spraying blood and bits of denim on the white wall behind him, that Gage saw that the shape was actually Zachary. He'd crossed half the distance between the hall and the killer before being shot, but now he was going down.

Now was Gage's chance.

He was up and out of the chair in a heartbeat, pushing off his bad knee, ignoring the pain. He knew he'd never make it there in time. He knew the man was too fast.

Which was why he was already throwing what was in his hand—the cell phone— even before taking a step.

It wasn't a run. It was a *wind-up*.

The cell phone streaked through the air. The man spun back as fast as a tiger, squeezed off a shot that blasted the stuffing out of the top of the recliner, but then the cell phone reached its destination. It smacked him right between the eyes, stunning him long enough that Gage managed two steps before the man recovered and brought his gun to bear once more.

Then Gage was on him.

They slammed into the vinyl floor, the man's back taking the brunt of it but Gage also taking a knee to the stomach. It didn't matter. He'd bear all the pain and then some. He concentrated on the gun, getting his fingers around the barrel, and he didn't quite manage to do that, but he did have his fingers around the man's forearm. A fist slammed into the side of his head. A knee pounded into his stomach.

He didn't let go.

He would never let go.

It might have continued like that, Gage holding fast to the killer's gun arm, the killer punching and kicking him in any way he could, but then Zachary joined the fray. He pinned the killer to the floor, allowing Gage to pry loose the gun. It took a bit of doing, the killer howling in frustration, but Gage finally managed to rip it free. He had the Ruger and he tossed it aside. Yet that wasn't the only danger.

The pill.

The tiny blue pill.

Gage lunged for the man's mouth, clamping his hands around the jaw, trying to force it open, the killer glaring with bug eyes. Zachary struggled to keep the killer still, even as he thrashed and bucked with all his might. Just had to pry the teeth apart. Fish out the pill. Stop him.

The was a crackle, like someone biting into a piece of ice, and the glare of the killer's eyes became triumphant.

Stunned, Gage relaxed his hold on the man's face. It couldn't end like this. The killer grinned with the satisfaction that only a psychopath could feel, and Gage, still with his hands on either side of the man's face, felt the unrestrained glee as well as saw it. An ember of hope snuffed out inside him, a dead lump going cold and heavy in his gut.

"I ... still ... win," the killer said.

With each word, he faded a bit more. Gage heard his own heart pounding, felt the sweat stinging his eyes, but he still felt himself separating from his body, because he did not want to be there, not going to be here as this happened. Yet he shook off the feeling and slapped the man hard across the face, but it barely got the killer to blink. He screamed in his face. He shouted for him to tell him where Tatyana was. A bit of blood trickled down the corner of the killer's mouth. The man was almost gone, and he was still grinning. Red teeth. Lots of red teeth.

Gage lifted the man's head and slammed his skull into the floor again and again, roaring against his failure, letting out all of his rage, each crack louder than the last. A violent man? Yes, he was a violent man. He'd show the world violence. This was how a violent man acted when he stopped keeping the darkness at bay. Again and again, he pounded the man's skull, blood splattering the yellow vinyl, the red growing darker, ever darker. He did this until the eyes were dead, until the killer was really gone, never to return.

If he allowed himself, he could have gone on taking out his frustration on what was left of the killer, but an image of a bound and gagged Tatyana brought him quickly to his senses. There was still a chance. Somewhere in Barnacle Bluffs, she was alive. He rifled through the man's pockets, praying that there really was an antidote, and found a second tiny vial in the second jacket pocket. A milky white liquid. Could it be? Yes, it had to be, a twisted sense of fairness carried to its conclusion.

This would save her life—if only he knew where she was.

Where?

Curled into a fetal position a few feet away, Zachary groaned. Gage scrambled on hands and knees to the kid's side. The kid, already on the pale side, was deathly white. He held one blood-soaked hand to his shoulder, another blood-soaked hand to his thigh. The wounds did not seem life-threatening, but there was a lot of blood. Gage cast around until he saw the cell phone, the object that only moments ago had been a weapon and now he prayed would once again serve its primary function.

He popped it open, and, when the cracked screen illuminated, breathed a sigh of relief. Something going right for once. He dialed 911 and glared at Zachary.

"What were you *thinking?*" he said.

"Couldn't ... couldn't let you do it alone," the kid said.

On the phone, the dispatcher started to answer, but Gage spoke before the words were finished, telling him someone was shot and bleeding, spitting out the address, and disconnecting while the man started to speak again. No time for chitchat. He had to think. He looked at the dead man on the floor, all that inert flesh, that monster who would never hurt another person but had hurt plenty enough already, and tried to will the body to give up the location.

Nothing. There was nothing.

He roared at the kid, "Did Zoe make you do this?"

"No, no."

"Why did you yell? You lost the element of surprise."

"Yelled ... yelled because ... stop you ..."

The kid's eyelids closed, and that was it, he was out. Not dead. No, not dead, just out to the world, the pain too much for him. *Stop you.* Of course. Zachary had yelled not at the killer, but at Gage.

He didn't want Gage to swallow the poison.

It was brave and stupid, and Gage admired every bit of it.

This was no time for any of those feelings, though. Tatyana needed him. He heard sirens in the distance, and some part of him knew if that ambulance got to his house before he figured out where she was, it would be too late. Think, Gage, think. Where would she be? There were clues, the truth was right there in front of him, it had to be. What hotel would a man like this killer stay at? The very best, just like Omar Koura? That would be the Inn at Sapphire Head.

If they'd been staying in the same hotel, it would certainly have made it easier for him to kill Omar without being noticed. Just duck in and out, then scurry back to his room. No, too obvious. He was too smart to be so obvious.

The sirens were growing louder.

Think harder. Concentrate. Look at the killer. Think about what he'd said. Was there some sign? The man's clothes told him nothing. He rifled through the rest of the pockets, both in the jacket and the jeans, and as expected, found nothing—no wallet, no keys. All right, something else. Wait. The bottom of the shoes. What was that? It was sand caked in between the treads of the soles. There was no sand anywhere near Gage's house, his drive made of gravel, then the highway below. Maybe the killer had not driven at all, but walked, walked from the beach. Why the beach? What was on the—

"Preparing for a cruise to Hawaii," the man said, *with a laugh.* Of course!

It hadn't been just a joke, but a little slip of the truth. What do you take on a cruise? A ship. What was the closest ship?

The one Miranda had sailed to shore.

Was it still there? Had to be. It was such a bold place to hide Tatyana that no would even think the killer would dare do it, which perfectly fit the man's personality. Gage sprang to his feet, ignoring the thousand shrieking demons in his knee. Pain unimaginable, but what was pain when the life of someone you loved was on the line? Gage had been there before, seven years ago, and this time he could not be too late.

If he was too late, then he might as well go back to the house and drink that special brand of bourbon the killer had concocted for him. He couldn't go through this again. He *wouldn't* go through this again.

Already running full out, he burst through the door. He clasped the vial in his hand like a baton. The night air was thick and heavy, cold in his lungs, wet on his face. The wail of sirens were so piercing that he knew the ambulance was coming up his drive even before he saw the sweep of red and blue lights on his arbor vitae, on his gravel driveway, on the side of his house. No, not an ambulance—a police officer, standard procedure when someone reported a shooting. Gage realized this right as the headlights were rounding the bend, coming into his view.

He ducked into the ivy, landing hard, making himself as flat as he could.

Kicking up bits of dust and gravel, the police cruiser roared past. Gage jumped out of the bushes, clothes wet, and resumed his sprint. A cop might have helped him, but more than likely would have only stopped him, asked questions, lots of stupid questions. There was no time for delay. How much time did Tatyana have?

Tick, tock, the poison was doing its work.

He reached the bottom of the driveway and pushed on, across the road, ignoring the blare of a truck's horn, and sprinted even faster down the road on the other side. To the beach. Be swift. Faster now. He knew he could be faster. He felt a throbbing on his right forearm and knew he must have cut himself in the ivy when he'd jumped, but it didn't matter. It was just more pain. His knee threatened to break in half. His ribs, aching from the blow he'd taken from the killer, were going to cave in on themselves at any second. This useless body of his was no good for this sort of thing, for any sort of thing, really, but it was all he had. He'd make it work.

He'd save Tatyana or die trying.

The way was so dark. Why did it have to be so dark? There was one street light near the road, but he'd long since passed that and the road turned into a black void before him. One wrong step and he'd go down and never get up. Another siren was coming up the highway and he prayed that it was an ambulance this time, for Zachary's sake, but he couldn't spare a glance backwards.

He'd been on this walk hundreds of times. Maybe thousands. So many nightly sojourns to try to walk away his guilt.

He knew the path by heart. He didn't need to see.

Placing his trust in his memory, he ran even harder. The ocean grew loud, and he smelled it too, that great salty expanse, the brininess of it, sharper because the wind barely blew. His nose guided him down the concrete steps. To the sand. On the sand, so lumpy and uneven. Running. Still running. Where was that gap in the rocks? He could barely see it. He stumbled over a log, went down, got back up, still moving.

Then he got a stroke of luck: a sliver of moonlight appeared in the clouds, like a crack in an opening door.

It was just enough light, the barest hint of illumination on the sand, but it was enough to show him the way. He dodged half-exposed rocks, crumbling logs, and tangles of sea kelp. He squeezed through the gaps in the rocks and there it was, the sailboat, still listing on its side, the tattered sails barely flapping in the breeze.

He ran full tilt. In the near darkness, the details of the boat were hard to make out, the white fiberglass hull gleaming like the sloped back of a beached whale. Beyond, the ocean was a black, invisible expanse, somehow even more vast because it could not be seen. Lights from the houses on the bluff behind him checkered the uneven sand with diffused yellow squares.

He was alone, but he was not alone. To his left, he saw a shape that he thought was a redheaded woman in a bikini, but no, it was just a log. Miranda was gone, lost, never to return. Up ahead and to the right, he thought he saw another woman, wading in the surf, her pant legs folded up to the knee, but he blinked and the image was just sea foam, dissipating with the next wave. He'd taken Janet to the eastern shore many times, but she was nothing but a memory now too. He'd failed her. In the roar of the ocean waves, he thought he could make out a hundred different female voices—there was Zoe, there was Carmen, there was Karen—all calling to him, beckoning him like mermaids singing sweet promises of no more pain and no more guilt, just a slow drift into the darkness until you met your fate on the rocks.

No.

There was a woman on that boat, a woman he loved. He splashed into the surf, the cold water soaking his shoes. Clutching the vial in his teeth, he clambered onto the deck. His feet slipped and he fell hard on his back, the edge of his back. More pain. What did it matter? He still had the vial in his mouth and he had not bit down. There was still a chance. A whole life stretched before him, the only one he could see, based on this chance.

He crawled on hands and knees to the hatch and tossed it open, the door slamming against the fiberglass. His left hand left a bloody print next to the door, suddenly vivid in the growing moonlight. The cabin was a wall of darkness. He ducked his head inside, blinking into that darkness. Was she there? Not waiting for his eyes to adjust, he scrambled inside. He felt the edge of a counter. The edge of a bed. Something rough, like burlap. Not a sheet or a bedspread. A sail? It smelled as if had been soaked in sea water. With a dry mouth, he felt upwards and found what he expected, that the sail was wrapped around a body.

A shroud.

Just like what had been wrapped around the body of Marcus Koura, these tattered sails were meant to be a shroud—only this time it had been the killer's sadistic game.

His heart pounded so hard he felt it in the edge of his fingers as he felt his way up the body. His eyes adjusted. He saw the face exposed, deathly white, far too white, the eyes closed in a sleep that might have been permanent. A bloom of blonde hair spread on the thin mattress. It was definitely Tatyana. He felt her cheek and the skin was cold. Dead? No, no, she couldn't be dead. He took the vial out of his mouth and leaned his cheek down to her nose and mouth, holding his breath, waiting.

A breath! It was faint, but it was there.

He shook her gently, then harder. No response. He told her she had to drink something. He told her it would save her. Still nothing. He shook her again and she released the feeblest of moans. Just as she did so, sirens blared up on the bluff, getting louder, closer. He uncorked the vial. He shook her again, harder, trying to get at least a little life in her. Eyes cracked open. Lips parted.

He held the vial to her lips and poured, just a little, a tiny bit, holding back even though his hands were shaking. She gagged and spat, but this was too be expected, and she was awake now. He told her she had to drink. He told her she had to drink it all. Without waiting for a response, he held it to her lips and started to pour.

This time she drank it. She drank it all, every last drop.

When the liquid was gone, what little strength she mustered to complete this task abandoned her. She lay limp. Gage tossed the vial to the side and held her tight. Was her body cold? Or was it warm? He could not tell through the sails. He might have been holding a body in a blanket or a corpse in a shroud. The sirens howled over the beach. He heard voices outside, shouts in the distance. He hugged Tatyana, pressing his forehead against hers, and whispered for her to hold on, just hold on a little longer. There was a life before them, a great life, a life with meaning and purpose, a life where violence could be a thing of the past, he just knew it. He just needed her to stay with him.

Stay.

Please stay.

Chapter 20

It could have been any beach.

Slouching in the wicker chair, a glass of bourbon in his hand, the screen door open to the warm breeze blowing into the hotel room, that's what Gage thought when he looked out at the yellow sun and blue sky and all that great stretch of gleaming turquoise ocean that lay before him. It could have been any beach—in Mexico, the Bahamas, the French Riviera. That was the thing about a beach. From a certain vantage point, and at a certain temperature and certain humidity, they were all very much the same. This was Oregon, of course, a little isolated spot outside Bandon that seemed a good place to take refuge for a few days, enough hours south of Barnacle Bluffs to put all that craziness behind them. The press had lingered far longer than he had expected, and it was impossible to find some peace within yourself with a microphone shoved in your face.

Three weeks had passed since that fateful night when a psychopath had strolled into his house, but it felt more like a year. The killer's name, they eventually discovered, was Benjamin Orvick, and, as they'd all expected, he was an operative for Islamic terrorists who'd been working with Omar Koura and eTransWorld to move funds to where they were needed. Miranda—whose real name had actually been Stephanie Planck—

had been his longtime girlfriend until she'd met Marcus Koura and the two of them decided to do something to bring down the company. What had happened to the money, nobody knew, and anybody who would have known was no longer alive. The FBI, the press, and the world at large would go on trying to sort it out, but as far as Gage was concerned, he was moving on with his life.

The calendar still showed that it was spring, not summer, but that was the thing about the Oregon coast. This kind of warm day could be had at any time of the year. A cold and blustery day could be had as well. Today, he was glad it was the former.

Outside, on the patio and to the left, he heard laughter. Voices. Zoe, dressed in denim shorts and a sleeveless pink top, stepped into view. Pink! What had the world come to, that she would ever allow herself to be seen in pink? Barefoot, she was gazing at the ocean and must have sensed he was watching, because she turned and grinned over her shoulder at him.

"You okay?" he said.

He held up the bourbon as an answer.

"No, really," she said.

"I'm okay," he said. She turned her head, and he noticed a tiny sparkle on her nose. "Hey. You're wearing your nose ring again."

She smiled. "Yeah. I kind of missed it."

"Me too."

"Really?"

"Yeah. Strangely enough."

"Huh. You seen Alex and Eve?"

"They went into town. Antiquing, I think. Whatever that is."

She nodded. Zachary, looking hesitant, stepped next to her, dressed in ridiculous purple swim trunks and a black cartoon shirt that depicted one of those yellow creatures from the latest animated movie. Gage saw the edge of the white bandage on his side peeking out from under the swimsuit. It was the only sign of his injury. He no longer crouched or winced when he walked. After only a few days of frolicking in the sun, his face had darkened and blond highlights had appeared in his hair. He looked at Gage, and, honest to God, a pink flush appeared in his cheeks.

"One of these days," Gage said, "you'll stop being nervous around me, kid."

"Yes, sir."

"Garrison."

"Right. Did you see the news, Mr. Gage?"

"Garrison."

"Right. Did you hear about all the charities?"

"No."

"Billions," Zachary said, too excited to even think about getting nervous. "It was just on CNN. Billions of dollars in donations at hundreds of different charities. Salvation Army. Red Cross. Doctors Without Borders. All anonymous, all wired from dozens of different overseas bank accounts. They're already saying it's about the same amount of money that took down eTransWorld, the same amount of money that's crippled the terrorists. You know what this means, right? Of course you know what it means. Who am I talking to? But it's awesome, right? Totally awesome."

"Totally," Gage said, smiling.

They all grinned at each other, perfectly aware of what it meant. It meant that Marcus and Miranda weren't trying to steal money for themselves. It meant their plan had been a good one all along, a plan to bring down a shadowy terrorist organization, a shadowy banking institution, and a couple of shadowy individuals as well. It meant that Marcus had intended to do this for a long time, which was why he had named his boat *Charity Case*. It meant that he and Miranda had not died in vain, which was something at least. Not everyone got to say the same thing.

Zoe took Zachary's hand. She led him away from the patio toward the ocean. He watched them go, watched as their details blurred in the warm haze that hugged the sand, watched them wade into the surf like one person, smiling and laughing at one another. He was glad he had brought them. This was good. He needed good.

"Can two fit in that chair?"

She'd whispered the words behind his ear, her warm breath sending a tingle up his spine. He looked over his shoulder and saw her, his Tatyana, blinking at the bright sun, blonde hair mussed and strands charged with static. Usually the picture of perfect composure, it still surprised him to see her in such a disorderly state, no eyeshadow, no lipstick, the wrinkled burgundy sweatpants not matching the purple T-shirt in the slightest. He knew she'd be back to her tidy, compact self before they all went to dinner, but he was glad she didn't feel quite the same compulsion to look perfect for him.

He put the bourbon on the floor. Climbing into the chair, she draped her arms around his neck and settled into his lap. He marveled at how warm, how alive she was. Zachary wasn't the only one who tanned quickly. Her face and neck had already taken on a bronze hue, so much better than the sickly yellow color she'd had while recovering in the hospital for a week. She'd been a terrible patient, of course, as most doctors were, antsy to get out of there as soon as they were sure she was able.

He'd figured the last thing she'd want to do would be to spend time with him. In fact, he'd feared she'd never want to see him again, after the close brush with death that was entirely his fault, but she'd asked for him as soon as she'd regained consciousness. She'd insisted on holding his hand, and she'd squeezed it so tightly that he felt the bones in his fingers grinding in her grasp.

"Good nap?" he asked.

"Mmm. Very good."

"I'm glad. I thought about joining you, but you were sleeping so peacefully, I didn't want to disturb you."

"You should have disturbed me. I like being disturbed by you."

"Ma'am, if I didn't know better, I would think you were subtly implying something other than me sleeping next to you."

She smiled. "Was I really being that subtle?"

They were looking into each other's eyes, but he couldn't help but let his gaze drift to her neck, to the absence there. Following his eyes, she touched the spot where the CK necklace would have been and ran her fingers over the empty flesh.

"You want to ask," she said. "I can tell."

"Wanting and doing are two different things."

"Still. You have been wanting for a long time."

"So far, I've resisted."

Her smile turned into a smirk. "Oh, Garrison, you just can't let something go, can you? If there's a mystery, you have got to get to the bottom of it."

"Well, I am a private investigator."

"It's more than that, and you know it."

"Hmm. Does this mean you're not going to tell me?"

She sighed, then nestled her head under his chin. They sat like that for a while, two warm bodies entwined, both of them looking at Zoe and Zachary frolicking in the surf. That was such a frivolous word—frolic—but it was the perfect word to describe the way they were splashing water at one another and laughing with glee. They could all use a bit more frolicking. Gage didn't know if he was capable of it, but he was willing to try.

"I was that young once," Tatyana said.

"You're still young."

"Not that young. I was very young, not even a woman yet, and I had a young man much like Zoe does. We were happy. We even knew each other as children. Our families knew one another. I can't think of a time I did not know him."

Gage remained silent, afraid that if he even murmured in acknowledgement, he might break the spell and give her a reason to clam up again.

"His name was Sergei," she said. "Strange, saying it aloud. I have not said it aloud in many, many years. You see, there is a reason why I ... why I do not love easily. The chemist I married was not the first man who knew how cruel I could be. Sergei, he gave me the necklace when we were sixteen. In Cyrillic, the Russian alphabet, his name is actually spelled with what looks like a C to you. Koshkov is his last name. He had a necklace too, but with my initials. He saved and saved to have them made. It was our promise to each other, that we would always be together. But when the time came ... I just could not do it. I could not stay there. Ukraine, there was no future. I had to leave, make something of myself. I left without even saying goodbye, because I knew I would not be able to leave if I saw him. He wrote letters. So many letters, so angry. I never wrote back."

Her voice became rough, a strange warble deep in her throat. Her face, nuzzled against his neck, had grown warm.

"I did not wear the necklace again until one final letter came," she said. "It was from his mother. It was a few years later, about the same time I was having second thoughts about my life in Atlanta. I was thinking of going back, maybe seeing if Sergei would take me back. But his mother ... she said he died in a bar fight, in an argument about the future of Ukraine. He had been spending a lot of time in bars, always drinking. She was not angry with me. She said she hoped I found the life I wanted. It was so much worse, her being nice."

"I'm sorry," Gage said.

"Now you know."

"You were very young."

"Please don't make excuses. I was cruel. I did not need to be that way. So I wore the necklace as a reminder. I decided I would never love again. I did not deserve it."

"But you took it off. You're not wearing it anymore."

"Mmm hmm."

"Which means ..."

"I think you know what it means."

They sat in silence for a while longer. It may have been a minute. It may have been an hour. To Gage, it didn't matter. This was the place where he wanted to be—with Tatyana in his arms, surrounded by his friends, a vast and unjudging ocean stretched out before him. He wanted to stay in this place forever. He knew it wasn't possible, that he wasn't built for it, but he wanted it all the same.

"Now that you know," she said, "you have to promise me something."

"Oh?"

"You're not going to try to fix this. Fix me."

"Hmm."

"Is that something you can do?"

"I can absolutely promise to think about that."

"Garrison …"

"I'm getting hungry. Are you getting hungry?"

"I'm not done with this."

"I hear there's a great Italian place just up the road. Let's round up the others."

She sighed and climbed out of the chair, offering him her hand. If she'd been tearing up, she hid it well, a shock of pink around her eyes the only sign. He got out of the chair and together they walked onto the beach. The sand felt rough and warm under his bare feet. Holding her hand, he found he did not need the cane. It wasn't so much that she carried any of his weight, keeping it off his knee, as it was her presence that made him forget the pain. That was something, at least. In fact, the more he thought about it, the bigger a something it was. Maybe it was everything, really, being with the right person who could help you forget the pain.

"How about Alex and Eve?" Tatyana asked. "We need to call them. Let them know where to meet us."

"Yes," he said, "we should absolutely do that."

"Oh no. You didn't already—"

"I'm afraid I did."

"You lost the new cell phone we gave you?"

"Lost is such a strong word."

"Garrison!"

"I prefer to think that it found a new home not in my possession."

"You know, you really are incredible."

"Ma'am," he said, "I will take that as the compliment I'm sure you intended it to be."

About the Author

SCOTT WILLIAM CARTER's first novel, *The Last Great Getaway of the Water Balloon Boys*, was hailed by *Publishers Weekly* as a "touching and impressive debut" and won an Oregon Book Award. Since then, he has published a dozen novels and over fifty short stories, his fiction spanning a wide variety of genres and styles. His most recent book for younger readers, *Wooden Bones,* chronicles the untold story of Pinocchio and was singled out for praise by the Junior Library Guild. He lives in Oregon with his wife and children.

Visit him online at www.ScottWilliamCarter.com.

Made in the USA
San Bernardino, CA
25 February 2016